A Merry Mistletoe Wedding

www.transworldbooks.co.uk

A Merry Mistletoe Wedding

Judy Astley

BANTAM PRESS

LONDON · TORONTO · SYDNEY · AUCKLAND · JOHANNESBURG

TRANSWORLD PUBLISHERS
61–63 Uxbridge Road, London W5 5SA
www.transworldbooks.co.uk

Transworld is part of the Penguin Random House group of companies
whose addresses can be found at global.penguinrandomhouse.com

Penguin
Random House
UK

First published in Great Britain in 2015 by Bantam Press
an imprint of Transworld Publishers

A CIP catalogue record for this book
is available from the British Library.

ISBN 9780593076569

Typeset in 11/15pt Giovanni Book by Kestrel Data, Exeter, Devon.
Printed and bound by Clays Ltd, Bungay, Suffolk.

Penguin Random House is committed to a sustainable
future for our business, our readers and our planet. This book is made
from Forest Stewardship Council® certified paper.

MIX
Paper from
responsible sources
FSC   FSC® C018179
www.fsc.org

1 3 5 7 9 10 8 6 4 2

Acknowledgements

Twenty-three years'-worth of thanks to the brilliant Linda Evans, who took me on back in 1992, has been my editor for all this time and who retired just before I wrote this book. The best editor, friend and mentor any writer could have. 'A glass? Well we could, but it makes more sense to have the bottle . . .'

For this book – thank you to my daughter Zelda for information on fabulous outdoor-based and alternative early years education. If only every child could experience this kind of school: www.zeldaschool.co.uk

Thanks also to the patient and helpful Kiran Johnson at Richmond-upon-Thames register office for answering my questions about getting married on Christmas Day.

And as always, love and thanks to my writer mates: for the mutual encouragement, listening to each other's grumbles, proper laughter and huge fun. You know who you are.

ONE

August

There are some phrases, Thea considered, that immediately lift the spirits – 'More cake?' and 'It's my round' being two of them – while others tend to depress the mood every time you hear them. The dreaded 'Back to School' was definitely on her heart-sink list, especially after such a blissful summer. Each year the phrase (almost always spelled as 'Bak to Skool') turned up the minute the term finished in July and lurked like a nagging little background downer all through the holidays. Meanwhile, every shop that flogged uniforms cruelly reminded both pupils and teachers that the summer holidays pass far more quickly than the weeks of each term, and that you slack off and avoid the purchase of new grey socks at your peril.

Thea was lying in the sun's soft warmth on the pale, dry sand dune at the top of the beach, trying not to think about the next day's long drive back home to London from Cornwall. The last day of her holidays, last day – for a while, till they could grab a precious weekend – with Sean, was not to be wrecked by thinking ahead to autumn and the onset of winter's inevitable chill.

'All this glorious beach, pretty much all to ourselves. Isn't it just perfect?' Thea leaned on her elbow and turned to look at Sean, who was dozing on a red and white Liverpool FC towel alongside her.

'Mmm,' he murmured, briefly opening one eye and smiling at her, then returning to his snooze. Thea sat up properly and looked along the sand towards the far side where the ground started to rise up to the cliff top. A pair of walkers tramped in sturdy boots up the hill along the coast path and a wetsuited surfer clambered sure-footedly across the shoreline rocks, heading for the next bay to catch that ever-elusive better wave.

Today, now they were just past the August bank holiday, it felt to Thea as if half the world had vanished overnight. For several weeks, and until only a few days before, this beach below Cove Manor had been a busy, bright encampment of stripy windbreaks and lilos and gaudy towels spread on the sand. Families joined up together to play cricket. Frisbees were hurled about and small children dabbled in the rock pools with nets, catching tiny creatures in buckets and racing to show their parents what they'd found. Older children shrieked in the sea, whooshing up the surf on body boards and tumbling into the water. Even on the inevitable cold, damp days that any British summer has, there'd been many stalwart sorts huddled in cagoules against the rocks with flasks of warming tea, determinedly getting the most from their precious time off. Now, apart from a few scattered groups revelling in the luxury of so much deserted space, all was quiet. Where the tide had gone out and left the sand dark-glistening and wet, there were no footprints, no half-built castles waiting for the waves to demolish them. All school-age infants had been scooped up and taken home. Right now their poor parents probably had them queuing for pre-school haircuts or were stressing over shoes that weren't stocked in *that* width because 'there's no demand'.

Sean sat up and put his hand on Thea's bare shoulder. It felt cool on her sun-warmed skin.

'It's that great annual moment of peace,' he said. 'The fabulous end-of-August exodus. Even though the holidaymakers earn me my keep, it's wonderful when they've all gone.'

Thea looked at him. 'But soon I'll be gone too. It's back-to-school time for me as well as the children. I should be there now really, getting the classroom set up and making a start on the new term's endless admin.'

So much for avoiding the subject. She hoped she didn't sound whiny. She didn't feel it, just a bit wistful. It had been so much fun, such a huge delight to be living for the whole seven weeks' school break with Sean (and his Siamese cat Woody) in the converted stable block beside Cove Manor, playing at being properly domestic without having to rush back after their usual too-brief weekends together. She'd been able to unpack properly, claim wardrobe space. They'd relaxed into simply existing, had cooked non-special-occasion food rather than trying to impress each other as they tended to during their more usual rushed time together. She'd got to know people in the village and made a couple of friends to hang out with when Sean was working. As owner and landlord of the beautiful Cove Manor, a luxury, top-of-the-range, eight-bedroom holiday rental, he had to be on call for anything the clients might need. Thea and her parents, brother and sister and their families had been the first people to rent it the previous Christmas after Sean and his business partner, Paul, had renovated it. They had been able to do a stunning job, thanks to its hugely profitable appeal as a film location. She remembered being rather startled when Sean told her that the house was much in demand for erotica on the basis that, 'The muckier the movie, the classier they want the set.'

Sean pulled her close to him. 'Ah yes – this year there's the gigantic downside to September. My woman done left me . . . I should write a song.'

'Actually, I think you'll find that one's been done,' she said, laughing in spite of the gloom starting to creep up on her as the reality of returning to what she thought of as Real Life took its place in her head. It had made her start to fret about things she might have forgotten to do, but she mentally instructed such thoughts to bugger off, along with the melancholy at the thought of separation from Sean. There was the phone, there were emails, Skype, weekends and half-term: it wasn't as if they really had to be apart *that* much. All the same, mostly she'd be waking up alone in the mornings, coming home after a day's teaching to her cute but empty little house in south-west London. At the moment, much as she'd always loved it, its best quality was definitely its closeness to the M3 and the road to Sean.

'No, really, I'll miss you so much. It's been brilliant having you here all this time, the best-ever treat. Just give me a while to deal with the last of the paying punters and I'll come up to your place for a few days. We got through the last couple of terms OK on long-distance love; we'll get through the next one.'

'I know, I know. Can't have it all and all that.'

'Now that *was* a great song, "Long-distance love",' Sean said. 'And back when that came out, keeping it all going over a distance was all about payphones and letters. They sure had something to grumble about then.'

'And long distance to an American wouldn't mean a mere hop of under three hundred miles.'

'Exactly.' Sean kissed her. 'It'll be fine. And then in a blink or two it'll be—'

'Ah, no, don't!' Thea warned, putting a hand over his mouth before he could say any more. 'Don't mention the X-word! Not before the first of December.'

'The X-word? Do you mean Christmas?' Too late, the dreaded word was out.

'Aaaagh!' Thea put her hands over her ears. 'No, not yet!' Even though that season now had a special place in her heart since that was when she'd met Sean, Thea couldn't be doing with the long, long run-up. It seemed to start earlier each year.

'But that's what autumn is really, isn't it? The great commercial run-up to . . . er . . . the X-word.'

'If I had my way, all mention of it would be banned till after the fifth of November at the very earliest. Or – at a pinch – after Halloween,' Thea told him firmly. 'It should be an actual *law*. And in the same legislation I'd also outlaw any talk of going back to school after summer till at least halfway through the last week of August and any features about getting that "essential" bikini body before . . . Well, no mention at all. They should just be off limits for ever. Who needs it?'

'You certainly don't. You can't improve on perfect.' Sean ran his fingers down her spine. His touch on her skin never felt anything less than thrilling. In fact not even just touch: his smile across a room full of people could light her day.

'I should say something like "Yuck, that's too cheesy" but actually just thank you,' she said. She was surprised to feel a bit tearful suddenly. She stared out to sea, blurrily watching two surfers lying on boards, waiting to catch the next promising wave. The sea was too flat today for good surfing but some, as Sean did, went into the water daily as if to check on the sea's mood. He'd been out there that morning, early. Thea liked to sit on the headland in front of Cove Manor, watching with the day's first mug of tea, as he jogged down the sand with his board before doing a few warm-up stretches and then racing to the water and plunging into the waves. After he came out he'd shake his head like a dog and his longish sun-streaky hair would dry in spiralled tendrils that were slightly salt-scented, even after a shower. 'I can't *not* surf,' he'd told her once back in January, soon after they'd first got together last Christmas, when she'd questioned whether it was too crazily cold to be clambering out of a warm bed to put on a wetsuit and head for the freezing sea. It was as if she'd asked him if he'd considered taking a break from breathing. When he'd been up to London to stay with her, she'd sometimes caught him looking at the sky, noting the direction of the scuttering clouds, as if thinking about how good or otherwise the faraway surf would be that day. It wasn't surprising, she supposed. For years he'd been one of the world's top surfers, spending much of the year competing all over the globe. If you cut him, he'd probably bleed salt water.

This time last year, she'd thought, as she lay back down on the sand, life couldn't get much worse. The baby she'd been delightedly surprised to be expecting had given up on her at only twelve weeks of pregnancy and she'd been distraught at the loss. Then shortly after, Rich, her fiancé of ten months, had packed up his possessions and his poodle and left. So much grief had clouded the months following all that. And yet now . . .

'What are you thinking about?' Sean's shadow fell across her face and she opened her eyes. He leaned down and kissed her. 'You look miles away.'

'I was just thinking about how awful last summer was and how brilliant this one has been. I'd never have imagined this could happen.'

'That you'd hook up with someone as gorgeous and wonderful as me?'

'Ha! Well, I'd say yes but it might go to your head a bit. Can't be having that. You already know how gorgeous I think you are.'

'It's not over yet, you know.'

'The summer? Well, it is nearly. I'll be up to here in bookbags and the shiny faces of thirty little seven-year-olds next Tuesday.'

'Nativity plays before you know it. Shepherd outfits, Wise Men, all that.'

'You're doing it again – that was *this* close to the X-word.' She prodded him in the ribs, feeling bone beneath her fingers.

'What you need is something about the X-word that you can look forward to, so instead of it all being four months of annoyance, you can celebrate it and get all excited about it.'

'Don't you have to be about ten to feel that way? All geed up about a new bike?' Thea knew she was being a bit of a grump but couldn't help it. The thought of those giant swaying inflatable Santas in the shopping mall greeting her with 'Ho ho *ho*!' for weeks on end was just that little bit too grim. A week or two of Christmas was a lovely and exciting time. Several months of relentless glitter and tat, less so.

'Maybe you could get excited about a Christmas wedding,' Sean said, rather quietly.

She sat up again quickly. He wasn't looking at her, he was staring out to sea. His hands were fidgeting with strands of the tough marram grass that grew on the dunes.

'What do you mean? Is there a wedding party booked into the manor for Christmas?'

He shrugged. 'Not yet. But, y'know, there could be.' He turned and smiled at her, looking slightly scared. 'It could be . . . maybe . . . ours?'

Thea didn't say anything for a moment. She could feel her heart beating faster. 'Oh. Er . . . are you . . .

um . . . ?' Had she just heard what she thought she had?

'I'm asking you if you'd marry me, Thea, yes.' He was concentrating on plaiting the strands of grass now, avoiding her gaze. His obvious nervousness was so endearing, she thought. She put her hand on his wrist. His pulse throbbed under her touch.

'Yes,' she said.

'Yes as in you realize what I'm asking, or yes as in the answer is yes?'

'Answer is yes. Yes, I'd love to marry you.' She leaned forward and kissed him lightly.

'What, really? Sure?' He laughed and hugged her to him.

'I am sure. I'm saying yes.' She hadn't had to think about it, not for a second, because there was absolutely no doubt: Sean was her soulmate, the for-ever one. It wasn't like last time when she had taken a few days, thinking about whether to say yes to Rich's proposal those couple of years ago, and it was her mother who'd told her that if you had to think about it, that should tell you the answer was absolutely a big fat 'no'. She should have listened. At the time, since Rich had been living in her little house for a while, it had seemed a fairly logical next step. It was only after he'd left her and she'd started to recover during last Christmas here at Cove Manor with her family, that she'd finally twigged that 'logical next step' was a hugely inadequate reason for signing up in front of witnesses for a whole life with someone.

Sean looked at her, his eyes gleaming. 'Wow, that was *way* easier than I thought it would be!'

'Did you think for even a minute that I'd say no?' she asked.

'I don't know! It's not something I've ever asked anyone before. I didn't know how it would go because I didn't even think of asking the question till just now. It just seemed . . . a moment. The right one. I haven't got you a ring or anything.' Both of them were laughing: the moment seemed so madly unexpected and wonderful. Thea looked at the beach, the sea, the sky, taking it all in so she could keep this perfect moment for ever. Who needed a ring?

Thea had had a ring before. A big fat diamond one that Rich had been so proud to tell her he'd bought at a bargain price at an upmarket shopping arcade frequented by cruise-ship passengers while they were on a low-season cut-rate holiday in Barbados. 'They were practically giving them away,' he'd said, as if that were its greatest charm. Nice. She'd given it back to him on the day he left. No doubt, in the same spirit of thrift, he'd one day give it to someone else and tell the girl how lucky she was that he'd kept it on the off chance rather than selling it on eBay and blowing the cash on a mini-break to Vegas.

'I don't need a ring,' Thea said. 'I don't need anything.

Just you. And you know what? Suddenly, I'm quite looking forward to Christmas this year. And *that's* something I never thought I'd be saying when it's not even September till next week.'

Sean took her left hand and looped the plaited grass over her third finger. 'I guess this will fade and fall to bits but with luck, we won't,' he told her. 'And before you say anything, I already know – that really *is* cheesy.'

TWO

The estate agent was bang on time. She'd rung the bell but followed up with a light rap on the knocker as well, probably well used to slack home-owners whose bells had given up the ghost. Anna, having had a quick shufti from behind the purple velvet curtain at the sitting-room window, was surprised to see how young the woman was, and wondered how both she and the agency she worked for had considered it safe for her to come to do this valuation on her own. You couldn't be too careful, could you? After all, how could she have known she was coming to the home of a pair of safe pension-age rockers where the only danger was having her ears blasted by Led Zeppelin being played at volume 11. She and Mike could have been anyone. She was so punctual that Anna reckoned she had probably been sitting in the car outside the house for a good ten minutes; that way she could show how reliable and on the ball the company was by not being a second early or late. Good ruse – after all, this area, Barnes in south-west London, was up to its roofs in estate agents; those, chic restaurants and artisan bakers. You had to keep standards up or sink under the hurtling competition.

'She's here! We're on!' Anna called to Mike, who was in the wicker peacock chair in the kitchen holding his guitar, looking as if he didn't quite know what to do with himself. He already seemed to be wilting slightly under the threat of the intense scrutiny he (or rather his home) was in for in the next hour. He was clearly taking this visit as an invasion and Anna wanted to give him a bit of a kick to perk him up. He was making the place look untidy and she suspected untidy didn't go down well when a house was being valued. Anyone could see it was a bit tatty (or would the term be 'well loved'? It had certainly been that) around the edges without Mike adding to the atmosphere.

'Mike, get it together, man, or she'll knock off a few grand for lack of smiles,' she said to him and went to open the door.

'Hello!' Anna was conscious that she sounded falsely thrilled. The beam she'd put on her face as she greeted the girl felt forced. Why was she so nervous? After all, this agent was going to be very well paid when (if) a sale went through. And it wasn't a commitment, not at this stage, only a preliminary what-if.

'Hello! I'm Belinda.' The girl held out a slim, pale hand. A couple of silver rings glinted, her nail varnish was a safe mid-pink and she was wearing the kind of office uniform of black trousers and jacket that was probably meant to look reassuringly professional. Like a banker, Anna thought as she ushered the girl into her hallway. That kind of corporate thing was another world to Anna, who was from the realm of art and sculpture and dressing as she pleased. How weird it must be to have to wear heels and full-scale make-up and something safe and dark every day but never colourful layers and shoes that didn't look as if they hurt.

'Would you like tea?' Anna offered as they reached the kitchen. She felt twitchy, even though she needn't, yet considering whether to sell a house you'd lived in for over forty years was a massive decision. Would the sitting room have been a better place to take this Belinda? It was big and light, had plenty of sofa space if a long sit-down preamble to the viewing was needed, and was as tidy and clutter-free as she could manage. Mike's paintings of exuberant nudes on the walls might be a bit daunting for her but there were other things she could look at: big old patchwork cushions, lots of colourful throws and the vast Moroccan rag rug in multitudinous shades of turquoise. On the other hand, the kitchen had useful distracting gadgets that would need dealing with while they got to know each other. Nerve-wise she sympathized with Mike, who had put his guitar down and was making a bit of an unnecessary palaver about getting out of his chair. Was he playing at being an old man or something? He wasn't quite seventy yet, not nearing ninety, and he had plenty of energy in him. He shook hands with Belinda and gave her a half-smile.

'Regular, camomile, jasmine or mint?' Anna said, opening a cupboard and checking what she'd got.

Belinda said, 'Oh – er, camomile would be . . . um . . . Well, I'm not sure. I've never had it. It sounds nice. I like to try new things.'

'It smells of cat piss,' Mike warned her with a sideways grin as he filled the kettle.

'Mike . . .' Anna gave him a look.

'Well it does. *And* it tastes of old hippies.' He was smiling but Anna saw a puzzled expression on the girl's face. Maybe she didn't know what an old hippie was. It was quite likely – she looked about seventeen (though surely couldn't be) and her voice was direct from the safe calm world of private school, ponies and violin lessons. Either way, Anna would bet the value of this house that she wouldn't know what a hippie tasted like.

'Take no notice of him, he's just winding you up,' Anna said, wishing the agent could go outside then come back in and they could all start again.

'Could I change my mind about the tea?' Belinda said. 'I'm actually fine, thanks. We are told to say yes even if we don't want one because it gives the home-owners something to do and we get to check out the kitchen. You can tell almost all you need to know about a house's value from the kitchen. Oh . . .'

'What's the matter?' Mike asked as Belinda faltered over her words. 'Do the pink kitchen units confuse the price issue? It was all done back in the days of fancy paint effect. The distressed look was very chic then. Not that we distressed it, I mean. The growing family managed that by themselves. Or are the walls and ceiling a problem? I was rather proud of my wispy clouds on a blue sky effect. You dab the colour on with a J-cloth and smudge it.'

Anna looked at him, willing him to stop. He was rambling and would unsettle the poor girl even more.

'No, no, that's er . . . lovely. And unusual. It's just that I'm not supposed to say things like that,' she admitted. 'It's not very professional of me. I do tend to *blurt*.' She smiled at him and bit her lip. Anna felt annoyed, recognizing a gesture that was meant to look charming and a bit helpless. It probably got results with most of the men it was aimed at. Belinda's pretty fingers tugged at the end of her long blond single plait. She was *that* close, Anna reckoned, to putting it in her mouth and giving it a childlike chew.

'Orange squash?' Anna offered.

'No, no, really, I'm fine. I don't need anything.'

Anna poured herself a glass of water, put it on the table and they all sat down. She was conscious that the surface of it was covered with old pale rings from years of mugs of tea carelessly placed. The table would be going with her and Mike when (if) they moved but did that kind of thing get noticed by those valuing a house? Belinda eyed the plate of Bourbon biscuits Anna had put out but didn't take one.

'So,' Belinda said, putting her iPad in front of her and switching it on. 'I understand you're downsizing?'

'Er . . . sort of. Possibly,' Anna told her. 'We haven't quite decided yet what we're going to do, but we do need to move. This place is far too big and keeping it going just for the two of us is an expense we could do without, frankly, now we aren't working so much.' The family weren't any good at helping them decide either, though Belinda didn't need to know the ins and outs of that. Emily had cried (she'd always been a crier, but was even worse now, being hugely pregnant) and told them they couldn't possibly sell her childhood home. Jimi had said it was a terrific idea – the place was way too big and they were being the household equivalent of hospital bed-blockers. As for Thea, well, they'd got no sense out of Thea since Christmas when she'd paired up with Sean and started to spend every other minute on the A303 whizzing up and down from Cornwall. Anna and Mike could tell her they were re-locating to Mars and she'd probably just smile and say, 'Great, fine.'

'The idea is to find out what we've got available,

money-wise, if we decide to sell up. Then we'll know what we've got to play with and we can think about options,' Mike said.

'I expect you're thinking of something like sheltered housing? My gran has just moved into a lovely place. Very safe and caring,' Belinda said to Anna in a low tone, surprising her by reaching across the table and gently taking hold of her wrist.

'Fuck, no!' Mike spluttered. 'How old do you think we are?'

'About the same age as Belinda's gran, I expect,' Anna told him. 'We probably are.'

'Only if she was a child bride,' he argued, then turned to Belinda. 'I share a birthday with Keith Richards. Though a few years later.'

She looked a bit blank.

'Guitarist? Rolling Stones? You must have heard that saying: when the world ends, the only survivors will be cockroaches and Keith Richards? I intend to cash in on the birthday connection and claim shared immortality.'

Belinda giggled and swiftly removed her hand from Anna's. 'My gran says the Beatles were better. Oops, sorry!'

'What I'm trying to say' – Mike's tone was softer now – 'and I'm sorry if I overreacted there, is that where we're going isn't relevant at the moment. We haven't decided yet. Could be Wales, could be West Wittering, could be Willesden. Don't know.'

'I'm ruling out Willesden,' Anna said. 'And possibly West Wittering. Isn't it all yachties in blazers? Not really our bag.'

'Just the valuation then,' Belinda said, tapping out a note on the iPad with the end of her nail. 'Though we do have some good listings for retirement . . . No, OK. So – um . . . shall I just wander round or would you prefer to come with me and show me over the premises?'

It felt so impersonal, having the home where they'd lived for over four decades, where they'd raised three children in a warm tumble of domestic chaos, described as 'premises'. Mike was being no help, rabbiting on about totally irrelevant things. He was now staring out of the French doors, focused on a fat magpie gorging itself on the contents of the bird feeder hanging from the apple tree. Anna had planted that tree shortly after Jimi was born. There'd been a plum tree at Thea's birth, a pear for Emily. And then there were the younger trees for the first three grandchildren. Emily's new baby was due in a couple of weeks – if they really were selling up, would it be worth continuing the tradition here and putting in a little quince after it was born? Or should they do that at the new place? If it had a garden, that is. Suppose they opted for a flashy flat with a swanky terrace instead? Would a quince thrive in a big pot?

'I think I'll come too,' Anna said, deciding that if this girl was going to be raising her prettily arched eyebrows at the undersea mural (complete with full-breasted mermaid) she had painted in the second bathroom and the embroidered crushed-velvet patchwork curtains which were getting a bit shredded but were still so beautiful, then she'd rather be there to see it and to defend her home instead of imagining the worst from downstairs.

'I'll just have a quick look to start with,' Belinda explained as she made a couple more notes on her iPad about the kitchen, 'and any measuring and so on will come later if you decide you really do want to sell. Today, I'll be able to come up with a very rough ball-park figure but I'll have to go back to the office and let you know from there, officially. Property round here is in huge demand,' she continued as they made a start in the sitting room. 'A double-fronted place like this doesn't come on the market very often, especially not one with a view over the playing fields. Nice big back garden, perfect for a young family.'

'Could a young family possibly afford it?' Anna asked, genuinely curious. She had a very vague idea of local property values. This corner of London had always been expensive. The house had previously belonged to Mike's parents and no way could he and Anna have afforded to buy it, even all those years ago.

'You'd be surprised.' Belinda continued to make notes as she prodded at Anna's terracotta-painted wall of built-in bookshelves. 'The area has a lot of media people, a lot of bankers. They're all the ones who want easy access to central London and as much green open space as possible. It's all here.' She flicked at the curtains, checking how far the old double doors to the garden went back, and she pulled up the rug to look at the broad oak floorboards beneath. 'Nice,' she commented but said little else and Anna could only guess at what she'd written on her iPad.

'There's lots of potential with a house like this,' she announced as they went up the stairs to inspect the bedrooms. She looked pleased by the scale of the rooms but grimaced at the emerald-green fittings in the second bathroom. Anna was glad Belinda managed to control her self-confessed tendency to blurt: the bath and basin had been a fabulous find, from the 1930s with art deco squared-off corners; she and Mike had been so delighted to get them.

'Terrific!' she exclaimed, looking at the ornate coving in the second of the two back bedrooms. 'You see, we emphasize the wealth of original features but the buyers like to know there's room for making their own mark. There are walls that can come down and space to extend the kitchen way out into the garden. The attic is ripe for conversion and this little space here' – Belinda opened a door and peered into the room where Anna put anything that needed ironing and then removed it when it had been there long enough to flatten itself under the heap – 'this could make a lovely ensuite wet room . . . just about, with a knock-through to the next room.'

Anna felt sorry for her house. If it were a person, it would be crying out for a reassuring hug by now. It must be like sitting in front of a famous cosmetic surgeon having your face tweaked this way and that as the face-changer to the stars decided that you were way too old and baggy to continue to present yourself to the wider world – and that, unless you accepted his offer to charge you a million dollars to be fixed, you should consider a life under a big balaclava.

'It's always worked fine for us as it is,' she said, by way of defence.

Belinda laughed. 'Oh, but the kind of family who'd afford this would want to *extend*. Everyone does. Ideally, they'll want a separate floor for the children, and of course proper live-in accommodation for a nanny. That, at a push, could go over the garage. And there's space at the end of the garden, if you knock down that big tatty old hut, space for a good-sized home office, which is so much a *thing*. Oh yes, I am certain this house will go for a jolly good sum.' Anna noted that she actually licked her lips as she wrote down another note on her iPad and the two of them went back to the kitchen. Mike wasn't there. Anna wondered if it was worth telling Belinda that he was probably in the 'tatty old hut' that had worked so brilliantly as their joint painting studio for the past forty years. Belinda had probably had posters on her wall at university that they'd designed. But it was true the hut was mostly held together by a crust of old oil paint and might well fall down with a good push. She thought of what could replace it: a stylish pod structure maybe, or a chichi shepherd's hut, decked out in Cath Kidston and bunting? Perhaps a small wooden pavilion with a verandah, which wouldn't look out of place on a village cricket green? She'd quite like one of those.

'So.' Belinda tip-tapped again on her iPad. 'I can tell you now, very rough ball-park-wise, that – given the fact so much *work* would be needed – I'm afraid we're actually looking at rather under the magic *three*. And also, timing . . . A lot of people are keen to get moving between now and Christmas. So, how soon would you want to move?' she asked.

'Er, not sure. And what do you mean, "just under the three"? Three what?'

'Oh, three mill. Million,' Belinda said breezily. 'Two point nine five, for asking, I'd say, though I'd have to confirm and you might have to be flexible on the final . . . Are you OK?'

Anna had sat down heavily in Mike's peacock chair. She pulled at a bit of loose wicker. So it looked like they were really going to move. They would be able to afford somewhere cheaper and smaller but still lovely and have plenty of 'change'. Like most artists, they hadn't managed to equip themselves with fancy pension schemes so the house would have to provide it. And oh, what a wrench it would be, how much clearing and sorting – and then the finding somewhere else. It was going to be a massive upheaval. But it was time. She was still in terrific energetic health but her sixty-eighth birthday wasn't far off and she'd quite like somewhere to live that was easier to care for. Five bedrooms, three bathrooms and a massive garden were far more than two people could possibly need and the expense of keeping it all going – the council tax, the ongoing maintenance – it was all becoming way too much.

'Um, I think so,' she said. 'Just a bit surprised, that's all.'

Belinda looked worried, clearly nervous that she'd got a potential fainting on her hands.

'Is it a disappointment?' she murmured, eyeing the kettle. 'I'm so sorry . . .' The slim hand was back on Anna's wrist. Anna let it stay there this time.

'No. Good grief no. It's not a disappointment. Not at all.'

THREE

They weren't real contractions, just the Braxton Hicks sort that nature sends to give you a rough idea of what to expect. Emily was certain of this because the baby wouldn't be born for another eight days, on a Friday, preferably early in the evening when Thea would be home from work and could collect Milly and Alfie and take them to hers for the weekend. That way Sam wouldn't have to worry about them and could immerse himself in the birth experience. He'd been drunk when Milly was born and had sneaked out for a quick cigarette just in time to miss Alfie's arrival, but this time she was determined he'd be there, doing back-rubbing and forehead-moistening and being the one who cut the cord, like a proper hands-on father.

She'd written the due date in pen in her diary: 5 September, and there'd never been anything in that diary in ink that didn't happen as and when it was supposed to – and thank goodness for that. Emily needed precision in her world because without it, all would free-fall into chaos. You couldn't run a home, two (soon three) young children and an accountancy practice on vagueness. If she wanted vague and un-reliable she'd got Sam for the role and, since she'd reluctantly started her maternity leave two weeks before, she'd been appalled at how much he left to chance, domestically speaking. Why, for one thing, did he do the food shopping so haphazardly, lugging home bags of random items on the way from collecting the children from their various summer activities? It was terrifying knowing this didn't leave him both hands free to steer them safely across the road – in fact, she could make a case for that being actually illegal. If it wasn't, it should be. After all, you couldn't trust two under-eights with micro-scooters to wait for the green man at the lights, still less anticipate the murderous idiot who's gone hurtling through on red. Also, she'd so often suggested planning the week's menus in advance so he could order online and not have to keep popping up to Waitrose, but no. He claimed it gave him 'thinking time' and that he couldn't bang out his humorous column for the biggest-selling Sunday newspaper on being a feckless father *every single week* if he never left his writing hut. That was the trouble with him being a journalist – he could find an excuse for anything, in the interests of 'research'. 'Besides,' he'd over-argued, 'Milly and Alfie have to learn that food doesn't just come in boxes from a delivery van. They need to see shelves being stacked, money changing hands, pleasantries exchanged. They must experience the joys of handling fruit, learning what's in season and so on.'

Her response (that Waitrose was a long way from being a jolly French *marché*, that availability of mange-tout from Peru in November was not exactly 'seasonal' and that the only likely pleasantries were a curt 'Do you need a bag?' followed by a 'No, thanks') seemed to make her – as too often – sound peevish and controlling. She didn't mean to; she just didn't see why everything couldn't be properly organized.

Emily leaned back on the sofa and put her hand on her stomach, feeling the muscles grow hard and the taut-stretched skin tighten. Definitely Braxton Hicks. Just a practice run for her muscles but all the same she was glad she'd thought to put the big stripy throw across the seat cushions. These contractions had been coming and going all morning and she was sens-ing that a bit of leakage might be going on. Nothing to worry about, just a *feeling*.

'Helloooo! Anyone home?'

Emily sat up abruptly, startled. That bloody Charlotte. Why did she always turn up by way of the kitchen and never just ring the front doorbell like a proper visitor? Since she'd turned up in Cornwall the previous Christmas as 'a friend' of Emily's father, and then been unable to leave because of the endless snow, she'd almost made herself an extra family member. She reminded Emily of a cat that has several owners and makes itself at home with all of them.

Awkwardly, she hauled herself off the sofa and went through to the kitchen, conscious she was actually waddling like a comedy pregnant woman, hand on her aching back. Just you dare bloody laugh, Charlotte, she thought, seeing her waiting by the door. Just you dare.

'Hi, Emily! I just popped in to see '

'Sam's not here.' Emily stood aside as Charlotte, not to be put off, clattered in past her with a selection of carrier bags, which she dropped on to the table. A couple of cans of lager spilled out and Emily caught them as they rolled to the edge. 'He can't come out to play with you because he's taken the children for a playdate with one of Milly's friends.'

'Oh, that's all right,' Charlotte said, unabashed by Emily's lack of welcome. 'I'm not just *his* friend you know. I'm a whole-family bargain bucket, me.' She laughed, but Emily didn't. Charlotte glanced at her distended front, 'God, look at you, you poor sod. No wonder you've got a face like a slapped arse. You're about ready to burst. Sit down, I'll make us a pot of tea. Shame you're not allowed anything stronger; you look like you could murder a glass of medicinal Merlot.'

She practically pushed Emily into a chair and started bustling round the kitchen. Emily told herself to loosen up – Charlotte was only being kind. But seeing her making free with her kitchen, opening and closing her cupboards, being familiar with where everything was, made it clear how often she'd been here in the house just hanging out, laughing, smoking in the garden, having lunchtime beers with Sam while she – Emily – had been up to her eyes in other people's tax returns and phone calls to HMRC. She loved her job, loved figures and finance and putting everyone else's fiscal houses in order, but she didn't do it so Sam could slack about at home with his father-in-law's ex-mistress.

'So you've finished with work then? Are you taking the whole year off or splitting it with Sam?' Charlotte asked as she plonked one of Emily's favourite mugs in front of her. A couple of drops spilled over the side. Emily scooped them up with her finger and licked it.

'Sam's always here anyway, so I suppose I *could* take the whole of it,' she told her. 'But I'm not sure I want to stay away from the office for that long.'

'You don't sound keen. I'd love it, all these children. You're so lucky.'

'I know, I know,' Emily said, rubbing her aching back. 'But I hate being away from work. Things might go wrong. Bad habits set in, you know?' She probably didn't, Emily thought. Charlotte was a self-confessed free spirit, late forties, blowsy, cheery and unsettled, lurching from singing gigs in anything from run-down clubs to quite prestigious theatre shows as and when she could get the work. *Not* having regular work didn't seem to bother her at all, whereas it would send Emily thoroughly frantic with terror. Look how she'd been last December, sacked from the pantomime in Plymouth she'd been booked for, only days before Christmas. Did it bother her? Not at all.

'Chill, Ems,' Charlotte said, scrabbling about in one of her shopping bags (not from a supermarket Emily would visit) and pulling out a pack of chocolate biscuits. She opened it with her teeth and offered the pack to Emily, who took one and nibbled the chocolate round the edge of it. Charlotte ate hers fast in two greedy bites. 'No lunch today,' she explained, spluttering a few crumbs on to the table. 'I'm on the 5:2 diet so I'm having five biscuits at a hundred calories each. If you've got to do near-starvation you might as well do it with stuff you love.'

'Are you sure you've got the hang of it? It doesn't sound quite right,' Emily asked, still halfway through her own biscuit.

Charlotte reached for another and looked pensive. 'Well, whichever way you look at it, it's cutting down, isn't it? I could give up these or I could give up whatever else I'd eat. I've opted for sin over sense.' She grinned. 'No change there!'

Emily couldn't disagree. There was something about Charlotte's honest exuberance for life's indulgences that she almost – but not quite – envied. What must it be like to racket around doing whatever you pleased and

37

not worrying about whether you were secure or had a pension or even a home of your own? Charlotte lived in a tiny rented flat overlooking the District Line. Emily had once said to her that it must be horrendously noisy but Charlotte, forever seeing an upside, had simply said, 'Oh, but come on, who doesn't love a train?'

'So when's your loved-up sister getting back from the sticks?' Charlotte asked. Her hands were wrapped round her mug and Emily could see that her nail varnish was several different shades of pink. She must have come here this morning via the House of Fraser make-up department, Emily thought. She'd once said you could get a whole manicure free by asking the assistants at various counters if you could try out a colour and getting them to apply it. Last Christmas in Cornwall Charlotte had given Milly a full-scale manicure and the child had got a taste for it; she was forever pleading with Emily to let her have sparkly nails. Emily would know exactly whom to blame if Milly was sneaking mascara into school by the time she was eleven and dyeing her hair purple.

'Tomorrow, I think,' Emily said. 'School starts on Tuesday so Thea will need the weekend to get ready.'

'Will she?' Charlotte looked puzzled. 'I thought that with proper jobs like that you just rocked up at the right time and got on with it. Why does it take three days to decide what to wear?'

'Teachers don't just "rock up",' Emily said, taking

another biscuit. What the hell – how much more weight could she put on at this stage? 'They have to prepare lessons and so on.'

'Oh I know, I know. But it's a long time since mine was at school, I've more or less forgotten. He's in Australia now. I'm lucky if he Skypes. You don't get them for long.'

Emily felt her eyes starting to brim. The thought of life without Milly and Alfie, with them halfway across the world, rarely thinking of her, filled her with deep sorrow. It occurred to her she might well become one of those women who ends up with eight children, just because she couldn't bear to be without a baby in the house. That was a vision that didn't fit in with her job, her life plans or her preference for cream sofas. She hustled the very notion out of her brain before it took hold.

'Still,' Charlotte went on, seemingly oblivious, 'so long as he's happy. That's all you want for them, isn't it? I suppose he might be home for Christmas but probably not. On which note,' she said, getting up to switch the kettle on again, rinsing the mugs and finding more teabags, 'what are you all doing for it this year? Last year's was a hoot, wasn't it?' She gave a deep and dirty chuckle. 'I bet you didn't ever think you'd end up snowed in miles from anywhere not only with your family but with both your parents' lovers. Hee hee.'

'I don't think Alec actually was Mum's lover. Not

when he spent most of Christmas in bed with you.' This was something Emily definitely didn't want to think about. The very idea was absurd. She'd guess Alec had been only in his mid-forties or so and her mum was . . . well, she'd had a bus pass for a few years now.

'No, dear, of course he wasn't.' She winked at Emily. 'Ah, but your lovely dad and me though . . . till he got second thoughts. Still, I can't grudge him sticking with his own wife. I really like your mum – she's a bit special. Not a word of rancour towards me. It was a kind of honour to give Mike back to her.' She gazed out of the window and Emily felt yet another cramp across her middle. She really didn't want to discuss the complications of her parents' sex life, not now they'd managed to shake off their mid-life madness, change their minds about a possible divorce and restore themselves to being a perfectly normal (for that hippie generation anyway) semi-retired couple with possible house-selling projects and a future together to get on with. Whatever blips, lovers, deviations from the path they'd had last year (and frankly it had all been a bit too *Jeremy Kyle* at the time), it now seemed calm again; their proposed divorce, the bombshell that they'd dropped on the family the previous autumn, was now a notion in the past. That Christmas at Cove Manor, with Charlotte and Alec as the unexpected interlopers, was long behind them, never to be repeated, thank goodness.

'So you didn't say. What *are* you doing this year? Or is it too soon to have made plans?' Charlotte persisted.

'Oh, it's never too soon for plans, not for me. We'll be home, here,' Emily stated firmly. 'I don't want to travel anywhere. And Sam promised that whatever happens, we won't have to . . .' A repeat of last year was not to be thought of, she'd decided the moment they were on their way home from Cove Manor after the previous Christmas. Being snowed in so spectacularly had been appalling. Emily still had nightmares about it. When Milly had fallen off her new bike on Christmas morning, Emily had been frantic with terror that she might have broken a limb. How would they have got her to a hospital when no traffic could get through? The nearest one had been over twenty miles away. The isolation, the lack of control over where she was: it had tainted the whole holiday and she never wanted to go through that again. 'I want to be in my own bed on Christmas morning with my new baby and my children and Sam and have a tree with only *our* decorations on it and Sam cooking the turkey and—'

'Being at home sounds lovely,' Charlotte interrupted. Emily looked at her quickly, checking to see if she was teasing but she wasn't. She was smiling and looking soft and gentle. She was quite beautiful really, Emily thought, in a blowsy sort of way. She liked to show plenty of plump cleavage and had a very sparkly taste in earrings but she had an underlying grace and a natural sexiness that lean, clean and carefully smart Emily just never could achieve. No wonder all men liked her. She had wondered about Sam for a brief moment but dismissed the idea. He'd once said of Charlotte, with a journalist's casual cruelty, 'You never know where she's been.' She hoped that was enough for him to remember to keep his distance.

'So how about you?' Emily felt she should ask but she was slightly dreading hearing an answer that might upset her. Was loneliness a reason why Charlotte had kept so determinedly in touch with them? She hoped not. Charlotte was always out at night, singing in pubs, and recently there'd been a four-month stint in a musical, touring what she still called the provinces. It hadn't made it to the West End but as Charlotte had said, 'An audience is an audience and it's London's loss if they can't be arsed to go north of Watford.'

'Well, it looks like it'll either be *Cinderella* at Woking or *Babes in the Wood* at Richmond.' She got up to put the now-empty mugs in the dishwasher, and turned to grin at Emily. 'I'm a bit long in the tooth for a Babe, aren't I? So I'll probably be channelling Cinderella, one way or another. As per. No balls for me.' Then she rallied and laughed. 'Not the sort you dance at, anyway.'

FOUR

It was the last day of August, and luckily the day was a hot one: they could have lunch in the garden, as Thea's house was a bit small to accommodate a lot of people for a sit-down meal. More than six could be done but it was then a matter of people squeezing past each other, of her warning them – as if they were small children – that if they wanted the loo then please go before they sat down so as to avoid everyone having to shuffle chairs around to get out of the way later. She counted up on her fingers: Emily, Sam and the two little ones; Mum and Dad; her brother Jimi with Rosie (if she hadn't got one of her heads) with their son Elmo (age sixteen, taller by the day) and herself. That made ten.

As she prepared salads, Thea briefly wondered if this whole-family lunch would be better waiting till Sean could be there too so they could make their big announcement together, but he had various glitches and repairs to sort out at Cove Manor before the next lot of renters arrived, and, besides, this was *her* family. It was her job to tell them what was happening: she didn't really need back-up. Surely they couldn't be anything other than delighted for her and her news? Or would they think it a bit soon? She hoped not – after all, she was in her mid-thirties, not a ditzy young thing, and she knew her own mind. They already liked Sean, which was a big improvement on how they'd felt about Rich. Not that it was their fault; goodness knows they'd tried. Rich had been invited to lots of family lunches and birthdays and so on over the two years they'd been together. But he'd never really gelled with Mike and Anna and he hadn't had much to do with her brother or sister. He'd kept himself very much on the periphery at the very few gatherings that hadn't coincided with one of his dog shows or some essential visit to his poodle-breeder sister, who had seemed to loathe Thea from the start for distracting Rich from the dog-show circuit. It had been a lucky escape, she realized now: a hostile, jealous sister-in-law was never going to make for a lifetime of cheeriness.

Thea was putting the chicken pieces and their piquant sauce into the oven when the doorbell rang. The crinkly outline of Mrs Over-the-Road's pinky-white perm was visible through the opaque glass in the front door.

'Hello, June,' Thea greeted her. 'How are you? Have you had a good summer?'

'It's not over yet; September's always the best bit.'

June sniffed the air and gazed past her along the hall-way. 'So you're back then.'

'Er – yes. Since Friday,' Thea said. 'Are you coming in? Coffee?'

'No. I won't, thank you. I just wanted to . . . er . . . to let you know . . .' June glanced behind her as if expecting an attentive audience to be agog for secrets. She seemed very serious – this could only be momentous news.

Thea looked across the road, suddenly filled with a kind of dread. She hadn't seen Mr Over-the-Road since she got back and he must be pushing eighty. Was June about to tell her the worst? What had she missed around here over this long and lovely summer? But she could see their front door was open and June's husband Robbie emerged from behind their cotoneaster, brandishing shears and clip-clipping away to neaten it up for the autumn.

"That young man of yours,' June half-whispered as if the street were listening in. 'He was here. You weren't in.'

'Sean? No, it can't be him. He's down in Cornwall. Or he was when I spoke to him this morning.'

'No, not your *new* one.' June was bright-eyed with the thrill of imparting information. 'The *old* one. The one you didn't marry. Not that you've married this one either.' She had another sniff and her lips pursed as if she was stopping herself from coming out with, 'Back in *my* day . . .' and a lecture about being ladylike and waiting.

'What, Rich? Are you sure? I doubt it was him. I haven't seen him all this year. It must have been someone who looked a bit like him. Probably someone selling something.'

'People selling things don't usually look through the letter box and go round and try the side gate.' June smiled and, with an expression of maximum triumphant drama, delivered her killer line: 'Nor do they have a great big orange poodle with them.'

Soon after she had seen that Thea was satisfyingly astounded, June went back across the road. Thea returned to the kitchen to deal with potatoes and think about what her neighbour had told her. What on earth could Rich have wanted? They hadn't spoken since Christmas Day when he'd phoned while she was with her family at Cove Manor, not to wish her a happy Christmas or to share the sad memory that this was the date their ill-fated baby had been due, but to offer her a poodle puppy at half the usual price. All heart, that man. If she'd had any lingering doubts that she was well rid of him, that call had demolished them for good. It would be nice to see the dog again though. Benji had been far too big for this little house but she'd loved his company. He'd been a great lolloping heap of curly apricot fur, gentle, affectionate and blissfully warm to snuggle with on the sofa in winter. He'd also been a champion show dog, Rich's pride and joy, and his offspring would certainly be future stars at Crufts if Rich and his dog-breeder sister had anything to do with it.

'Hello – are we early?' Jimi came in through the back door carrying a bottle of wine, which he put straight into the fridge. 'I thought white wine, assuming we'd be in the garden. I don't know why food in the garden doesn't suit red but I can't get it out of my head that it just isn't right. Is that mad?'

'Probably. But I do agree. Anyway, we're having chicken and various salads, so I think white is a top choice. But there is red as well, in case.'

'Oh yes, there's Dad. I think he'd drink red with anything. Ice cream, soup, oysters, you name it.'

Thea laughed. 'You're not wrong there. Red wine and also Jack Daniel's. Is Rosie with you?'

'She is. She and Elmo are in the car having a difference of opinion over Elmo's jeans. Rosie has told him he shouldn't be showing the world what brand his underwear is and he is pulling a full-on teenage sulk. I'm leaving them to it and they can come in when they've agreed to differ. So,' he continued, helping himself to a stick of celery, 'good summer? You've got quite a tan.'

'It's been a great summer, thanks.' She smiled ridiculously broadly. She couldn't help herself – who knew you could be *this* happy?

'Oh, *that* good, was it? Ooh-er! You're looking great on it, whatever it is. And I think I have a good idea what "it" is.'

'Stop it! But thank you. And yes, it was wonderful to spend so long with Sean without having to rush back here for work and stuff. Shame it's over.' She chopped at a large handful of parsley, adding, 'For now, anyway.'

'Oh? "For now" sounds interesting. Or did you just mean you'll be back there for half-term?'

'Something like that, yes. Jimi? Can I tell you something?'

'Er, I dunno. Is it, you know, *girl* stuff? Because if it is . . .' He looked quite nervous and she laughed at him.

'No! Nothing serious. It's just Mrs Over-the-Road, June, she was here a few minutes ago and said that Rich had called by, looking for me. It was definitely him because he'd got Benji with him.'

'Great dog, shame about the bloke,' Jimi said.

'I don't suppose he phoned you or Mum or anyone, did he?' she asked, realizing immediately that it was probably a daft question. Rich had had little enough to do with them when they were together; he was hardly likely to start ringing round and asking after everyone's well-being at this point. Unless there was something he wanted.

'Me? I don't think he ever had my number, so no. Can't speak for Mum though. But wouldn't she have called and told you?'

'Not if he asked her not to.'

'Oh, I think she would. She'd probably tell him to piss off. She always knew where her loyalties lay when it came to Rich.'

That was true. Anna had been wary of Rich, and although when he'd left she'd been sympathetic and generous with the tissues to mop Thea's many tears, Thea couldn't help thinking at the time Anna was suppressing the urge to do a triumphant air-punch. The words 'I told you he wasn't a keeper' remained tactfully unsaid. That must count as quite an achievement for her.

'Didn't he leave a note or anything? You didn't miss a phone call?'

'No, nothing. It was only last week apparently. I'm wondering if he's still around.'

'Would you *want* to see him?'

Thea thought for a moment, standing by the sink with a pan full of potatoes ready to boil. 'I don't think so. There's nothing left to say. I wouldn't mind giving Benji a cuddle though. Of the two of them, he's the one I miss.'

'There you go then. Might as well forget about it.'

Emily was very quiet. Thea noticed that she didn't eat much but kept stroking her pregnancy bump and shifting about in her chair. She'd chosen the softest of the seats and she was in the shade but still looked hot and uncomfortable. It wasn't surprising, Thea supposed. This was what nine months pregnant looked like and it seemed as if it felt a lot worse. At least the children weren't playing up. For once, there were no arguments between them: Alfie and Milly were down on the swing quite amicably taking turns and not screaming at each other.

'Are you OK, Em?' she asked, pouring her some more water. 'Do you want to go inside and lie on the sofa for a bit? I could bring you some pudding. It's Eton mess.'

'No thanks, Tee. I'm fine. Just a bit achy. It's only a few days to go now. I hope you're ready for having the children to stay on Friday?'

'If it *is* Friday,' Anna said. 'Could be any minute, I'd say. You're looking pretty twitchy.'

'No, it'll be Friday. And even if for some crazy reason it isn't, it's got to be after today because it's not the first of September till tomorrow.'

'What's that got to do with it?' Mike asked. 'What have you got against August?'

'School year,' Sam told him. 'Em's determined this baby will be the oldest in its year, not the youngest. Me, I'm not bothered about that. It can come out as soon as it likes. It's been like sleeping next to a radiator – just what you don't need in a hot summer.'

'Well, you know what you should have done at the time, don't you?' Jimi said, laughing. 'But hey, it's a bit late now.'

'Jimi, shut up. Not in front of *children*.' Rosie nodded her head in the direction of Elmo, who put his hands over his ears and rolled his eyes skywards. 'Anyway,' she went on breezily. 'Er . . . this table is all very jolly and Cath Kidston, isn't it? Does nobody have matching crockery any more?'

'God, Mum,' Elmo groaned. 'You didn't need to change the subject quite so thuddingly.'

'I'm only saying. All these flowery cushions and the spotty tablecloth look gorgeous and festive and I love the pink and purple water glasses. But if you'd actually got married, Thea, like you were going to, you could have had proper matching plates and things too. The best thing about a wedding is the present list.'

'Oh, nice one, Mum, even better,' Elmo said, doing a sarcastic slow handclap.

'Yes, well done, Rosie. One of your better efforts,' Jimi said.

'Hey, it's OK, I don't mind,' Thea reassured them. 'I couldn't be happier, in spite of my tableware failure.' The moment was perfect. She must tell them *right now*, just as soon as she'd been inside and fetched the pudding. She got up and collected the last of the finished dishes together and carried them into the kitchen, took the big bowl (a car-boot sale oddment, blue with pink spots, probably not to Rosie's taste) out of the fridge and came back out only to find that Anna had decided it was a good moment to announce something too.

'OK, all of you,' she began once Thea had started passing the dishes of pudding along the table. 'I know we vaguely mentioned it last year but now we've decided it really is time to move. The house is way too big for us, far too expensive to run and we could do with an adventure and some travel. We'll have a bit of a look round, start thinking of what we'd like to do in the next however many years we've got left and when we find somewhere we like then we will sell the house.'

Thea mentally stashed her own announcement away for later. It could wait a little bit, even though she was dying to tell them.

'That's a bit sudden, isn't it?' Jimi said. 'What brought this on?'

'Well, it's not *that* sudden. We talked about it last year, first off. But what really brought it on was having it valued,' Mike said, helping himself to more of the creamy goo that was rapidly turning sloshy, even though Thea had kept it in the coldest part of the fridge for the last hour. Perhaps June Over-the-Road had been right and September was going to be glorious. She'd give a lot still to be in Cornwall with Sean and felt a little stab of missing him. He should be here, right now, sitting beside her with his hand resting on her thigh and warming her through her dress.

'Oh, you can't move away!' Emily's voice was close to a wail. 'What about us?'

'It's not that big a country, Emily,' Thea said. 'Look at

me and Sean. We manage to see each other absolutely loads. And they might not go far away anyhow. Could be just up the road if they find the right thing.'

'But they might go off to France or Ireland or something. People do, especially old hippies like them.'

Mike laughed. 'Not so much of the old, thank you!'

'Sorry, Dad, but you're not thirty any more, are you? And, Thea, you're single and only have yourself to think about. You can just fling a few things in a bag, get in the car and off you go without any hassle,' Emily told her. 'You try organizing a load of children for a trip. Even getting them into the car is a nightmare, let alone packing and sorting for them and all that.'

'Hey, calm down, Em, we haven't gone yet. It won't be a rush job. And of course it all hangs on someone liking it enough to part with the folding money we're after,' Mike told her. 'Great pud, Thea. In fact, lovely lunch all round.'

'Well, I'm glad it won't be a rush,' Emily said. 'Because with a new baby and these two, I don't want to go *anywhere* that isn't my own home for absolutely years.'

'Not even at Christmas?' Thea asked, feeling nervous. She could say it *now*.

'Christmas?' Emily managed to stretch the word over several octaves. 'Definitely *not* Christmas. *Especially* not Christmas! And anyway, why are you even mentioning it? It's months away. It's not like you. You only like last-minute talking about it.'

This was the moment, even though Emily had already taken her spanner out of the bag and shoved it firmly in the works.

'I'm talking about it now because . . .' Thea began, conscious that they were now all looking at her and sensing there was something big to report. She hesitated one more second, still wondering quite how to come out with her news and rather enjoying the suspense of the moment.

'Ooooooh!' Emily gasped. 'Oh bloody hell!' Everyone turned to look at her and she grinned.

'What is it? Emily, are you all right? Is it the baby?' Anna got up and rushed to her.

'I must apologize to Thea about this very pretty cushion I'm sitting on,' she said. 'It seems my waters have just broken and I've made it all soggy. Sorry to interrupt, Thea, but I seem to be in labour.'

FIVE

'The bag. Where's the stuff, Sam? And the birth plan – it's in the bag, which should be in the car boot. You did put it all in, didn't you? I did ask? At least three times?' Emily, who had sounded so laid-back about the waters and the cushion, had gone into instant organizing mode and was directing operations from Thea's garden bench, waving her arms around as if she were conducting the last night at the Proms.

'Everything's in the car.' Sam was calm and reassuring. 'Jimi's got the house key and he's going to pick up the children's overnight kit so they can stay here with Thea.'

'Yes, I'll be off there in the next half-hour,' Jimi said. 'Shouldn't you be on your way, Em? Maybe *go*?'

'Yes, do go, darling,' Anna chivvied her. 'Sam's phoned the hospital and they're ready for you.'

'It's OK. Whatever happens it can't be born till after midnight. It just *can't*.' Emily stayed where she was, seemingly in no rush to get going. Thea tried hard to assume that after two previous babies, Emily knew what she was doing, but there were a lot of long moments in which Emily did huffy breathing and the intervals didn't seem very far apart. Even she knew that meant something fairly momentous when it came to childbirth.

'The children's things are in another bag in the hall-way,' Emily, in one of the between-breathing breaks, told Jimi. 'Apart from Alfie's toy rabbit which is on his bed. He *must* have his rabbit.' She turned back to Sam. 'We should have brought *everything* with us this morn-ing, not just the hospital kit. Why didn't you just fling all their things in the boot as well as mine?'

Sam shrugged and took another sip of the coffee that Thea had brought out for them, along with more water for Emily. 'Because you insisted this baby wouldn't be born till Friday. I've thought all the time that seemed a bit late because I'm sure it was after that Halloween party at number fourteen—'

'Sam, please! Nobody here needs those kind of details! Owwwww!' Emily got up from the bench and leaned forward, gripping the edge of the table and doing slow, noisy breathing followed by a low, long groan.

'Why is she mooing? It's like the sound she made that time I saw her doing yoga out in her garden, but louder and worse,' Elmo murmured to Thea. He looked fright-ened. Thea was keen for Emily to go *now* – she wouldn't wish the possibility of giving birth in a lay-by beside the A4 on her or anyone. How fast could the arrival of a third baby be? You heard of people who took only half an hour and the baby was born on the kitchen floor. Perhaps this would be the day she found out what all the boiling of water, such a feature of any soap-opera birth, was for.

'It's a nature thing,' Thea explained, giving him as much of a hug as she trusted a boy of only just sixteen could tolerate from an aunt. He didn't squirm away. 'You have to breathe your way through the contractions. It's to make you relax.'

'She doesn't look relaxed.'

Thea couldn't argue with that. Emily, who had gone back for a refresher course of childbirth classes in the belief that something must have changed since she'd had Alfie six years before (she wasn't about to miss out on any innovations), was now letting her mouth hang loosely open. Her head was back and her eyes were closed. Anna went to put an arm round her for support but Emily wriggled free.

'Mummy?' Milly prodded her mother's arm. 'You look all funny. Are you going to die?'

'Definitely time to go.' Sam – at last – discovered a sense of urgency and gave Milly a hug. 'Be good for Thea and be nice to Alfie. We'll call as soon as we know whether you've got a baby brother or a sister. Emily? Come *on*. You can't have a baby on a damp lawn.'

Emily, who was now wearing a pair of Thea's leggings

and the baggiest long top Thea could find that would fit over the baby, waved a goodbye to them all and headed for the house, leaving behind a chorus of good-luck wishes. By the time she'd reached the front door she had to stop again for another session of mooing, this time while bracing herself against the post at the bottom of the stairs.

'I hope she makes it in time,' Anna said, looking anxiously after the two of them. 'Should you go too, Thea? Or maybe me or both of us? Suppose she ends up having it in the car?'

'Sam won't let that happen. He's very proud of those smart leather seats,' Mike said, chuckling.

'I can't go – I've got the children here for the night. Don't worry, Mum, she'll be fine. It's not far.'

Thea crossed her fingers in the hope that what she said was true. She felt excited for her sister but also tense. Although she'd watched several episodes of *One Born Every Minute*, she'd never actually seen anyone in labour in real life before and had been startled at how *earthy* Emily had suddenly become once nature took over during those contractions. Emily, who was normally quite prim and controlled, had turned positively animal. Thea felt a surge of hope and delight about the idea that one day she and Sean might have a baby of their own. They hadn't talked about it yet but she remembered that time on the beach last Christmas, before they'd properly got together, when he'd said that he'd like some children one day. Would he cope with seeing *her* like that? It didn't seem to bother Sam in the slightest; he'd been more concerned with borrowing a towel for his car seats.

Just before she, Elmo and Jimi left, Rosie helped Thea take the last of the dishes into the kitchen and loaded them into the dishwasher. 'I see Emily's managed to make this afternoon all about *her*, as usual,' she said. 'I mean, I don't want to be horrid about your sister but she is always a bit of a drama queen.'

'Well, she could hardly help the timing,' Thea said, resisting the urge to take over with the cutlery; she hated the knives being loaded blade-side up. She had visions of someone accidentally tripping and landing on one. Maybe she wasn't so unlike Emily after all.

'No. Well, that's true, I suppose. But whatever your news was going to be just faded into the background after the soggy-cushion event. I'm dying to know what it is. Is it hats or knitting?'

Thea laughed, trying to work out what she meant. 'Hats or knitting? Knitted hats?'

Rosie plonked a saucepan into the dishwasher. 'Oh, you know what I mean.' She stopped and had a quick look over her shoulder to check for anyone who'd overhear, then went on in a dramatic half-whisper, 'Is it something to congratulate you for? Hats for a wedding, knitting for a baby . . . Or . . .' She stopped suddenly. 'Sorry. Oh God, I'm being really tactless, aren't I? Suppose it's neither but you wanted both? Maybe you've been promoted to head teacher, or you were going to say you've won the lottery or something. Sorry, Thea, just delete everything I've said. I'm an idiot.' Rosie flapped a tea towel to cool her reddening face, and Thea was very tempted just to blurt out the wedding plans to her but managed not to. If she couldn't tell the whole family all at once then she really wanted her parents to know first and Rosie, as she'd just proved, was something of a blurter. She would never keep it in till Thea found the right moment for the rest of them. It would have to wait. Besides, with Emily having the baby, they'd all got plenty to think about. She and Sean would tell them together – he'd said he hoped to be up to visit her at the weekend.

'Rosie, really you haven't said anything idiotic, not even close. And what I was going to say, well, it can keep for another day.' She went to the fridge and took out a can of Coke. 'Here – go and give this to Elmo. He was looking a bit shell-shocked about Emily mooing. I expect he could do with something to cool him down.'

Rosie laughed. 'OK. Though I have to say it isn't such a bad thing for him to see. Now he's coming up to the age of . . . well, possibly getting it on with a girl, or at least considering it possible, perhaps he'll remember Emily going into labour and it'll make him think twice about taking daft risks. I've already bulk-bought condoms in case. Jimi says it'll only encourage him but

I remember teen boys. They don't need encouragement – their hormones do that for them. They just need practical solutions.'

Thea, thinking this was possibly too much information about her lovely nephew, took mugs of tea out to Mike and Anna, who were on the garden bench with the Sunday papers. Then she sploshed the remaining dishes about in the sink, and had a quick look out at where Milly and Alfie were lining up some snails they'd found and were trying to make them race across the terrace by waving lettuce leaves at them.

'Are you two OK out there? Do you need anything?'

'A biscuit?' Milly asked quickly.

Emily preferred them to have fruit rather than biscuits, Thea knew, but she was their aunt not their mother and, besides, she wanted them to be happy staying overnight with her so they'd want to come again. She wanted to have a baby of her own, but if – and she tried not to think like this, and the doctors had given her no reason to but occasionally it crept up – if that miscarriage had been only the first of several, then she'd want to be the best aunt she could be and at least have the delight of seeing (and helping as far as possible) her sister's and brother's children grow up.

'Jammie Dodgers?' Thea took the packet out of the cupboard and Milly and Alfie skipped into the room looking far more thrilled than ordinary biscuits deserved.

'Yeah! Wow!' Alfie gasped as if she'd offered him priceless truffles and an array of top-class pâtisserie.

'Mummy says biscuits will break all our teeth and they'll fall out and we'll have to eat with our gums and only have horrid soup for ever and ever,' Milly said, chomping into a biscuit. Thea felt a tiny moment of guilt. Perhaps she should have respected their mother's views and given them more strawberries instead. There were still some in the fridge so she took them out and put them on a plate with a couple more biscuits each. 'I'm sure that just for once your teeth will be safe. You can give them an extra good scrub at bedtime.'

'Will we have our new brother or sister before we go to sleep?' Alfie asked.

'I don't know, darling. I suppose you might. If it comes, your daddy is going to call to tell us.'

'Will the baby want a biscuit? Should we save one for it?' he went on.

'Don't be stupid.' Milly gave him a scornful look. 'Babies don't eat *biscuits*. They haven't grown any teeth yet. They just have juice and stuff.' She thought for a moment. 'They have milk. From *breasts*.' She looked down and pointed to her own chest.

'Ugh, that's *'gusting*,' Alfie spluttered.

The two of them went back outside to line up their snails again, leaving Thea strangely emotional at the thought of Alfie already wanting to include his as-yet-unborn sibling in the biscuit allocation. He was only just six and it seemed so sweet and automatically loving to accept – without question or jealousy or any sense of being displaced as the family baby – that there'd be someone else to consider. When her phone rang, she had to take a few seconds to blow her nose and wipe a silly tear away before answering.

'Did you tell them? What did they say?' Sean sounded anxious, excited to hear her family's reaction to their plans. Thea took her phone up to her bedroom and opened the window to let in the scent of the roses that were still blooming generously on her wall. A small chill breeze sneaked into the room, a reminder that although the day had been hot and sunny, autumn was out there, getting closer. It would be almost dark by eight too. In Cornwall, Sean would get half an hour longer of daylight but darker mornings. On some nights in early July, it had hardly seemed to get dark at all there.

'Sorry, Sean, I was desperate to but I didn't get a chance,' she told him. 'I was just starting to tell them, but then at the crucial moment Emily scuppered it by going into labour, so the moment passed and everyone was busy making sure she got off to the hospital OK. As a lead-up, I did slightly mention them all possibly going to Cornwall again at Christmas but Emily was definite that she wasn't planning on going anywhere but her own home and that she'd hated it last year so I feel a bit up in the air now. I expect it'll be OK. Somehow.'

'You want her to be here with us though, don't you?'

Thea felt a bit choked up all over again, 'Well, of course I do. How can I get married without my awful grumpy sister being there to be picky about what I'm wearing, about the venue, the flowers, to criticize my hair and so on?' She sniffed and reached for a tissue from the bedside table. 'Yes, I want her there. But I'm just being selfish. She's got more to think about right now than whether to buy a hat or not. I've got the children here for the night. Also Mum and Dad are still here being all nervy about Emily. We all are.'

'Of course you are. She's the priority right now – her and the baby. How's Sam?'

'Ha, Sam! He's being pretty cool about it all but in the end he hustled Emily off to the hospital as fast as he could.'

'I'll be able to come up next weekend. Maybe we can talk to them all then, together. Would that be OK?'

'Oh yes, way more than OK – brilliant! It's only been a couple of days but I miss you *so* damn much!'

'And I miss you too, Elf. Is it all right if I bring Woody? I could leave him at a cattery but I think he'd rather be with us.'

'Definitely. I can't wait to see him again.'

'More than me?'

'Of course. *Far* more than you!'

Once back in the kitchen Thea found Anna switching on the kettle for the third time that afternoon and rinsing out the mugs they'd been using.

'It doesn't matter how old you all get, it's the default setting of a parent never to stop worrying about their offspring.'

'You could have gone to the hospital with them,' Mike told her. 'Sam said he didn't mind. He even actually invited you.'

'*Sam* might not mind but I caught the look on Emily's face when he suggested it. And I can't say I blame her – I'd have hated my mother being in the room when I was giving birth. She'd probably have told me I was doing it all wrong.'

'You wouldn't do that with Emily,' Thea said. 'And you wouldn't have needed to go into the actual delivery room.'

'She'd have worried I could hear her. *I'd* have worried I could hear her. There's nothing worse than your child being in pain, even if they aren't far off forty. No, I'll wait it out. Shall I bath the children? How about making up their beds? I need something to do.'

'The beds are done – I did them yesterday. And Jimi will be back soon with their overnight things. You can read them a bedtime story if you like. I've got a heap of books for them.'

'I'll do that then,' Anna agreed. 'I just want to keep busy. Oh, and Thea?' She turned back just as she was going to round up the children. 'What was it you were going to tell us? It sounded important.'

Thea smiled. 'Oh, it's fine, it was nothing much,' she said. 'Nothing that won't keep.'

SIX

September

Emily couldn't stop looking at this strange new tiny person who lay in the transparent plastic crib beside her bed. His plump, pink little face was half-submerged in the clumsily knitted blue blanket that Charlotte had insisted on making for her. 'I know it'll be a boy,' she'd said as she handed it to Emily. 'So I wasn't going to bother with some daft neutral just-in-case colour.' Emily had decided then and there she'd manage to 'lose' the blanket somehow, and would wrap her baby in the soft old cream cashmere one she'd had for Alfie – but Sam had put this one in the bag at the last minute and she now found she felt very fond of it. Something handmade, however ineptly (the thing had several dropped stitches and one very wobbly edge), with affection and care could only be full of warmth and love: a baby, all instinct and no knowledge, would surely sense that.

Emily couldn't sleep, although she knew she should try to. She was desperate to go home even though it was only 5 a.m. The hospital hadn't let her go earlier as she'd hoped to because her son had been born at 11 p.m. and the staff insisted on her staying until the morning to be sure all was well with the two of them.

One more hour, she couldn't help thinking as she gazed at him. That's all it would have taken to get him to 1 September. But whether those sixty minutes had blighted his future chances of getting into a top university eighteen years from today didn't matter at all at the moment. There he was, all fresh, pink, perfect and asleep. Soon he'd wake for feeding, changing and a lifetime of needing her. No one could *not* love being needed.

Like most of her new class, but not quite like the scary-looking shorn-headed little boys, Thea had had her hair cut for the start of the new school year. That Tuesday morning, she'd washed it in the shower, flicked it up, tufted it out and secured bits of it with gel. In the interests of not getting glared at by the traditionalist school head, she'd washed out the few pink and lilac streaks that had jollied it up over the summer, but she still kept it short and spiky as she had since she'd had ten inches cut off after Rich had left her a year ago. It had been a small act of defiance at the time, since he had preferred her with long hair, but she'd decided it suited her far better like this. She could always grow it again in the future when her jawline sagged and she needed something to hide behind.

'Elf,' she said to herself in the mirror once she'd finished tweaking her hair, but it didn't sound the same as when Sean said it. Only a day after they'd first met, he'd pulled at one of the sticking-up fronds, laughed and said she looked like a little elf. If a woman had said it, especially one taller than her, she'd have felt patronized. When Sean did, even that first time when they'd barely spoken more than a few sentences to each other, the term simply felt warmly fond.

The day was hot and still summer-dusty but on the drive to the school Thea passed more than one restaurant and pub that had a board up on the pavement, advertising early-booking terms for office Christmas parties. Not yet, too soon, Thea thought, as she did each September. It felt wrong, all this fast-forwarding too far; it was too much like wishing one's life away. Still, this year Christmas was something to look forward to – that is, once she had the family onside. Otherwise, well, she and Sean might as well elope. They could run off to get married among hotel strangers on a tropical beach somewhere. She didn't fancy that at all, though she could imagine many would. However glorious and sunny the weather, for her there'd be something cold and a bit sad about having no one from home to celebrate with.

'Hey, welcome back to the madhouse,' Thea's friend Jenny greeted her as she walked into the school's staff-room. 'Did you have a good summer?'

'Pretty much perfect, thank you. The only downside was coming home.'

Jenny laughed. 'So it's all going well then. You two are still at the icky romantic stage. Yuck!'

There was still time for a mug of tea before facing her new class and the onslaught of anxious mothers ushering them in, each one of them wanting 'a word'. Thea had already thoroughly checked reports on her incomers from their previous class teacher – one child was a selective mute (although not in the playground), another was terrified of birds and there was one who couldn't be separated from his toy giraffe, a stuffed animal that was almost as big as he was. There'd be several more with problems – imagined or otherwise – whose parents hadn't mentioned them before but who were sure to think that day one of the new school year was the perfect moment, so a bit of fortifying wouldn't go amiss.

'We seem to be. And, er, well, actually, guess what . . . !' And Thea couldn't help herself: having failed to tell her news at the weekend, it was just dying to break free. 'We're getting married!' It was safe enough to tell Jenny; her family weren't likely to run into her any time soon, so no chance of it getting back to them on any gossip grapevine.

'Wow, you don't hang about. Congratulations!' Jenny gave her a hug. 'So when? Next summer?'

'No, not summer. We thought Christmas would be good. It sort of goes with how we met, you know? I always think we had such a lot of help from the magic of a massive bunch of mistletoe, so it feels like the perfect time to do it. The day we met, Sean asked me to sneak out after dark on a secret mission to get a huge bunch of the stuff. I had to hold the ladder while he went up and cut some down. He got spooked by an owl and nearly came crashing down.'

'Bit bloody lucky for you that he didn't then. So, Christmas next year? Great idea.'

'No, *this* Christmas. No point in waiting, is there? Neither of us are teenagers or anything.'

'*This* Christmas? Like, only about fifteen *weeks* away?' Jenny stared at her, wide-eyed and with her mouth a bit gapey. Thea fought an urge to reach forward and push it shut.

'Well . . . yes. Why not? What's to wait for? Now we've decided, we just want it to happen, as soon as possible!'

'Why *not*? Thea, do you have *any* idea how much planning a wedding takes? There are *so* many things to consider. My cousin had a whole website and database thing full of plans and projects when she got married. She had a huge fat folder just for napkin options for the reception.'

'Oh, but I do know. Remember I started organizing one before, when I was with Rich? It was his idea to have some chintzy hotel reception and everyone done up in morning dress and so on. That is till he changed his mind about that and about me. I don't want anything like that this time round. Definitely not. We only want a teeny event, nothing mad, definitely nothing elaborate. I hate a massive fuss. I want just Sean and me and a few others. That would feel just *right*. I can see it now, all soft light and evergreens, muted colours – no glary white frock or anything.' Thea poured the boiling water into two mugs. Jenny was looking as if she could use one as well.

'Well, you say that but there's still your dress to consider, the reception, bridesmaids, *their* dresses, catering, cars, invitations. It's why there are things called wedding planners.'

Thea handed Jenny her tea and laughed. 'Oh, Jen, we won't need all that faffing about. It's going to be a family thing in Cornwall. I can find a dress easily enough. It's not as if I'm planning on a fairy-tale outfit of feathers and white velvet. Just something . . . lovely. I'll give it some thought, obviously. But I'm not the fairy-princess type – it won't be from a wedding shop kind of thing, not this time. Been there, done that. It wasn't me.'

'If you get stuck, I could help find one or has your sister volunteered for that?'

Ah – the cloud in the perfect blue sky. Thea could almost feel a real one passing between her and the sun. 'No – Emily has just had a baby, on Sunday. I had the family round for lunch and she went into labour as I was about to tell them about the wedding plans. So the announcement never actually happened, what with everyone rushing round making sure Emily and Sam got off OK. And that's fine and as it should be. But it means I haven't actually quite told them yet.'

'Oh – that sounds a bit sad. Lovely about the baby, obviously, but it's a shame you didn't get to make the announcement. Still, they'll know soon enough and they'll be thrilled for you. After all, what's not to look forward to?'

'Well, that's the slight fly and ointment thing. The one thing Sean and I really want is to get married down in Cornwall because of it being where we met and because we want to involve the sea and the beach for after the ceremony. And there's the fabulous accommodation for everyone too, right there. We can even get Christmas Day itself for the ceremony, in this place called Pentreath Hall which belongs to his friends Paul and Sarah, and that'll be fabulous. But the one thing *Emily* said she would absolutely *not* do this year is have Christmas anywhere but at her own home.'

'I can't *not* sympathize, to be honest. New baby, small children and all that,' Jenny said, finishing her tea and rinsing her mug. The staffroom was filling up

now with post-summer conversations and a welcome
to two new staff members.

'I know. I can understand how she feels. I don't want
to have our wedding without Emily being there but I
don't know how to change her mind, or if I should even
try. Maybe we should change *our* plans rather than expect her to go along with us? But it would be so exactly
what we'd love and Sean said he's kind of booked the
venue now, though I suppose it could be unbooked . . .'

'I'd leave it for the moment,' Jenny advised. 'When it
comes to it, she won't want *not* to be there for you, will
she? And she might get over the travelling thing once
she knows the reason for going.'

'I hope so. I really do. But I can't be sure,' Thea said.
'Other priorities and so on. Anyway, into the fray – let's
meet this year's tiny terrors.'

Anna got off the bus in Chiswick and went across
the road and up a side street to the address she'd
written in her diary. It was Miriam's turn to host the
book group and she'd managed to get everyone to
agree to an afternoon meeting instead of the more
usual evening ones. 'We'll have tea and scones,' she'd
promised, but Anna had brought a bottle of white wine
as that was what they usually had at their meetings and
sometimes, given how heated the discussion could get,
you just needed something calming. It was surprising
how vehement people could get over whether Jane Eyre

was a put-upon mouse or deep down a scheming gold-digger.

She felt slightly nervous, even though she was 90 per cent sure Alec wouldn't be there. He wasn't a book-group member but he was Miriam's son, lived fairly nearby and might have called in for a quick visit. In her head, Anna practised being casual about seeing him again. It would be the first time since Christmas, when he'd mistaken a flippant remark of hers for an actual invitation to join them all in Cornwall. OK, he'd been, briefly, her good-fun lover, but what on earth had he been thinking of, arriving out of the blue like that? He knew she was still married, even though – back then – she and Mike had been planning a divorce and were going through a bit of a play-act that involved pretending they didn't mind each other having other relationships.

Miriam's garden path was a hazardous tangle of overgrown lavender, trailing nasturtiums and morning glory that had spilled down from its trellis and was snaking across the paving. Typical Miriam, Anna thought as she gently pushed the foliage aside with her foot. Miriam was exuberant, colourful of dress and un-coordinated of movement. If a garden could mirror the person, this had got it just right.

'Come in!' Miriam opened the door before Anna reached it and ushered her in, waving a full wine glass rather dangerously. Her hand hit the wall as she moved, but she salvaged the glass's contents with long-practised skill. 'Everyone's here but *some* haven't read the book. It's not much to ask, is it?' she said as she took Anna into the kitchen to get her a drink. 'After all, the clue's in the name: Book Group. It involves a group. And a book. You've read it, of course?'

Anna had. The person who last got to choose what they read had opted for *Tess of the D'Urbervilles* so Anna, who had last read it as a teenager but had recently seen the film, wasn't completely lying when she said yes.

Women of a Certain Age, rereading the classics they hadn't gone near since their schooldays, Anna thought as she took her glass into Miriam's sitting room. It was like something from a Barbara Pym novel; all they lacked was a shy archdeacon to simper at. There they all were, eight or nine still-energetic lady pensioners doing their best to keep their brains active. Anna had a bit of a heart-sink moment. Was this what it came to, in the end? Finding things to do to keep you away from a couple of decades of daytime TV and a lonely decline? Mike had his music and she had her painting but even so . . . She told herself not to be so ridiculous. People of all ages met to discuss books. It was a *thing* and, besides, she enjoyed it. And yet, just as Miriam opened the discussion with a question about whether Hardy, if writing today, would come under the genre of *domestic noir*, Anna had a wistful recollection of the afternoons she'd spent in bed with Alec the previous year. Twenty years younger than her and so exciting to be with at the time – at least until she'd had to spend that Christmas week in Cove Manor with him and he'd turned out to be a bit mopey and wet. (Although, as it turned out, not so wet that he hadn't managed to spend the nights secretly shagging Charlotte.) She'd never thought of herself as a woman who was brave or wild enough for an affair but it had been such fun, and, in the end, essentially pretty harmless, as Mike had been up to the same at the time with Charlotte.

'You can hardly put Hardy in any "domestic" category, surely?' Miriam said, waving her hand about. The hand contained a scone and crumbs and a blob of strawberry jam fell on the rug. A black cat rushed across and licked it all up and Miriam took no notice at all.

'Well – it depends. I mean—' Anna began but the doorbell rang and Miriam whirled off to open it.

'Hello, Mum. You said it would be OK – I'm not intruding, am I?' And there, in the doorway, stood Alec. Hair longer, a bit greyer, possibly a little less of it. He was wearing a cream linen jacket and old jeans and looking, well, probably what Thea would call 'totes buff'. Anna could feel her face going pink. 'Hi, everyone,' he said, 'I hope you don't mind me joining in but *Tess* is one of my favourite books. Mum said I could come if I promise to behave.' There were a few giggles and a general murmuring of approval. Then he crossed the room and sat beside Anna on the fuchsia velvet sofa. 'Hello, Anna. You're looking well. It's been a while.'

SEVEN

'So how was day one back at the chalk face? Survived?'
Sean called Thea just as she was beginning to water
the big pots of Japanese anemones in the back garden.
They were flagging in the heat and deserved a long
cool drink, as did she, and she'd brought out a glass
of ginger beer to have on the terrace once the watering
was done.

'It was fine, just. Two who wouldn't stop wailing –
they kept setting each other off. But there was only one
pair of damp knickers, which is pretty good for day
one.'

'Were they yours?'

'No!'

'Oh. I'm disappointed. Does that mean you weren't
thinking of me at all?'

Thea giggled. 'You are so naughty! And of course I
was thinking of you but I'm not going to tell you that.
It'll go to your head.'

'Or to my . . . No, sorry. I just can't help it. I'm missing you like crazy here. I have to keep getting in the sea. Woody is looking well fed up with me running down the beach the whole time. He's bored with following me down there and stands on the top of the dune, miaowing crossly.'

'Aw, sweet. I miss him. You too, of course, but definitely him more.'

'Heartless woman. I'll be up at the weekend to remind you what you should be missing most. But anyway, how is Emily and the sprog? Have you seen them yet?'

'Not yet. She wants a few days of settling, she said, but on Friday night she and Sam have invited us all there for a takeout supper and some baby-gazing. Will you be here by then? And if you are, could you bear to come too?'

'Of course. Can't miss an opportunity to show your folks what good husband material I'll be, can I?'

'Brilliant. Just don't go mentioning things like damp knickers though, OK?'

'Oh go on, just once or twice? Please?'

Before Thea could answer, she heard a click and the side gate opening. She was sure it had been locked that morning when she'd left for work but maybe she'd forgotten. She looked round quickly, suddenly nervous that she'd be face to face with an on-the-off-chance burglar but instead a dog came racing towards her. A big apricot poodle. Benji. He woofed a delighted greeting at her and she reached out to pat him. He leaned against her, thrilled to see her, his big woolly head lolling and his tongue hanging out.

'What was that? Did I hear something?' Sean asked as Thea looked beyond Benji. He wouldn't have arrived alone.

'Oh, er . . . nothing. A dog just got into the garden. I'd better go and shoo it out,' she said. 'Shall I call you back later?'

'Yes, do. Love you, Thea. Can't wait for the weekend.'

Rich came through the side gate and was in the garden as if he had every right to waltz in as he pleased, a year after he'd moved out.

'Love you too, madly, deeply and always,' she said to Sean, slightly more loudly than she normally would. Whatever Rich wanted from her, he definitely wasn't going to be left with the impression that she hadn't moved on.

'Hello, Thea.' Having breezed in through the gate as if he still lived there, Rich now waited by the kitchen door.

'Did I miss hearing the doorbell?' she asked him. 'I was watering the plants.'

'Er . . . no, actually. I didn't ring. It just seemed natural to come in this way, like I always used to.'

Thea didn't say anything, neither did she smile, nor did she move towards him.

'Sorry. Another time I'll remember to ring the bell,' he said, getting the gist of her body language.

'And I must remember to keep the gate locked,' she replied. 'Anyway, what are you doing here? I don't think you left anything behind when you moved out.'

'No . . . er, I was in the area and just wondered how you are?' He looked awkward and Thea had to admit she was rather enjoying the situation. This was, after all, the man who broke her heart but could no longer get to her. The man who had said that her miscarriage had been 'just as well', because he didn't want children. What a difference a year made – and whatever had she seen in him?

'You wondered how I *am*? I've still got the same phone number, Rich, same email address. You could have phoned, emailed. Why turn up out of the blue?' Benji was running around the garden, scrabbling at any bare patches of earth he could find, just as he always used to when he lived here. If he dug around a bit he'd probably find old toys of his that he'd buried, and possibly even her pink espadrille that he'd stolen from under the bed.

'We were together a long time,' he said. 'I'm allowed to remember we had some good times, aren't I? I always hoped we could end up as friends.' He smiled and added, 'Your hair is pretty drastic, isn't it? What made you cut it?'

Thea put a hand up to it, feeling as if it needed protecting from him.

'I like it short. It's more fun.'

'It suits you. I like it too. It's just so . . . different. I don't suppose you fancy a swift one? For the old times?'

'*What?* Are you *mad?*' Thea backed away.

'I meant a drink. At the pub. Early-evening glass of vino, like we used to,' he said, pushing his fingers through his hair, smoothing it back. She'd never noticed before what a girly gesture that was. Or maybe it was a typically male one – checking for a receding hairline, possibly.

'Oh, I see. Right.'

He laughed. 'You surely didn't think I meant—'

'No, I didn't; don't be ridiculous.' Of course she *had* thought he meant sex but only for a millisecond. She also knew he'd been deliberately ambiguous, which would be his idea of being funny, perhaps testing her. But even Rich, whose instinct for tact and diplomacy was pretty much absent, wouldn't seriously suggest a bout of sex after so long without even a conversation. He looked hot and bothered. He was wearing a dark blue suit and a shiny silver tie and an air of someone who'd spent the day doing things that involved tedious meetings and getting overheated in the London dust. She thought of Sean, who existed pretty much entirely in T-shirts and flip-flops, his longish curly hair wind-blown and sun-bleached at the ends. She was pretty sure he didn't own a tie apart from a black one for emergency funeral use.

Thea was about to tell Rich it was an absolute 'no' but Benji came running up and nuzzled her hand. It was definitely good to see this lovely dog again. So many times they'd walked the few hundred yards to the pub with him on his lead, pulling them in through the bar-room door as if he knew the drill exactly. He'd liked the pub; Benji was the sort of dog that drew complete strangers to come up and talk and he loved attention. Rich had always been a bit short with those who did this but Thea had enjoyed it. What was there *not* to like about anyone who approached to express admiration for such a gorgeous dog?

'Well . . . OK, maybe just for half an hour,' she agreed, giving in to what she had to admit was overwhelming curiosity about why Rich had turned up. 'Hang on there for a minute and I'll get my bag and keys.'

He may have lived here once, shared her bed and her home, she thought as she locked the back door after her a few minutes later, but she really didn't want him inside the house now, somehow sullying the air that Sean would be breathing at the weekend. No – he was out of her life, and he could stay out of her house.

'So who is he?' Rich asked once they were settled in the riverside garden of the Old Swan with glasses of wine.

'Who is who?' Thea asked.

'The person you were telling you loved down the phone.'

'How do you know it's a "he"?' she teased.

'Ah – well, if you've joined the other team that would go with the short hair, I suppose.'

'Working the old stereotype then, Rich. You'll have noticed I'm wearing sensible shoes too.'

'But not dungarees.' He was looking her up and down, appraising her dress, her body. It felt a bit uncomfortable.

'Anyway, it's nobody you'd know,' she told him. This evasive tone was a mistake and she felt like a sulky schoolgirl. But she didn't want to tell him about her new life with Sean. Rich was firmly on the outside of everything she did now.

Rich chuckled. 'OK, as you like. Good to see you've moved on though.'

'Are you surprised? Did you think I'd pine for the rest of my life?'

He shrugged. 'I don't know. I suppose not. I just know . . . and I'm sorry . . . but I realized at the time that getting married, living with someone as a couple on a for-ever-and-ever basis, children and all that . . . just wasn't for me.'

She relented a little, as he actually looked quite regretful about it. 'Well, I'm glad you decided before we got married rather than after. Simply packing and walking out like you did was at least pretty uncomplicated. How is your sister, by the way?'

'Oh, you know Elizabeth . . .'

'I don't really, though, do I? She never wanted to be close enough for us to get to know each other. I don't think we ever had a conversation in which she didn't tell me I wasn't good enough for you.'

He frowned. 'Well, your family are pretty much a closed shop too, I seem to remember.'

Thea thought about the spring just past: of Sean teaching Elmo how to fish in the sea down in Cornwall; of him coming up to London and helping Mike shore up the tumbledown back wall of his painting shed; and of him and her mother laughing crazily together over a whole evening of old *Yes Minister* repeats they'd found when flipping through TV channels. Not *so* closed shop. Not at all.

'So what are you doing down in London?' she asked. She took a large glug of wine, eager to get home. It was getting chilly now and she was starting to feel hungry.

'Er . . . just a bit of work stuff. Meetings and so on.'

'And you took the dog with you?' She watched Benji paddling in the river's shallows, eyeing the ducks, which kept safely out of reach.

'Oh, there's always a willing girl on reception who'll mind him for the duration.'

I'll bet there is, she thought. Good old Rich, putting on the suave charm. She could imagine him, all big toothy smile, handing the lead over and saying, 'Would you mind? I'll only be half an hour.' He might even call her 'sweetie', gambling on her being the sort who'd smirk at this and not glower and want to clout him. And it would all be a done deal before the girl could even think of protesting that she was scared of dogs or allergic to fur or simply had too much to do.

'Wouldn't it have been easier to leave him with your sister?'

He frowned. 'Not really. I don't actually live up in Cheshire any more, you see. It didn't work out. So that's what I was doing in London – I went for a new job and I'm moving back down this way. I'm bunking down in a mate's flat over in Kingston till I find a permanent place to rent.' He smiled at her and raised his glass in a mock-toast. 'So you see, we're practically neighbours.'

'That Belinda from the agency phoned,' Mike said to Anna over supper. 'She's got some people who want to see the house – or "effect a viewing", as she put it, if that's OK with us. What do you think?'

Anna thought for a moment. It had jolted her a bit, that afternoon at Miriam's. She'd seen the future and wasn't sure she liked it. The gentle pursuits of the retired lay in wait, looking far too much like the horribly patronizing ad for insurance for the 'elderly' she'd seen on TV. It had featured a smiling grey-haired man in a yellow V-neck jumper, saying that 'the missus loves pottering in the garden with the grandkids'. Pottering. Would life really come down to 'pottering'? It wasn't that she'd even been tempted to think of rekindling the old affair with Alec but seeing him had left a wistfulness, a feeling that such excitements were unlikely to be available to her in the future. After all, the queue of men hoping to woo women in their sixties was a very short one. She could see herself with a wallet full of cards that would tell anyone who went through them after she'd been run over by a bus that she was a Friend of every worthy art gallery. There'd be discounted pension afternoons at the local theatre. Books. Poetry readings. Her painting. None of these were unappealing in themselves, not at all, but so far in her life she'd preferred to be doing rather than *viewing*. And she definitely didn't potter.

'Mike, would you ever consider going on one of those European river cruises?'

He laughed. 'What, the ones that are advertised during old episodes of *Morse*? No, I don't think I would. My idea of hell, actually, though I'll admit the scenery looks great. And, besides, we're not old enough.'

'The thing is, we are.'

'We can't be. We're the generation that saw the Stones in Hyde Park the first time round and you could sit in a tree and watch for nothing. We went to the first-ever Glastonbury. Hell, I *played* at the first-ever Glastonbury. Our lot don't do old.'

'It creeps up,' Anna said. 'Those godawful ads for funeral-insurance plans and tooth fixative, they're about us.'

'But we've still got our own teeth.'

'That's not what I meant.'

'I'm not paying for my own fucking funeral while I'm still alive. I can think of better uses for a couple of grand.'

'Can you? What?'

Mike thought for a moment. 'Whatever it is, it won't be a river cruise. Or any cruise. I wouldn't mind a trip to New Orleans. And I'd love to go to Nashville and buy a Dobro.'

'A what?'

'Steel guitar, like the one on the front of that Dire Straits CD. As played by Ry Cooder and others – you know that rich, twangy sound. I've been wanting one of those for bloody years.'

'You see, we can do that, Mike. Once the house is sold we can do anything. We can put everything in storage and just travel. There's no need to settle to living in one place immediately, is there? We can even rent if we want to.' Anna was starting to feel excited at the prospect of being rootless. Ageing, gracefully or otherwise, in the same suburban area, the same *house*, they'd occupied since they'd met all those years ago, was not compulsory. Well, the ageing bit was but not the staying put. It was an exhilarating feeling.

Mike poured them both some more wine. 'Are we going to be wanderers? At least for a while? It sounds fun. Studenty, young.'

'Yes. After all, wherever we are, we won't be more than a plane-ride away from the family if they need us.'

'Or if we need them.'

'And they've got each other. And Thea's got Sean now, so she's not on her own any more, not that she wasn't perfectly capable when she was, but it's great to see her so happy.'

'It is. And he's so much more "her" than that Rich bloke ever was. So what do you think? One more Christmas here and then we're off?'

'I think so, yes.' Anna sighed, glad that they were on the same page on this. 'Though I think we need to start looking for alternatives to this place, as soon as we can. Maybe out in the country, or by the sea. I'd love to have somewhere smallish and cosy by the sea as a base. I don't think I'll be comfortable without one to come back to, from wherever it is we're going.'

It was five thirty in the morning and Thea was only half-sleeping. She was having a dream in which she was wearing an ancient lace wedding dress, yellow-faded with age and tattered and ripped. She was clambering through deep snow, clutching a bouquet of brown-edged drooping roses and she was painfully out of breath. The church was in sight, only a hundred yards away, but no one was around and however hard she tried to tread her way through the snow, she was making no progress. More thick snow started to fall and she struggled to stay upright, pushing against the drift that was now engulfing her, preventing any more movement.

'Aaaagh!' she spluttered, waking herself. There was something white and soft all over her and it took several moments to realize she was trying to free herself from the duvet that had got twisted tightly round her. She lay still for a few minutes, gasping, gradually waking, and then she reached over and switched on the light. She sat up and ran her fingers through her hair, trying to push the dream out. Miss Havisham, she thought, remembering the age-mottled lace, the faded flowers: the bride in *Great Expectations* whose wedding never happened. But this was only a dream, not an omen. And just because last Christmas at Cove Manor had been a crazy, snowy white-out with the whole village cut off, it didn't mean it would happen again, probably not in their lifetime, let alone only twelve months later. And even if it did, everything would be fine, really it would.

But as she got out of bed to go downstairs and make some reviving coffee, she had a little twinge of guilt and confusion. When Sean had called late in the evening to wish her a loving goodnight, what had stopped her from telling him she'd been out for a drink with Rich?

EIGHT

'Oh bloody 'ell, what a day. I'm *so* glad it's the weekend.' Thea slammed her bag down on the staffroom table and went to run herself a glass of water. 'I wish this tap dispensed wine. I could drink it dry,' she said.

'What's up?' Jenny was there, sorting some paperwork to take home. 'Can it be that bad in only the first week?'

'I know. Who knew? The children are great, they're over their first wobbles and settling in fine. It's not them, it's . . .' Thea pointed in the direction of the head teacher's office. '. . . it's *her*. Sodding Melanie. *Completely* inflexible. I mean, *why*? Just cos she's the school head, surely it doesn't mean *everything* has to run the way she says? What about a bit of class-teacher freedom to make decisions?'

'You'll have to tell me, Thea. What's she done now? And here' – Jenny went to the tin that was kept by the kettle – 'if you can't have wine, have an emergency Hobnob.'

Thea took the biscuit, sat down and waved a hand

towards the window. 'The weather. I mean, look at it! How fabulous and hot and stunning is that? And for how long? All I did was take the children outside this afternoon and had them sitting under the chestnut tree for story time because I thought it was too great a day to waste cooped up inside. But oh no, apparently that's not allowed. Melanie comes storming out and asks for "a little word", so I left Chrissie to carry on with the story and Melanie starts telling me off and says there are "safety issues" about being outside and that it's not on and I was to take them back inside, *immediately*. It isn't as if they hadn't been outside all lunchtime so what's the difference, safety-wise? I felt as if I was one of the seven-year-olds and I'd just kicked a football through a window. Honestly, has she never heard about outdoor classrooms? They're a *thing*? Or about how children respond to nature and how being outside has a massive effect on their ability to concentrate and absorb information?'

'I do sympathize. Melanie would have them all completely silent in tidy rows of desks with tests every week if she thought she could get away with it. Talk about old school, literally.'

'It's made me feel like quitting. I mean, what am I doing *here*? I've just spent the summer in Cornwall with the gorgeous, lovely man I'm going to marry and I came all the way back here to work just to be told off for giving my class a bit of fresh air. It'll be winter in a few weeks and they won't even notice a change in season unless they get out there and *experience* it. I want them to sniff the air, feel the differences in the days, not just have autumn coming on with them in centrally heated oblivion.'

'You sound like you're on a mission,' Jenny said. 'Maybe you should get a job in a Forest School? Don't they have the children outside almost all the time?'

'If I could find one round here, I think I'd love to,' Thea said. She gathered her bag up again and took a few deep breaths. 'Anyway, it's the weekend. Wheee! Sean's on his way. Can't *wait* to see him. Have a good one, Jenny.'

'Hey, hang on, Thea – why did you say round *here*? Do you need to carry on living here?'

Thea hesitated, her hand on the door. 'Well, no – of course not! Sorry that must have sounded mad! Actually we haven't even talked about it. But I think I'll have to see out the school year here, won't I? I mean, I can't leave my class – and all of you – in the lurch.'

'That's very noble of you, but what will Sean have to say about that?'

'Good point. I'll talk to him. It seems ridiculous that we haven't given it that much thought. In fact there's masses of stuff we haven't really thought about – we just drift along in a soppy haze.'

Jenny laughed. 'Well, that doesn't sound so bad, does it?'

'No, it's bliss, but at some point we'll have to get a little bit practical. Sad, but true!'

She was here again, had been for a good hour, being helpful with the children. Emily could hear Charlotte singing 'Mockingbird' in the kitchen as she clattered about with cutlery and plates. Emily presumed she would be staying for supper. She hadn't been invited but it would be horribly rude not to include her. Not that Charlotte tended to need asking. Did the woman do anything at her own home except sleep? And even then, who knew where she spent the nights.

Emily had her feet up on the sofa and was trying to remember not to cross her ankles (danger of thrombosis) as she fed the baby. He was a calm little soul and did nothing but sleep between feeds and nappy changes so she slightly felt she didn't quite know him yet. Milly had been a busy sort even at this age, already alert and looking round and protesting at being put in her crib after feeds. Alfie as a baby had been a bit calmer, but Milly had been so curious about him that she would slyly prod him awake, so Emily had spent a lot of time trying to soothe him. Milly, she remembered, had been so envious of the attention he got that she'd forced her toddler body into his newborn-size knitted jackets and mittens and stretched a tiny hat over her hair. With this new one, both the older children had lost interest the day after she'd brought him home.

'He doesn't do anything. When can he play with me?' Alfie had demanded.

'Babies don't *play*,' Milly had told him scornfully. 'They just have sucky-yucky milk and then they *poo*.'

'Ugh, smelly poo-poo!' Alfie had been delighted and ran round the house pretending to be a train while bellowing 'Poo-Poo!' till even Sam ran out of patience and parked him in front of CBeebies.

'Just for the sake of ten minutes' peace,' he said when Emily was about to protest. 'I thought you could do with some quiet time.' She couldn't argue with that but wished he'd sat down with the boy and some Lego or a story instead of using the TV as a baby-minder. It set a precedent. In the end, of course, thank goodness for Charlotte.

'What time is everyone coming? Shall I do the children a quick stir-fry?' Charlotte appeared in the sitting-room doorway holding a wok.

'Would you mind awfully? It's a lot of trouble for you.' Emily shifted the baby across to the other breast and he snuffled close, his mouth panicking around the nipple till he found it and latched on, sucking greedily.

'No trouble at all.' Charlotte beamed at her and pointed the wok at the baby. 'Isn't he good? I had endless feeding trouble with Louis. It used to get embarrassing out in public, flashing a massive tit at the whole bus when he wouldn't get on with it. One old colonel-type once yelled, "For goodness' sake, cover yourself, woman," at me but he didn't think about looking somewhere else. He kept turning round for a good eyeful.'

Emily, who wouldn't dream of breastfeeding on a bus (or even travelling on one unless it was an emergency), smiled to show solidarity.

'I hope Sam's given you a glass of wine, Charlotte,' she said.

'Ho, yes, we're well down the bottle, don't you worry.'

We? Emily thought as Charlotte bounced back to her chores. She could feel tears prickling. They came even more easily than usual at the moment and although she knew it was hormones, she still felt a bit left out. Sam and Charlotte and Milly and Alfie were being a unit of their own out in the kitchen and she was isolated here on her sofa, still sore and stretched and flabby and uncomfortable and not yet quite as mobile as she'd expected to be. Still, only an hour or two and the cavalry would be there – her family knew how to make her feel better. It seemed silly at her age but what she really needed was a hug from her mum.

'Mmmm. Do we really have to get up again?' Sean stretched out in the bed and pulled the duvet back up from the floor and snuggled it over Thea's naked body. 'Couldn't we just cut out the middle bit and stay where we are for the night?'

'Sounds very tempting,' she said, thinking about

how she was slightly dreading this evening. She was a little bit nervous about holding a tiny baby without feeling sad all over again for the one she hadn't had last year. She hoped she wouldn't cry. 'But in another hour you'll be starving and wishing we'd gone to Emily's for that supper after all.'

'True. And it's gift-horse *stylee*. We don't even have to wash up. OK. We'll go, of course we will. And when we tell your folks about the wedding plans, let's hope it goes down better than it did with my mother.'

Thea sat up abruptly. 'What? Doesn't she approve? I thought she quite liked me. Oh, bummer. What did I do wrong?'

'No, no, she likes you a lot. But when I said we wanted a really small simple wedding in Pentreath Hall she got a bit funny. I told her about it being Paul and Sarah's pretty-much-stately home, only a mile from Cove Manor – she's met them and liked them – and that it was beautiful and had lots of atmosphere. But she was still a bit sniffy, said it wasn't a "proper wedding" without at least a hundred people and a sit-down do and she wasn't travelling three hundred miles from Lancashire to have a sausage on the beach and no confetti. She also requires . . . er, a church.'

'But most people don't get married in a church these days, do they? Especially people like me who haven't been in one since their nephew's christening.'

Sean laughed. 'Hey, me neither. But don't worry

about it. She'll come round. It's just that every now and then her Catholic roots start to show. She also hasn't been in a church since her ancient Auntie Dot died and even then she grumbled about the lack of a proper requiem mass. It'll be fine. She'll rock up in the end, I know it. She was just putting in her three p's' worth.'

Thea reached down to the floor for her robe, which Woody the cat was now lying on. He rolled over and purred as she tickled his ears. She felt quite a lot like purring herself just now. Everything felt so wonderfully perfect. 'And with any luck, we'll tell my lot we're getting married and maybe there'll be no unexpected hitches and they'll all be pleased. Apart from Rosie and Mum, nobody has thought to ask what it was I was going to tell them when Emily went into labour, so now I've got this really juvenile urge not to mention our wedding plans and just tell them very casually a week before it's going to happen.'

'And don't forget, there's always eloping. Or does that only seem a dramatic option if you're both teenagers?'

'Like the old days with running off to Scotland? Probably teenagers. If we do it, it'll just look like a massive sulk. At least, that's what Emily would say. Jimi would just say, "Oh cool." I think his vocab has regressed to Elmo's level.'

'He'd have made a good surfer. You can't be a pro surfer without the forever-young vibe.' Sean sighed and stared at the ceiling.

'I'm not even going to ask about how much you mind not being one any more. I can see it.'

'It's a young dude's game. However much you've still got the sea fever in your head, your body knows different. There'll always be some twenty-year-old carving a massive bomb with that hundred per cent fearless thing and superhuman skill. But at some point, and definitely after thirty, you don't see Hawaii's Pipe-line as an exciting challenge so much as something that might just kill you. You look at it and think: Hey, if I'm rag-dolled in there I might never see the surface again.'

'Mortality,' Thea said, climbing out of bed.

'Yep. That's the bastard,' Sean said. 'The grim reaper in a wetsuit. Not a surfer's best friend.'

Sean and Thea were the last to arrive at Emily and Sam's house.

'Whoo-hoo, I don't need to ask what kept you, do I?' Charlotte's laugh as she opened the front door to let them in could only be described as filthy. 'You've got that naughty glow.'

'You're absolutely right,' Sean said as he hugged her. 'But let's not tell everyone. We don't want unseemly displays of envy.'

'Too late in my case, sweetie, I'm already seething with jealousy, you lucky, lucky bastards. I haven't had carnal shenanigans in ages. Anyway, come in. They're all here, baby-prodding and making the right cooing noises at the poor kid.'

Thea took in the scene in the garden before they got to the kitchen doors. Anna was holding the baby and her face looked decades younger than usual as she looked on him with fond softness. Mike was down at the end of the garden with Jimi, pushing Milly on the swing. Jimi stood to one side, trying to cup a sly cigarette out of sight of Rosie.

'Ah – here they are,' Emily said. 'About time – didn't we say seven? The food will be here in a couple of minutes. I wouldn't have kept it waiting – nobody wants it cold.'

'Lighten up, Emily,' Sam told her. 'They're not late. Drinks? Who's driving?'

'Neither of us,' Sean told him. 'We got the train and we'll get a cab back.'

'In that case, we can all give the baby's head a thorough soaking,' Sam said as he poured generous glasses of champagne.

'Are we doing a toast?' Thea asked, hesitating before drinking.

'Not yet. Not till later, if at all. Depends on Madam's mood.' He indicated Emily and then said in a near-whisper, 'She's a bit up and down, to be honest. If she's snappy, don't take it personally. Anyway, come out and have a proper look at the little sod. See if you approve.'

Thea took her time approaching Anna and the baby.

Her mother looked almost Madonna-ish holding him. Maybe it was all the shades of flowing blue she was wearing, and her straight, shoulder-length hair pushed back. She doubted that the Virgin Mary had worn twenty silver bangles, though, and scarlet feathery earrings.

'Ah, Thea, come and see. He's absolutely beautiful.'

Thea held out her hands to take the baby from Anna, slightly scared of getting the handover all wrong, but suddenly there he was, in her arms, hardly weighing more than one of Alfie's soft toy animals. She sat down at the garden table, feeling the need to be safe from any risk, however minuscule, of falling. The baby snuffled and half opened his eyes and briefly looked at her. 'Hello, you,' she said. 'Aren't you just lovely?' And he was. She took in his perfect tiny features, his mouth that was making little sucky sounds. 'Oh and your fingers, so long and so perfect. Nails like tiny pearls.' She'd held babies before, been the first to see Alfie at the hospital after his birth six years before, but this one – he was the first since she'd actually contemplated the possibility of having her own one day.

'It really suits you,' Sean murmured close to her.

'Suits you like a dress?' Milly popped up between them, having overheard.

Thea laughed. 'Not a lot like a dress, Milly-love, no.'

'Cos you can't wear a baby. Unless you put him on your head like a hat. But then he'd wake up and fall off all the way to the ground and then he'd—' She stamped her foot hard on the grass.

'Milly! Time to get your 'jamas on,' Sam interrupted just in time.

Thea looked up at Emily, who had come out of the house and gone wide-eyed. She was holding out her arms for her baby. 'I'll take him inside and put him down. I don't want him to get chilled – and also the food has arrived,' she said, quickly taking him from Thea.

'What's his name?' Sean asked, taking hold of Thea's hand. Emily looked puzzled.

'Erm . . . I don't know. Ned. I think Ned.'

'You don't *know*?' Jimi was laughing at her and she went pink.

'Yes, of course I do. It's Ned, isn't it, Sam?'

'I like Ned. Yeah, Ned Michael,' Sam agreed.

'Not Edward?' Mike asked as they went into the kitchen and sat at the table.

'No. I just want one syllable,' Emily said. 'I can only cope with one.'

Thea saw Mike and Anna give each other a look. Was Emily being odd? It was hard to tell. She could be spiky at the best of times and maybe every woman went a bit funny after a baby. Thea had been heartbroken after her own miscarriage, especially as well-meaning friends and family had said all the wrong things, misguidedly sure they were being comforting. 'You're still young

here, why don't you, Thea? After all, you're the bride. You get to choose. That's of course if the wedding actually happens. You've been engaged before and with plenty of fancy wedding planning half done and it all came to nothing.'

'I *did* choose. Or rather, we chose *together*,' Thea told her, pushing back her chair and standing up. She could feel her eyes filling with disappointed tears. It was time to go. 'And you know what, Emily, whatever you think about the venue, if you can't even be arsed to be just that *teeny* bit pleased for us, not even give us *one* word of congratulations, then really, I don't think we need you to be there at all.'

NINE

October

It was now more than halfway through October and only nine weeks till Christmas and still Thea hadn't sorted out a wedding dress or any catering and so on. It was as if she'd put the whole idea of the wedding on hold since the row with Emily. They hadn't spoken to each other since and although her mother kept urging her to talk to her sister and make it up, she felt stubbornly that it was for Emily to apologize, even if she didn't actually change her mind about Cornwall.

'She's just had a baby, Thea; her hormones are all over the place,' Anna had reminded her, as if she needed to. 'She'll come round when she's got herself a bit more together. Be kind. She won't miss your big day, not when it comes down to it.'

What Anna didn't know was that Thea had gone to see Emily two days after that supper, taking flowers and a little pair of sheepskin mitts for the baby. She'd hoped the two of them could have a quiet talk and she could tell Emily how much it would mean to her to have her there at her side when she got married. But she'd been told by Sam at the front door that Emily was resting and wasn't feeling like seeing anyone. He'd looked apologetic and a bit shamefaced – and well he might because she could hear Emily calling out something to Milly in the kitchen. So she'd handed over the presents, told him to send love and tell Emily she'd like to see her soon. But she'd had no contact from her since, not so much as a cursory thank you. Her gesture had been completely ignored. It hurt, but she didn't want Anna worrying about it. This was between her and her sister.

At school, the children were starting to buzz about Christmas and each morning there was at least one of them bragging that they were getting an iPad for Christmas and another upset because they weren't.

'They're a materialistic bunch, aren't they?' Jenny commented in the staffroom. 'It's all about *stuff*.'

'That's kids for you,' Thea agreed. 'I remember thinking the world would end if I didn't get a Cabbage Patch doll one year. I think Mum had to trawl every toyshop in London to find one for me. They were *the* present that year.'

The days were getting colder and greyer but with those delicate touches of soft autumn sunshine that light up the changing leaves and make you want to get out in the fresh air. The shops were filling up with Christmas stock and shelf after shelf in every super-market was labelled 'Seasonal' and crammed with the kind of food that nobody really eats, like candied ginger and preserved mandarins.

'So you've started your shopping then?' Mrs Over-the-Road was walking her West Highland terrier as Thea unloaded groceries from her car boot, ready to take them into the house and sort out what was to stay here and what was to go with her at the weekend for half-term with Sean in Cornwall.

'Shopping? Nothing special, it's only the usual from the supermarket,' Thea replied, wondering what June was referring to.

'The cards have been in the shops for weeks now. Wrapping paper too. You have to get in quick with paper. Leave it last minute and they're clearing the shelves ready for Valentine's,' June warned, peering into Thea's shopping bags.

'Oh, *Christmas* shopping, you meant. Sorry,' Thea said, the fog of incomprehension beginning to clear.

'Yes, of course I meant Christmas. What else would I mean? They've been having a visiting Santa in Asda for weeks now. You can feel it in the air, can't you?' June pulled her coat close round her and shivered a bit to emphasize her point. 'In the mornings, it's properly dark. I like dark in the mornings. I don't trust those long summer days. You shouldn't be getting up hours after it's already broad daylight. It's all wrong.'

'You'd be a happy bunny in the Caribbean then, June,' Thea told her, trying to gather as many carrier bags together as she could so as to avoid making two trips into the house and back. 'It's pretty much twelve hours of day, a quick sunset and a precise twelve hours of night, all the year round. Very organized.'

June sniffed. 'Organized but very hot. We British aren't meant to be hot. It makes us itch. It's why we like Christmas: lots of woolly things to wear and plenty of good traditional food.'

'So you'll have got your Christmas cards already then?' Thea said, slamming the car boot shut.

'Me?' June laughed. 'Oh, of course, dear. I always buy mine in the January sales and most of the presents as well. You can't be too far ahead of yourself, that's what I always say.'

'Christmas is ages yet, June. There's plenty of time,' Thea said.

June gave her a look that told her she was in serious Season Denial and started to haul the little dog over the road to her home. 'It's not ages at all. Especially at my age. Time races on and it's all you can do to keep up with it. But if you don't, you fall off the edge. And you're not getting any younger either; before you know it, time will have caught up with you too. Make sure you don't leave everything to the last minute.'

Well, thanks for that, Thea thought, feeling a bit unsettled as she trundled her shopping through to the kitchen. Thanks for the big reminder that the old biological clock was ticking ever more loudly in both ears. If that's what June actually meant. She probably did. Once a woman was into her mid-thirties people seemed to think it was perfectly acceptable to comment on her lack either of a husband, baby or both. Only a week ago, the head teacher Melanie had told Thea that if she was thinking of leaving the job, then to remember to give a full term's notice. Thea hadn't even hinted about leaving: as she'd said to Jenny, she wouldn't want to leave her class halfway through the year. It would feel irresponsible not to take them through the full three terms. So where did that comment come from? Anyone would think they were back a hundred years ago when women had to give up teaching if they married. She was on the lookout for jobs in Cornwall though, and if the perfect one came up then maybe she'd just have to jump at it.

With or without Emily on board, if they were to go ahead with getting married at Christmas, she needed to get on with preparations. She'd heard that Emily was not only refusing to go to the wedding but was now hardly venturing out of the house. Thea had tried texting and emailing her – she wouldn't respond to phone calls – but had had no response.

She and Sean were opting for the lowest of low-key events because neither of them liked fussy weddings, but even this would need some effort. Paul, Sean's partner in the Cove Manor rental business, had taken over the running of his father's ancestral home, Pentreath Hall, and its wonderful orangery was booked for the actual ceremony, which would be quite early on the morning of Christmas Day as the registrar had plans to go on to help out at a homeless shelter later. Afterwards, they were planning to have a beach barbecue as a sort of wedding breakfast instead of a full-scale reception, but that still needed a bit of organizing, even if it was only a matter of deciding whether to go for sausages or kebabs and how much drink to get.

Lists, Thea decided, she must make lists, and immediately. However simple and rustic the wedding, what kind of useless bride hadn't made so much as a list of guests so close to the event? Ah yes: one who had fallen out with her sister, big time.

Three sets of people had looked over Mike and Anna's house but as yet no offers had been made. The agent Belinda had said they were wanting 'IBC', which apparently translated as 'In by Christmas'. Maybe, Anna thought as she tried to look at her house with coolly objective rather than forgiving eyes, they'd concluded that just too much needed doing. After all, not everyone finds the walls of a sitting room painted Book Room Red as cosy as she and Mike did. Some probably found its terracotta shade quite oppressive, especially in a fading October light.

One lot had included a young woman with swishy blond hair who Anna recognized from television but couldn't put a name to. She'd begun various sentences several times with 'Of course in my job . . .' without actually coming out with what the job was, so Anna had been none the wiser as to whether she read the news or was an Olympic athlete. One couple had been a brittle forty-something pair who found fault with every single thing from the size of the rooms to the locations of the bathrooms. As Mike had commented after, you'd think they hadn't even looked at the agent's details. All the room layouts and sizes were on there. They'd also found fault with each other, hissing '*darling*' at the end of every sentence when disagreeing on which bedroom would be right for 'the twins'. She and Mike hadn't heard from them again and Belinda the agent said they'd decided to move to France instead. 'These are not words I ever imagined I'd utter,' Mike said when Belinda called to tell them this, 'but God help France.'

It had been Mike's notion to look at a few possible ideas for a place for themselves fairly locally but on a smaller scale. 'We can at least see what kind of thing we might like,' he reasoned, and Anna didn't disagree.

'Nothing that needs work,' she told him. 'If I want to strip wallpaper, I might as well stay here.'

'If we stay here, we can't afford to strip anything, or at least not to put stuff back up again,' he said. 'I've been adding up what we'd save by buying something half this size. Heating, council tax, replacing that iffy boiler that probably won't see the winter out . . . it's endless. If we sell this, we'll be able to afford to eat, and quite well too, for the next few years.'

And so now, curiosity tweaked by a flashy ad in a Sunday paper's property section, they somehow found themselves in the marketing suite of a new riverside block of swish apartments sitting across a desk from a slick young man in a suit jacket that Anna could see was way too tight for him. The sleeves seemed to end halfway up his wrists and the fabric pulled across his skinny chest. Fashion, eh, she thought. Whoever had decreed that a cool look for young men was to truss them up so tight they ended up looking like Norman Wisdom?

'So, Mick and Annie . . .' Mr Slick said, looking up from the form he'd insisted they fill in to list the requirements they could easily have told him in two sentences.

'Mike and Anna,' Mike said. His knee was twitching – a sign that he was already bored and a bit grumpy.

'Sorry – right. So I see you're looking at a possible two bedrooms and some outside space.' He looked up and smiled at them. 'You do know these are, like, flats?' he said. 'No gardens?'

'We know?' Mike said, only slightly mocking the upward lilt of the young man's voice. 'But the ones at the top have large terraces? We could see them from outside?'

'Oh, the *penthouses*.' He smiled. 'I should tell you, those are the top of the range, price-wise?'

Mike twitched some more. 'It's fine. We did see the prices.'

'Oh right, er . . . OK.' He had a good appraising stare at Mike's leather jacket and blue bandana and Anna's long velvet skirt and said, 'Sorry, I'd have thought you might be looking for something a little more . . . compact. So you've looked at the finer points?' He handed over a fat glossy brochure. 'This kind of place attracts mostly young professionals, what with the basement pool and gym and a bar and restaurant on site.' He cast another thoughtful look at the two of them, who were so clearly the opposite of 'young professionals', and turned his iPhone over and over on his desk.

'Couldn't we just go and look at one of the penthouses? Please?' Mike asked.

'Oh absolutely. Of course, if you're sure.' The young man jumped out of his chair, rummaged in a drawer and pulled out a card. 'No keys here, all computerized, electronic, state of the art.'

The lift was entirely mirrored, which Anna didn't like. Face on, at home, in a good light, she would see herself reflected and not be too depressed at what she saw. Now she couldn't avoid herself from all angles and noticed that her neck was not as long as she was sure it had once been, and that her upper back was a bit rounded. She pulled her shoulders back, standing as straight as she could to deny evidence of the advancing years. Thirty-something professionals. How did they afford places like this? Even the smallest, barely bigger than a cupboard, was well over three hundred thousand pounds. She imagined them as neighbours she would probably never see, or if she did, it would be in the lift. They'd be looking tense in running gear, fiddling with a fitness wristband and avoiding eye contact. She'd be in her multiple colourful layers and wondering how terrified they'd be if she said hello and wasn't it a lovely day.

Floor ten: the lift stopped and opened on to a caramel-painted corridor. A light flipped on, the agent zapped the keycard and they were in.

'It's like a hotel suite,' Mike said, frowning, looking at the pale grey sofa, the carefully placed ornaments, the uninspiring paintings of vague riverside scenes. 'No character.'

'Actually, that's rather what I like about it,' Anna said as they toured the space. 'Especially the bathrooms.'

'Of course it's obviously a show flat, designer-led decor, an example of what you could achieve,' the agent told them. 'It's to reflect that you're actually buying into a *lifestyle*. Though of course . . .' He hesitated. 'I can see this particular style might not appeal . . .'

'Buying into a *lifestyle*?' Mike spluttered. 'Bloody hell, man, I'm pushing seventy. If I haven't got a "lifestyle" sorted by now it'd be a pretty poor show.'

'Mike . . .' Anna warned, worried about his blood pressure. 'Come on, let's look at the outside space.'

The agent slid the massive glass doors open and they went out to the terrace, which was broad and generous and paved with dark stone. 'Obviously pots are key,' he told them, indicating a pair of olive trees tethered to a rail and blowing fitfully in the wind. 'Pots and the view.'

'Bloody splendid, I'll give you that,' Mike actually agreed. 'But now I'm thinking it's just too high up. I know it would be next to impossible but I can't help imagining the grandchildren falling off.'

'Oh, I don't think they could do that,' the agent tittered. 'Not unless they dragged a table over to the edge and climbed up and over the barrier.'

As he laughed off what he'd said, Anna shivered, imagining Milly and Alfie doing exactly that and plummeting to the car park below, becoming nothing but blotchy, bloody splats. 'Look, thanks and all that but, you know, it's not for us, this. Sorry. Let's go, Mike. I can't live here or in any high-up place. Not now that thought has got into my head.'

Safely out of the cruelly mirrored lift she took hold

of Mike's hand as they went across the road to get a reviving drink at the riverside pub. 'At least that's one option ruled out,' she told him when she'd recovered from the horrors of her imaginings. 'It's got to be something with the garden on the actual ground. Do you agree?'

'Definitely,' he said. 'But it was useful to go and look, wasn't it? But oh dear' – he laughed – 'it looks like we'll just have to make do with the lifestyle we've already got. I didn't know you could "buy" them but I think I'd prefer not to.'

'I've been thinking . . .' Anna told him as she sipped her spritzer. 'Maybe we should look a bit further away. Get something small so we can do the travelling thing but have it to come back to. Something that would be easy to rent out if we want to stay away for a longish while, perhaps.'

'How far away? Please tell me not somewhere cold like Scotland.'

'No, not Scotland, though the scenery is worth some visits. I was thinking somewhere arty and by the sea and where there are lots of people like us. A place that isn't full of "young professionals" pounding for hours in gyms in the few hours they're not squashed on to commuter trains. Somewhere with great light and—'

'I hope "people like us" isn't a euphemism for "old" and that you're not meaning Worthing? We went there once, remember, and it was closed. On the plus side, though, I do remember seeing about fifty bikers, none of them younger than me.' He looked quite cheered by the thought.

'No, I'm coming round to thinking perhaps Cornwall. I'm thinking St Ives.'

'Ha! Cornwall? The cursed county Emily swears she'll never visit?'

'Ah, but having *us* there could be one way to change her mind, don't you think? I know it wouldn't be in time for Christmas and the wedding but if we plant the seed that we'll have a lovely base down there that they can all use for holidays whenever they like, then maybe she'll have a bit of a think about it. Surely the idea of a place by the sea where the children could run free on the beach any time of the year would tempt even Emily over the Tamar? It's just an idea, but it's a good one, I think. I've always loved Cornwall. I hate it that she and Thea aren't even speaking. I know they're both miserable about it and I want us to be all together when Thea and Sean get married. Thea's offered to put it off till summer but that's Cove Manor's peak renting season with lots of repeat visitors already booked in, and Sean's already turned down bookings for Christmas so they can accommodate us all. It isn't kind of Emily to be so anti. After all, she surely didn't hate it *that* much last year. I thought it was only the snow that scared her, and that was a real once-in-a-century event. So what do you think?'

Mike considered for a moment. 'It's pretty devious thinking but I like it,' he said. 'And at the moment, we only have to let her know we're seriously considering it; we don't actually have to go and live there.' He sipped his beer and looked thoughtful for a few moments. 'But, you know, I've always liked St Ives . . .'

TEN

'Melanie is on everyone's case about Christmas and wants ideas for some version or other of a nativity play,' Jenny told Thea in the staffroom. It was two days before half-term and there had been mutterings all week about various class Christmas shows. 'She's called a meeting for lunchtime and said "no excuses", so I guess we're under orders.'

'A nativity play? Again?' Thea said. 'Oh, groan. Starring parts for four children, to include the innkeeper and the Angel Gabriel, plus three support-role kings and a couple of shepherds and just about everyone else has to be an ox or a donkey with very little for them to do on the stage except fidget.'

'Don't forget the supporting cast of many angels.'

'Ah yes, many, many angels and all the parents coming into class to complain that their little star has been sidelined. It's a difficult one, isn't it? I mean, who doesn't love a proper nativity play? You can't beat the baby Jesus being dropped on the floor and one of the shepherds forgetting he should have had a wee before the show rather than during. But when it's every single year you get to the point where you need something a bit more inclusive. I've been thinking about something with more scope for them all to join in.'

'Excellent. You tell Melanie. Go ahead,' Jenny said with a giggle. 'I'll be right behind you.'

'She's off me at the moment so I don't hold out much hope.'

'She's off everyone, so you mustn't take it personally.'

After the lunchtime bell, Melanie was to be found sitting at the end of the staffroom table, tapping a pen on her notepad. The rest of the staff took their seats and waited for her to begin.

'Christmas,' she said. 'I think in these difficult political times we need to get back to basics. Do we have any ideas for a seasonal play?'

'Yes, I have,' Thea said, clicking on her iPad.

'If it involves anything from Disney, I don't want to hear about it,' Melanie said.

'Disney? No, it definitely doesn't. I was thinking it would be fun for the children to put together a drama enacting the story of Yule, of how the year is turning from darkness to light. The great earth mother giving birth to the new sun king.'

'I don't think so, Thea. That sounds way too pagan. There would be complaints. Anyone else?'

'Oh, I rather like Thea's idea, actually,' Jenny said. Thea smiled at her.

'Thanks, Jenny.' Thea seized the moment and continued: 'And I'd make sure it's not so much pagan as about nature. We can tie it in with a study of the earth turning and the movement of the planets and talk about the tradition of bringing in evergreens. They can sing carols like "The Holly and the Ivy". We can talk about the magical powers of mistletoe and . . .' Thea stopped, realizing she was gabbling into a disapproving silence. Melanie was glaring.

'Sometimes, Thea, I wonder if you're teaching in the right sort of school.'

'Sometimes, I wonder the same,' Thea murmured but not quite far enough under her breath. There was a collective gasp. She pressed on, feeling she might as well at this point. 'But you asked us for ideas, Melanie. Wouldn't you even consider this? It could include so much about the natural world and the seasonal cycle and wouldn't upset any of the more religious parents at all. It would be completely inclusive.'

'No. Thanks for your input but it's out of the question. I think we need a proper nativity play,' Melanie declared. 'One that will firmly ground the pupils in the story of what Christmas is really about.'

'Apart from what Christmas is about to the many pupils here who aren't Christian, that is,' the deputy head put in a rebellious bid and smiled at Thea across the table. She smiled back at him, grateful for the support.

There was a general muttering and shuffling and after only a very brief discussion Melanie declared that there would be a traditional nativity play with those who weren't in the main roles being cast as various plants, animals and angels. She then moved on to asking who had got the manger that they'd used the previous year and would they please return it immediately.

'Why did she bother asking for ideas if she'd already made up her mind?' Thea asked Jenny as they went off to take the afternoon classes. 'It was a complete waste of time. And we had a nativity play last year, and the year before, so they must have got the hang of the Bible version of Christmas by now. I thought something a bit different, maybe every other year, would be more dramatically challenging for the children. I'd got a whole set of lesson plans mapped out too. I was going to take them out to look at how the dead-looking trees and shrubs were already forming spring buds and tell them the story of how mistletoe came to be associated with thunder and was thought to protect against fire and lightning.'

'Boxes to tick, forms to fill in,' Jenny told her, giving her a brief hug. 'You've got great ideas but Melanie hasn't really got the imagination to give you scope to use them. You can still do the nature thing though, can't you? It's a good project.'

'I've started wondering what's the point of carrying on here, to be honest. These children are being taught by numbers, pretty much. There are other ways.'

'But if you hang on in, you'll be head of a school in a couple of years and then you can run things your way.'

'I *could* be head if I toe the line but I'm not sure I want to . . . I think you had a point about Forest Schools. There are so many ways for children to learn; they could be so much more proactive. They all start here burning with eagerness to learn and by eleven, too often the fire's half out.'

'As I said, box-ticking and Ofsted and SATs – they've all got so much to answer for.'

'Well, thank goodness it's half-term at the end of the week. I'm off to stay with Sean. I feel a bit sorry for him – I'll probably spend the first four hours ranting at him about work.'

'Oh, don't do that. Just drag him off to bed. That'll sort you out!'

'Have you made it up with your sister yet?' Charlotte let herself in through Emily and Sam's back door and surprised Emily, who was cooking pasta for Milly and Alfie.

'What do you mean "made it up"? It makes it sound like we've had a childish spat.'

Charlotte's eyebrows went up. Emily noticed they

looked a bit pink round the edges and guessed she'd had them threaded that afternoon.

'And you haven't?' Charlotte went on. 'What would you call it then?'

Emily drained the pasta and shrugged. 'It's nothing. Just . . . I don't know, I can't even remember. It was nothing.'

'It was *not* nothing – it's about her *wedding*, which is massively important and the longer you leave it, the more *not* nothing it'll get. After all, shouldn't she be able to count on you to help her find a dress and decide if she wants bridesmaids and whatever else weddings have?'

Emily sighed. 'I did all that with her last time and then it all fell to bits. She probably wouldn't want me around anyway.'

'Last time?'

'When she nearly married that one who left her. Rich. It was only a few weeks before the wedding. She's better off without me interfering.' Emily divided the pasta between two dishes. A couple of tubes of penne fell to the floor and she ignored them as she dolloped on some sauce (blobs on the worktop) and grated cheese over the top. Charlotte frowned and as soon as Emily put the plates on the table and went to call the children, she picked up a J-cloth and wiped down the granite surface and picked up the stray pasta.

'Oh, come on now, it doesn't sound like your input

made the difference.' She shoved the floored pasta in the bin.

Emily shrugged. 'Well, if she *did* ask my opinion, she knows I'd be saying not Christmas and not Cornwall. I was *so* unhappy there last year. That snow, that *trapped* feeling . . .' She shuddered.

'But that's not your decision though, is it, love? With weddings, we just have to go along with the bride and groom's choice. Can't you think about how much fun the day will be? How lovely to see your sister so happy?'

Emily shook her head slowly. 'I just can't,' she said.

Charlotte looked at her closely. 'You look terrible, Emily, if you don't mind me saying. I mean, you're all droopy and don't-careish. It's not like you. Just look at your hair.'

Emily glared at her and said, 'I do mind you saying, actually.' And then she burst into tears, thumping her body into a chair at the table between the two dishes of pasta and sobbing into her hands.

'Oh shit. Sorry, all my fault. Hang on, I'll get Sam,' Charlotte said. 'Give me a sec.' She went out to the garden office, clattered open the door without knocking and surprised Sam in the middle of some sneaky computer Minecraft. 'Get in here quick, Sam, and help me take care of the kids. Emily's not happy and I can't stay more than a few minutes. I've got a job audition.'

'Oh, please tell me she's not crying again,' he said,

slowly putting his feet down from where he'd been resting them on the desk. 'She's like a leaky tap.'

'She's depressed, you idiot. Any fool can see that.'

'No she's not,' he said. 'She's always been a crier.'

'Just come in and give her a hug or something. It's not as if you were up to your eyes in work, is it?'

'I've got a mega-deadline – can't you look after her?'

'Deadline? Yeah, right. I could see. And no, I can't, not this time. I only called in for a wee. As I said, I've got somewhere to be.'

'OK. You won't say anything though, will you?' he said, nodding back towards the now-closed computer as he locked the office behind him.

'About you diddling about doing sod all? Not unless I have to,' she told him. 'Now come and give me some back-up. The poor woman needs a break and a hair-wash and blow-dry. It might sound frivolous but it'll perk her up a bit. All the small things help.'

Sam trailed into the kitchen with Charlotte, and Emily looked up at him, her face blotchy and streaked with tears. She didn't protest as Charlotte hauled her out of the chair and led her firmly into the sitting room, pushing her down on to the sofa. Baby Ned was sleeping in his Moses basket under the window.

'When did you last get out of this house?' Charlotte asked.

'Dunno,' Emily told her. 'A while.'

'Not even to the shops?'

'Ocado delivers,' Emily said, picking at a small hole in her sleeve. She didn't like being questioned but understood that Charlotte was being kind. Kind upset her though. It made her want to cry. Actually, almost everything did: a handmade get-well card from Milly and Alfie (she hadn't even claimed to be ill); a homeless cat on the internet; Christmas adverts with everyone looking so carefree and happy. Anything could set her off.

'Look, honey, go and wash your face and I'll drop you off in the car. You're going to get your hair properly done.'

Emily laughed as she brushed away some more random tears. 'My hair? Bloody hell, what's the point?'

'You'll feel better, is the point. However awful you're feeling, if you can make yourself feel a tiny bit better about the bits of you round the edges that are easily sorted then it won't do any harm. Sam will look after the children.'

'I'm taking Ned,' she said. 'I like him to be with me.'

Charlotte eyed her. 'You won't leave him even for an hour?'

Emily slid up the sofa, closer to the basket, as if Charlotte were about to take him away. 'Not for a minute. It's just in case, you know?'

'Listen, I've got to go to a thing, a work thing, but I can drop you off on the High Road and you can go to that Blow and Go place in the precinct where you don't need an appointment. Or nails. Would you prefer a manicure?'

'Nails? Er . . . no. No point.'

'OK, hair then. But I do insist.'

Emily smiled. 'You're very bossy.'

'I am. And I'm also very right. You've dug yourself in here and you need to start tunnelling out again. Before you know it, it'll be Christmas.'

'Yes, that's soon,' Emily half whispered, 'and I haven't done anything.'

'Of course you have. You've had a baby. Get the children to make a list for Santa and Sam can sort it out. There's plenty of time. Now, let me have a quick wazz and we'll go.'

There were too many people in the shopping mall and Emily felt nervous as she pushed the pram through the crowd. Where did they all come from, late afternoon on a weekday? She wished Charlotte had been able to come with her because since she'd got out of the car and clicked the Bugaboo's seat into place on the wheels, she'd felt weirdly unsafe and vulnerable, all soft-edged, like an unshelled egg. The shop windows were Halloween-themed with orange and black everywhere and flashing scarlet devil masks and green fright wigs. Each sound, all the echoes of voices, the music blasting from shopfronts, was far too jaggedly loud and Emily pulled the hood of the pram up so that Ned wouldn't be overwhelmed by clamour. The garish masks and oversize plastic spider webs and witch outfits looked extra cheap and pointless and she feared for his new little spirit being contaminated by tat.

Outside Blow and Go, she hesitated and peeked inside. There was tuneless rap music playing, harsh and angry. The young hairdressers were wearing black tunics over spider-web leggings and most of them had green and white face paint and witch hats or horns. One girl had vampire teeth and a fake blood trickle painted from her mouth. Emily shuddered. Two large boys on skateboards raced past, almost colliding with the pram, and, in a panic, she reached into it and took Ned out, wrapped in his blue blanket, cuddling him close to her, stroking his soft, sleepy head. His fingers spread out like little starfish as he half-woke and then he drifted off again, tucked inside her coat.

'It's all right, baby. We'll go home. It'll be safe at home.' She murmured to him, kissing his fuzzy little head. There were more skateboards and a shouted commotion and a woman behind yelled, 'Hey, you!' Emily pulled away, pressing against the salon with Ned safely between her and the glass till the jumble of noises subsided. When she looked back again, she had a confused moment of wondering what was missing that should be there and then she realized. The pram had vanished.

'Oh God,' she whispered to herself. 'Oh God, that fucking interfering Charlotte.'

ELEVEN

'For heaven's sake, what kind of twat would steal a *pram*?' Mike asked Sam. He and Anna called in to see Emily as soon as they heard about the theft. Emily was curled up in a corner of the sofa, saying very little, clutching Ned to her even though he was fast asleep. She'd put a cosy lavender throw and some cushions over her legs and gave the impression of having built herself a barricade.

The day was a dark, rainy one and Sam had lit the wood-burner. With the lamps glowing, the place looked cosy and pretty and yet also a little unloved. Last week's papers were piled up near the front door, too late for that week's recycling. Anna had seen a trail of children's clothes up the stairs and a pile of clean clothes was balanced precariously on the banisters, ready to be put away. All was a long way from well.

'Anyone with an eye to a few quid,' Sam told them. 'They cost a bomb, those fancy buggies, and Em insisted she needed the most state-of-the-art gizmo for this baby. God knows why, but it's the must-have for all the smart mummies. The big fat four-by-four of prams. Anyway, it's probably on eBay as we speak. I'd have a look and go and grab it back but Emily won't let me. Says she never wants to see it again.'

'It would feel cursed,' Emily chimed in. 'Ned could have been in it. He was in it only seconds before. What would the evil thieving bastards have done with him? Thrown him out on to the concrete floor or in the road? Suppose they'd taken him and kept him or *sold* him? Or worse, he could have . . .' Her eyes filled with tears.

'But he wasn't in it.' Anna put her arm round Emily. 'And they only wanted a valuable piece of kit, not a baby. You can't sell babies.' She wasn't entirely sure about this but it was the safest thing to say. Emily's imagination was quite capable of conjuring up awfulness without back-up from her own mother.

'I could see it all, like a huge fast flash.' Emily sobbed into a piece of kitchen roll. 'If they'd got him, the whole thing from then on went through my head: the press, the "Oh, the careless mother, letting a child go from under her nose while she looked in a shop." Blame, hate, the horror, all *my* fault. Stupid, feckless woman, doesn't deserve a baby, it should be taken into care . . . People can be so vile.'

'Oh, come on now, Emily, none of that happened,' Mike told her. 'Not even close. Some yobs mugged you.

They probably hoped you'd left your bag in it as well so they could get cash and a couple of credit cards at the same time. In fact that's all they would be after. The pram was probably abandoned somewhere by the river, or even in it, like a nicked car.'

'I hate London. I loved it and couldn't imagine being anywhere but here in this house but now it's spoiled. I don't want to live here any more. I need to feel safe. I need to be somewhere the children can feel safe,' Emily said through more tears.

'That's a bit of an extreme solution!' Anna told her, getting up from the opposite sofa and heading for the kitchen. 'Though I can see how you might feel that at the moment. I promise you it'll pass. You need another cup of tea,' she said firmly. 'And you're no less safe today than you ever have been so don't start blaming an entire city.'

Sam followed Anna. He switched the kettle on and then took mugs out of the cupboard, 'Go easy on her, Anna. She's not herself. She won't let go of Ned. She's got him sleeping in our bed at night now.'

Anna smiled. 'Emily used to sleep in ours when she was that age. It was very much the thing to do back then. Now of course everyone panics about accidental smothering but it's only in our western cultures that a baby occupying its own cot is the norm. Don't worry about it, Sam, it won't be for long. He won't still be sleeping with you when he's twelve.'

Sam laughed. 'Is that supposed to be a comfort?'

'I'm doing my best here, Sam,' Anna said, grinning at him as she poured boiling water into the teapot.

'But really, it's bad and getting worse. She didn't want Alfie and Milly to go to school this morning. Luckily, for once they really wanted to go because both their classes have started on a Halloween lantern-making mission and they didn't want to miss out. But if they'd only got a regular school day to look forward to it would have been a battle and I'd be on my own there.'

'Hmm, that's not good. Emily really is very down, isn't she? She might need help that's beyond what we can offer. Has she seen the health visitor or a doctor?'

'She says she doesn't want to see anyone. I was think-ing it was really great that Charlotte nagged her into going out yesterday but it's done more harm than good. I keep telling Em the theft was just a form of mugging, an opportunity grabbed, nothing personal, but she's like a scared little animal and thinks the world has got it in for her.' Sam, who was usually so laid-back and cheerful, was looking half-chewed with worry. Anna felt sorry for him, for his inability to reassure Emily and make things right for her.

'Has she talked to Thea? Maybe this is a chance for them to bury the Cornwall hatchet.'

'Only if it's buried in each other's heads,' Sam said, putting two spoonfuls of sugar in his tea. He tasted it and grimaced and added one more. 'Thea called her yesterday, all worried about the theft, but Emily wouldn't speak to her. She's blaming her along with Charlotte.'

'Blaming *Thea*? Whatever for?'

Sam shrugged. 'Who knows. That's just what she's like right now. Irrational. Stubborn.'

'Depressed. You need to get her to see someone about it, Sam. And fast.'

Now the autumn was well under way, the leaves were daily cascading from the trees and road-sweepers were leaving them in heaps along the pavements, waiting for them to be bagged and taken away. Thea wondered, each time she went out to the shops and passed the mounds of foliage, how old you had to be before you stopped wanting to jump into the middle of a dry leaf pile and kick them around. She and Sean had done just that in the park only a couple of weekends ago, giggling like the infants she taught and racing each other to the café for hot chocolate. It had been one of the few blissfully carefree moments that weekend; just for a little while she'd managed to put the row with Emily out of her mind and simply relish the precious time with Sean.

On the first day of half-term, Thea had got the car packed and ready to go in the early-morning darkness. It was close to freezing outside and she breathed silvery clouds as she went down the path with the last of her bags. The lights were on in Mr and Mrs Over-the-Road's house and any second now the door would open and either June or Robbie would be sure to come out, dragging the half-asleep terrier as an excuse to find out where she was going and for how long. In Thea's opinion it was rather early for conversation so she closed the car boot as quietly as she could, then dashed back into the house to double-check she'd locked everything. The house phone was lying on the sofa so she picked it up to put back on the charger but as she checked to make sure that it was switched off she realized it was doing the fast beeps that indicated a voicemail message. No one, she reasoned, could leave one unplayed merely in the interest of gaining thirty seconds' time – after all, it could be some emergency news or a friend with fabulous gossip – so she sat down on the stairs to listen, the front door wide open.

'So I wondered if you'd do me a massive favour and have Benji over the second weekend in November. Otherwise I'll have to put him in kennels for the duration and I thought you probably wouldn't want me to do that to him.'

Rich's message gave Thea a jolt. He was a sly sod, she thought after she'd heard it. He'd left a message deliberately loaded with emotional blackmail when he could have called her on her mobile and they could have had a conversation about this. She knew what he was up to: he was avoiding her arguing that he surely had other arrangements that he usually made for the dog, and pushing him to think if he had anyone else he could leave him with. And great timing too – it was weeks now since he'd suddenly appeared in her garden and told her he was moving back down south. How sunny and warm it had been then; it seemed as if they'd moved on a whole season since, rather than only a couple of months.

After Rich's visit she'd been nervous that he'd keep turning up unexpectedly but she hadn't seen him since. She'd just got used to not leaping a mile high whenever her phone rang in case it was him; she'd finally been convinced that when he'd said 'We must have dinner and a proper catch-up', it was simply polite code for him having no intention of seeing her again. She certainly didn't want to see *him*. But Benji was another matter. The weekend after the end of half-term, Sean would be away visiting his mother up in Lancashire and she'd be alone and, really, she could have the dog to stay quite easily. Saying no on principle and condemning Benji to a cold and lonely kennel with possibly not enough opportunity for long walks and exercise seemed horribly unfair. She would call Rich halfway to Cornwall and say yes, but she'd have to make it as clear as plain glass that it was a one-off.

The road this early was good and clear for Thea had managed to get away before the main body of half-term travellers was on the road. As the sun came up behind her, she looked at the trees and hedgerows at the sides of the road and took in just how much they'd changed since she'd last driven on this route. Only a few weeks ago they'd still been green. Not with the vivid new brightness of spring or the warm variations of midsummer but a selection of gentle, fading shades going sandy in places, a little sparse here and there. Now all was russet and shades of chestnut and deep golds and there were gaps and near-naked branches showing through. She whizzed past Stonehenge and on through the rolling Wiltshire fields, which were now ploughed and earthy, some of them greening a little in places with winter crops. Sheep had grown back their fleeces after the summer shearing and were looking plump with growing lambs. The turning seasons: Thea thought about her class of infants. How many of them had even seen sheep apart from on TV? She would (in spite of the huge amount of paperwork that such things now involved) get a school outing organized to the nearest urban farm in the spring, try to connect the little ones with where their food came from and how sheep and goats and piglets actually felt to touch. And if they all ended up as vegetarians because they'd assumed meat was something factory-made for supermarkets and nothing to do with actual sheep, then that was fair enough.

The journey was a long one but Thea was excited to be seeing Sean again and stopped only briefly a couple of times for a sandwich and some reviving coffee, so when she arrived she wasn't surprised to find that Sean wasn't there. She let herself into the converted stable block by Cove Manor and took her bags into the bedroom that overlooked the sea at the end of the building. She hadn't needed to bring much with her in the way of clothes: over the past year she'd accumulated plenty of basics that stayed in the chest of drawers: knickers, tights, spare jeans and a couple of jumpers that she only wore here. Her shampoo, another toothbrush and various cosmetics also lived in the adjacent bathroom: the place definitely felt almost as much like home as her house in London did. She was – of course – excited about the prospect of moving down here permanently once the school year was up, but was concerned about how hard it might be to find a job in the area. Would friends come all this way to visit? Would the excitement of this slightly nomadic life fade away? How would it be when they had to deal with what Sean called the 'potatoes' of life, its essential mundanities, every single day together? Summer had been wonderful, all those weeks, but at the back of her mind had been the awareness that their time together was still limited and it reinforced the excitement of kind of playing house. The real thing would be soon though; after Christmas it would only be just over six months till the end of the summer term and then . . . a whole new life.

'Anyone home?' As Thea went through to the kitchen the door opened and Paul came in.

'Ah you're here!' he said, hugging Thea. 'Welcome back. I was looking for Sean. I've just brought over a couple of essentials for the manor before the half-term clients rock up. It's a bit last minute but we can't have them lacking a bedside rug. It can be a deal-breaker on TripAdvisor.'

'Hi, Paul, how are you doing? Love the sweater,' Thea said. 'Lilac is definitely your colour.'

'You can't beat a good mauve cashmere,' he said, stroking his own front. 'And it makes a change from all the mud coloured stuff the farming lot wear around here.'

'You are always an absolute beacon of chic,' she said, switching the kettle on. She remembered how when she'd first met Paul, the previous Christmas, she'd assumed he was gay. It wasn't entirely her fault: not only would he easily qualify as the best-dressed man in Cornwall – all soft fabrics and sugar-almond colours – Sean had introduced him as his partner, somehow managing to omit the word 'business'. It had been quite a surprise that he'd turned out to have a lovely wife, Sarah, and three children.

'Thank you – how sweet of you. Now – the thing I wanted to ask you both: supper at ours tonight? Sarah has made a massive boeuf bourgignon and the children are off on a sleepover so you'll be doing us a favour. If you don't come she'll make me eat it again tomorrow and lovely as it is, well, you can have too much of a good thing.'

'That would be gorgeous, Paul, thank you. I'll say yes but obviously I'll have to check with Sean and let you know if he was intending to surprise me with some other plan. I expect it will be fine.'

Paul gave a naughty chuckle and grinned. 'Ah, you loved-up young things,' he said, 'I am deeply envious. Long may it last. I can't tell you how excited Sarah is about you and Sean getting married at our place. It'll be our first one so I hope we all get it right. I expect you've got masses of organizing done by now, haven't you? We'll want to hear all about it over supper. So, see you later then.' And he was gone, leaving the faintest waft of expensive and hugely classy aftershave.

It wasn't hard to guess where Sean would be. If he wasn't in Cove Manor welcoming new renters then he would be in the sea. There hadn't been any cars outside apart from Sean's, so Thea took a mug of tea out on to the terrace overlooking the dunes below and sat on the bench alongside Woody the Siamese cat to see if she was right.

Sean was down on the shore, just coming out of the water, carrying his surfboard. She watched as he shook the sea out of his hair in the manner of a dog that's retrieved a ball from a river. How beautiful he is, she thought as he strolled up the beach, and she felt a great wave of peace that she hadn't been able to access back in London for the last few weeks. It was as if she were sloughing off a carapace of anxiety, out here in the chill afternoon air with the fading sun glinting on the iron-grey sea. And as Sean looked up, saw her, waved and broke into a sprint across the sand, she felt a rare moment of calm. Here just might be where she belonged.

TWELVE

'You got here pretty damn fast,' Sean greeted Thea at the top of the rocky steps from the beach. 'Couldn't wait to get to me, then?'

'Something like that,' she told him, hugging him tight in spite of the cold, soggy wetsuit. How fabulous to see him, she thought; this more than made up for the horrible rift with Emily and the daily annoyances of school life under the dictatorial rule of head teacher Melanie. And even though his hair dripped cold seawater on to her face, his mouth tasted of love and deliciousness. Also of salt, but that was OK.

'You must be in need of a reviving nap after such a long drive,' he murmured, pulling her close to him. 'And all that surfing tires a bloke.'

'So we're going to have a sleep?' she teased, unable to stop smiling as they went into the house. Oh, it was so good to be back, to be away from work, from the row with Emily, from the uncomfortable awareness of Rich and a new strange feeling that she was being watched by him, even though he'd only turned up that one time.

He laughed and his fingers stroked down the length of Thea's spine, which made her tingle. 'Possibly, possibly . . . it's not as if we have anything to rush off to.'

'Ah – well, we do, sort of. Supper at Paul and Sarah's. He stopped by to invite us just after I got here. I hope it's all right – I said yes.'

'Definitely. You get spared one of my inevitable pasta concoctions and I get extra time to diddle about with you. Bliss. Come on, Elf,' he said, pulling her towards the bedroom. 'Come and help me fight my way out of this wetsuit. The temperature out there is getting to the point where it feels as if it could freeze itself on to my skin.'

As Sean went to run the shower and rinse the sea off him and the neoprene, Thea's phone buzzed with a message. She had a little moment of anxiety in case it was Rich asking again about the dog but it was Anna.

'Hey, Sean?' she called to him over the sound of the running water. 'My mum just texted. The folks are on their way down.'

'Really?' he replied through the shower's steam. 'Are they wanting to stay here? They're very welcome. The spare room isn't too shabby, or it won't be if I move a few spare boards and stuff round.'

'No, they're heading for St Ives but asked if it's OK to

come over one day this week and see us. Lunch, Mum says. Shall I tell her just to pick a day?'

'Sure – any except Friday, changeover day. We can take them to the Rick Stein place in Porthleven. And to be honest, I'm not too sad that we'll have the place to ourselves for the whole week.' Sean came out of the shower naked and rubbing his hair with a towel. His body was so damn gorgeous, Thea thought. In spite of Emily's hostility and Rich's . . . well, existence, there were just so many blessings to count.

He put his arms round her and pulled her over to the bed. 'I think we've got plenty of time for a proper hello. And we can do some talking catch-up too. Later.'

'You see we could do as much of this as we like once the house has gone,' Mike said to Anna as they parked outside the Sloop galleries in St Ives. 'You can't even get into the town in the summer holidays but out of season it's a total luxury.'

'It is half-term though,' Anna said, looking around at the groups of families dragging bored small children behind them. 'I think we were just lucky.'

'Well, OK, but even there we've got an upside: it means we can go round the Tate without tripping over parties of schoolkids.'

'I thought we'd come to look for a place to buy? Will there be time for both?'

'Of course there will. And anyway, we've already

whittled it down to a few from looking online so it's not like the old days of peering in agents' windows. I'll admit St Ives is a bit more hilly than I remember. We might have to extend the search. But first, I think an ice cream. Fancy one?'

'I think so, though it's not really the weather for it,' Anna said, pulling her coat close round her. 'But we're at the seaside which means it's got to be done. So long as the gulls don't attack. I'm sure they didn't use to be this big or this menacing – I mean, look at them, dive-bombing anyone who's got a bag of chips. Are they bigger or am I shrinking? I dread the shrinkage.'

'Of course you're not!' Mike said, laughing. 'Why would you think that?'

'My mother did,' Anna said as they reached the ice-cream stall. She ordered a 99 with an extra flake. 'She got smaller and smaller like Alice after the potion. Every time I saw her during those last years, her skirt hem seemed closer to the ground. I wonder if that's part of why older people think they become invisible. They – or should I say "we" – start to disappear, literally. It's too depressing.'

'It's an illusion,' Mike said, paying for the ice cream. 'Blimey, three pounds fifty. How come?' he grumbled quietly. 'And nobody needs to do the invisibility thing. We already agreed we're not going to vanish into garden-pottering and snoozing. You're still out there enjoying life, aren't you? Seeing mates and doing stuff?

I'm still playing with bands in pubs and everything. Nothing has to change – we simply join in and do it all somewhere else. Neither of us is exactly an introvert so it'll be OK, trust me.' He handed her the ice cream. 'Those chocolate flakes are looking like they're doing a v-sign. That'll be in protest at the price.'

'That's the one thing worrying me about the idea of living down here,' she said as they went and sat on the harbour wall. 'Losing contact with old friends. That and whether it's really possible to find new ones without the long-term in-common stuff. In the end there'll probably only be the children at our funerals, not people we've known half our lifetimes, because we'll have drifted away. The first they'll know of our going is when they don't get a Christmas card. Some of them have packed up their homes already, gone to do the retiring-to-the-country thing. It's making me nervous.'

'The ones we care most about will still be there,' Mike said. 'And new ones, well, they'll be a bonus. And really, who cares who's at our funerals? We won't be. Well, not at the second one anyway.'

A gull swooped and, with swift and canny efficiency, stole one of Anna's chocolate flakes. 'Cheeky bastard!' she shouted at it, flapping her hands to stave off a second attack.

'We could keep a tiny London base though, I don't see why not. After all, you don't get gulls nicking your lunch in Richmond Park.'

'Not yet. But it'll come. Gulls or those screeching parakeets.'

They set off up the narrow lanes in the direction of Porthmeor beach.

'You're right about it being a bit hilly, Mike. And the prettiest cottages here round the back of the town – where you'd really want to live – don't have any place to put a car. Are we being idiots? I know we think we'll live for ever but I'm reluctantly coming to the conclusion we need to be practical. I wouldn't want to lug supermarket bags all the way through the town. Well, I might not mind now but in ten years, no way. I'll end up with a tartan shopping trolley.'

'Rosie's got a trolley but it's got a pic of Elvis on it and she says it's "ironic", whatever she means by that,' Mike said. 'But look, when you get a view like this . . .' They stopped at the end of a row of old art studios where the view opened out over the beach and sea. The sky was a rich blue-grey and the vivid turquoise sea was thrashing up the sand. As the sun broke through the clouds the beach was lit up with splashes of wet pink. 'There's nothing like the light in this place, is there?' he said, turning to Anna and smiling.

'No, that's true. And I hope we can find something with a view of the water.'

'I'm sure we can. Not necessarily direct sea frontage and not necessarily even over this side of the county but definitely we'll make sure we can see it.'

Anna and Mike carried on walking along the beachfront to the white Tate St Ives building. Anna thought about Emily and her new terror of going out, distrust of crowds and uncertainty about her children's safety. If they had somewhere, a bolt-hole away from London, surely she'd want to escape as often as possible? Who wouldn't have their mind soothed by being beside the ever-changing ocean? Perhaps this could be a good idea after all. She hoped so.

Pentreath Hall had seen better days but they'd been glorious ones and it showed. As homes go, it was possibly a bit too small to merit the term 'stately'; it would never be host to visiting coach parties and the grounds were more *au naturel* than those looking to sneak cuttings of prize specimens would be keen to visit. However, it was pretty impressive all the same, in spite of needing its paintwork touched up and the wisteria being out of control. It was a low-fronted Georgian oblong of a house like a piece of smooth gold bullion dropped into parkland, with a pair of grand columns supporting a wonderfully ornate porch and a broad set of steps leading up to double doors that opened into a large square hall with a black and white tiled floor and a stunning curved wooden staircase.

'It'll look good in the photos,' Sean said as he did a sharp handbrake turn on the sweep of gravel outside. 'Are we having photos? I mean obviously we will but I didn't mean the sort taken by a posh wedding chappie who takes thousands of us under a gilded bower or arty views of us in silhouette looking soppy on the pond bridge.'

'I wouldn't want that either. Elmo's doing Art A level and he's volunteered so I think we'll get something a bit more normal. Unless he wants us to climb a tree. He might think that would be arty, or "like, totes rad", as he'd put it.'

'Up a tree in a wedding dress?' Sean said, laughing. 'Now that I'd love to see. You'll be wearing the traditional hideous meringue, of course?'

'Of course!' she said. 'And you, I expect full kilt and frills and a sword.'

'I'm not Scottish,' he protested as they got out of the car. 'I was thinking more along the lines of my best wetsuit.'

'Thought you might. No tie though, promise me not a tie. I really hate them.'

'Oh, I think I can promise that.'

'Good – and I can promise *not* a meringue.'

'Hello, you two. Come on in!' Paul opened the door before they had chance to ring the bell and ushered them inside. The temperature fell a couple of degrees as the door shut and Thea pulled her old sheepskin jacket closer round her. 'Sorry, the boiler's buggered again,' Paul said. 'But the nice clever man will be here tomorrow and I promise it's a lot warmer in the kitchen.

Come through and say hello to Sarah and we'll sort you out a drink. And then' – he grinned cheerily – 'we'll show you what we've done with the orangery. I hope you'll think it's up to wedding standard because you two are going to be our first customers. We're experimenting on you.'

The kitchen was bigger than the footprint of Thea's little house. A massive black Aga occupied a vast old chimneybreast at one end and various dressers and worktops occupied each side. None of the chairs matched and the blinds at the window that had looked rather shabby last time Thea had been to the house were now missing altogether, leaving odd bits of ironmongery sticking out of the walls, waiting for something new to support. A couple of shabby ancient rugs covered some of the flagstone floor and a massive wolfhound lay on one of them under the table, barely bothering to flick his tail by way of acknowledging the visitors.

Paul's wife Sarah was chopping herbs by the sink and she came over to kiss Sean and Thea, still clutching a knife.

'Hello, both of you, I'm so glad you could make it. You must be exhausted, Thea, all that driving. These days, when I drive anywhere beyond the Tamar I have to pull over into a lay-by for a little nap. I even manage to cut out the sound of the children squawking, "We're not there yet," at me. It's a matter of survival for all of us.'

'Ah, but don't forget, Thea's younger than us,' Paul said, opening a bottle of champagne and pouring four glasses.

'Hardly at all,' Thea protested.

'It's the hair,' Sean said. 'She looks about fifteen.'

'Double it and add some,' she said, clouting his arm. 'I don't even *want* to look fifteen. That would be weird.'

'Uh-oh, lovers' fight,' Paul said, handing out the drinks. 'I just gave you half a glass, Sean, as I assume you're the driver tonight. And let's raise the fizz to you two and a very merry wedding. Cheers!'

'Here's to you both,' Sarah said. 'And when will you be moving down here, Thea? I assume that's the plan?'

'I'll need to find a job and there doesn't seem to be much going in teaching at the moment. I think I should see out the school year where I am but after that . . . well, it can't come soon enough. This term is being a nightmare. The head and I don't see eye to eye.'

'Really? What's the problem?'

'I think the children are too cooped up indoors and I keep trying to find reasons for teaching them out in the open, to give them a chance to be physical as well as using their poor little over-stretched brains.'

'I couldn't agree more,' Sarah said. 'You must come and see my school. It's exactly that – as much time out-doors as possible. I think you'd love it.'

'Oh, I would! I don't suppose you've got any vacancies?' Thea said, laughing.

'Sadly not at the moment. I wish.'

Paul topped up the glasses and said, 'Look, let's go and see the orangery. Is that all right with you, Sarah, or do you want us to wait till after the pud?'

'No, let's all go now. Come on,' and she led the way back through the hallway and across to the drawing room. Beyond that was a doorway through to a long room that ran the entire end wall of the house, with glass on three sides and an ornate cupola ceiling. It was too substantial to be called a mere conservatory, but still small enough to be intimate; it could accommodate a good fifty people on dark wood padded chairs which at the moment were stacked up against the wall. Glass doors all along the longest side led out to the paved terrace planted at intervals with urns.

'It's a shame it's dark because you can't see the view out over the sea just now but look . . .' and Paul switched on a light that flooded out over the terrace and beyond to the grassy slope that led down to the lake. 'We've had the lake cleared and it's almost grand enough to deserve to be called one now rather than a sludge pond. The water lilies won't be there at Christmas, of course, but the reeds are always pretty. And there's a wall between the lake and the terrace so children can't just run into the water.'

'It's stunning, isn't it?' Thea said to Sean, impressed at the amount of garden preparation that had been done.

'It is so long as the guests stay in the vicinity of pretty much what you can see from here,' Sarah told her, laughing. 'Just out of our sightline is the usual jumble of the wrong sort of rhododendrons and a tangle of trees that fell in last year's gales that nobody's got round to chopping up and clearing. There's always so much to be done and, as you know, we've had to take this on after years of gentle decline. So,' she asked Thea as they went back to the kitchen and sat at the table, 'do you think it'll be your perfect wedding venue?'

'I love it,' Thea told her, feeling suddenly a bit tearful. 'It's just beautiful.'

'Oh, Thea, don't get upset, darling!' Sarah said, squeezing her hand. 'I expect you're overwhelmed with preparations and so on.' As Paul served the boeuf bourgignon, she asked, 'Now the important question: have you got your dress yet? I expect you have so if you don't think it's bad luck, can you give me an idea what it's like?'

Thea decided to go for distraction rather than admit the truth. After all, what kind of daft prospective bride is so untrusting of her good fortune that she hasn't even looked for a dress to be married in, only two months before her wedding?

'Well, Sean says he's going to wear a wetsuit and bring his favourite surfboard to be his best man. So obviously I have to wear something that will match.'

'Hell, why not?' Sean interrupted. 'Seems a good idea to me. My board is my best mate.'

'And are you having bridesmaids, Thea, or keeping it uncluttered?' Sarah asked.

'We want it to be very, very simple. There'll be both our families and you, of course, and friends of Sean's from the village but otherwise just . . . us, really. And all a bit – you know – sort of homemade and unfancy. I can't do *fuss*.'

'Not even a best woman?' Paul asked. 'Isn't that the thing women have these days?'

'I . . .' To Thea's horror her eyes filled with proper big fat tears. 'I was supposed to have my sister Emily. But . . .' And she couldn't say any more apart from, 'She says she won't come all the way down here.' She sniffed. Sarah passed her a box of tissues and Sean put his arm round her.

'She will, in the end. She will,' he said.

'But why not?' Sarah exclaimed. 'It's not as if it's . . . I don't know, Australia or something!'

'She's just had a baby and she's not . . . not quite her usual self. But it's not only about that. Being so completely cut off by the snow last year had a really bad effect on her. She hated it; it really got to her. She was absolutely terrified! Really shaken by that isolation. Sam – that's her husband – promised her he'd never make her go away at Christmas again and she's making him stick to it.'

'Oh heavens, snow? Is that all?' Paul said, laughing. 'Seeing as that was the first proper snow in about a hundred years and made the national news, I think you can reassure her that she's more likely to drown in the eternal Cornish drizzle. You're her sister. She'll change her mind before the day, I bet you any amount of folding money.'

'Is this the right way?' Thea asked Sean as they drove his old Land Rover out through the hall gates and turned left, which wasn't the direction they'd arrived from. 'Are we taking a detour?'

'It's a mile or so longer but I wanted you to see something,' he said to her. 'It can't wait; I've been dying to show you ever since I first noticed. I was going to keep it for later in the week – not to mention in daytime – but I think you need to see it now. It'll cheer you up.'

'I'm sorry about earlier,' she said. 'Stuff's just been getting to me. School's tricky – the head is constantly on my case and Emily won't even talk to me. Mum says she's really depressed and I'm worried for her. It's kind of frozen any urge to get anything weddingy done at all. Maybe asking her to come down here at Christmas really is too much. But—'

'It'll be fine, trust me. And if you don't trust me, trust this . . .' He turned the car down on to a narrow track in the woods and it bumped over potholes and rocks.

He stopped the car and told Thea to hop out and together they stood under the trees.

'Look up there,' he said, pointing through the bare branches, black and stark against a pewter moonlit sky.

'Ahhh – yes, I see it! Wow – huge clumps of it!'

'And still growing too. So you see? The mistletoe was lucky for us last year; it will be for this. All will be well.'

THIRTEEN

'Mummy. Mummy? Wake up, Mummy.' Emily felt a jabby little finger prodding her shoulder and as she opened a weary eye she found she was nose to nose with Milly. What huge, intense blue eyes she had, Emily thought as she surfaced from a deep doze.

'What is it, sweetie?' Emily murmured, automatically gathering the sleeping Ned beside her into her arms. Milly could be a bit heavy-handed and had once got hold of the baby's wrist to drag him into place on the sofa so she could prop him up in a line with her soft toys.

'I want to be in your bed too. It's not fair.'

'You've got your own lovely bed with a pink princess duvet cover on it. You don't want to be in here. It's too crowded.' Emily yawned and glanced at the clock. It wasn't six o'clock yet and was less than an hour since she'd last seen it. She'd woken up to feed Ned at five and then hadn't been able to doze off again, as usual. Nights had become slow, monstrous hours of closed eyes but little sleep. It was as if every time she tried to let go, a zillion worries would take the chance to invade her head and shake themselves about, each one taking its turn at the front of her thoughts. Whenever she got close to banishing one, another would slot neatly into the vacant place until all she was left with was a frazzled, anxious gloom. It was, she decided in one of her more lucid midnight moments, like mixing paint on a palette. If you put too many colours in, you always ended up with mud brown. What sleep there was, was punctuated by the snuffling breath of Ned, his tiny wriggles, the jerking herself wide awake when he became still and silent, as she panicked that his breathing had stopped. And then there was Sam, who snored and shifted and was an ever-present danger to the baby of flailing arms and thoughtless turning. But if Ned slept in his crib, even though it was right by their bed, he might be taken. Emily wasn't sure what by, but the worst imaginings alternated between evil demonic sprites and bizarre cannibalistic burglars.

'Having your baby in bed with you is safe enough if you're careful,' she had been told by the nurse at the clinic. It wasn't exactly the most enthusiastic endorsement. The implication was loud and clear that if anything happened to him, it would be entirely her fault. But Emily wasn't a smoker, or overweight (not by much, anyway; after all, who was at maximum slenderness two months after childbirth apart from the Duchess of

Cambridge and Victoria Beckham?). She wasn't doping herself to a stupor with alcohol and as she barely slept between feeds and nappy changes nobody could accuse her of lack of vigilance.

'There *is* room. Daddy isn't here.' Milly scrambled eagerly across Emily's body and flumped herself down on the far side of Ned. 'See?'

So where was he? Sam wasn't a great one for early mornings and recently when he'd been doing the school run she'd had to shake him awake while the children brushed their teeth. Sometimes they'd be waiting by the door, coats on, and he'd be stumbling down the stairs still pulling on a sweater. 'You look like those awful women you see in the tabloids who rock up to school in pyjamas,' she'd told him only last week.

'You could always drive them yourself,' he'd grouched, his voice still just-woken deep and croaky.

'And what about feeding Ned?' she'd snapped back, but they both knew that wasn't the reason.

Emily left Milly snuggled under the duvet, put Ned into his crib and went down the stairs. There was no sign of Sam in the kitchen but she could see through the half-closed slats in the plantation shutters that a light was on in his office and images on his computer were flickering. She left the light off, carefully opened the back door and, taking a deep breath and crossing her fingers in case of dangers, swiftly crept across the terrace to catch what he was looking at before he noticed her. She was being a bit sly and sneaky and she knew it, but sometimes, sometimes, you just had to keep an eye on things or they'd slide.

'Sam? Why are you looking at property?' Emily whipped the door open and got her question out before he could close down the site. It seemed to feature a country cottage with the obligatory roses. The details would almost certainly mention 'an abundance of charm'. Her head whizzed through possibilities in the milliseconds before Sam could come up with an answer. Was he leaving her? Running off to live somewhere more peaceful and sane with . . . well, who? He quite liked Kate, a magazine editor up the road – they laughed a lot about shared journalistic in-jokes. How about Charlotte? No – he was wary of her and had once said sex with her would be like shagging an emperor-size duvet, maximum tog. Emily tried to remember if he'd said this as if it were a bad or good thing. After all, duvets were soft and comforting, although even the heaviest wouldn't have the crush-potential that Charlotte had.

As she'd anticipated, the website was abruptly shut down and Sam wheeled round in his chair. 'Do you have to creep up on me, Emily? I don't look at porn and I don't do online gambling, so can you please allow me my own space to diddle about on my own computer?'

Emily stepped inside and shut the door behind her – the morning air was close to icy and it was getting in and making her feel unsafe as if the slightest breeze could whisk her up to the clouds. 'I wasn't prying. I just wondered why you were up. It's early.'

'I couldn't sleep. You were extra-fidgety in the small hours.'

'So it's my fault.'

'I didn't say it was a "fault",' he said, making quote marks in the air with his fingers.

'No. But everything is, isn't it? My fault, I mean.'

Sam rubbed his eyes and ran his fingers through his hair. It was thinning, she noticed with shock. Oh God, he was ageing. They both were. Here was a new thing to worry about. Getting older could mean getting ill. Dying, even. She'd felt safe from that as her parents were still alive and surely there was a natural order to these things, but perhaps she shouldn't trust in that after all? Who would take care of the children? She must add something about it to her will.

Sam sighed and reached for her hand. 'Nothing is your fault. You're just not . . . yourself yet. If you'd only—'

'I'm not taking pills, Sam. Not while I'm feeding Ned.'

'Counselling then?' His voice was gentle but she could sense an underlying exasperation. She didn't blame him. She didn't like living with herself at the moment so there was no reason to expect him to like it either.

'I'm sorry.'

'About no counselling?'

'What good would it do? It's not as if I'm unhappy. I'd feel guilty taking up the time that someone else could use. I've got nothing at all in my life to complain about apart from being scared of the area I live in.'

'Oh, Em, come on now. You know it doesn't work like that. There might be some, I don't know, trick of some sort? Behavioural therapy?'

'Next you'll be saying I should get one of those so-called adult colouring books to *relax* me,' she snapped. 'I'm not six.'

'I wasn't going to say that, of course I wouldn't. But, you know, whatever it takes. Let's try. Mindfulness might help, maybe? Or back to your yoga?'

'Sorry,' Emily said again. She felt helpless and weak-light and when she tried to move towards the door she found she didn't seem to remember how to walk. She stood anchored to the spot, numb. It was cold. There was ice forming on the outside of the windows. She felt she might be freezing to a block and felt a small rise of panic.

'No, don't be sorry, it's probably my fault for not being able to sort you out. I'm fairly useless, I know, but I've never been faced with something that seems unsolvable,' Sam said.

Emily tried a few deep breaths but could only manage tiny shallow ones. For a few long moments she couldn't feel her limbs, couldn't feel how her feet connected with the ground. Was she floating? The illusion passed when Sam stood up and gave her a hug.

'I'd better go and get the kids off to school. On with the day and all that.'

'But it's half-term,' Emily said. 'Didn't you realize?'

'Ah – forgot for a moment. Look, Emily, you're doing a great job with Ned but . . . you know there are two others as well. Alfie asked me the other day if you were going to get better soon. I could see what he meant. When he's ill he lies on the sofa under the purple blanket. And now you're doing it. Can't we . . . I don't know, take them to the park today or something? If I'm with you, you'll be perfectly safe, I promise.'

Emily gripped his hand tightly as he opened the door and led her back to the kitchen. 'I'll try. OK, I really will try. This afternoon. But you have to tell me why you're looking at houses. Are you thinking we should move? Is it because I said I don't feel safe here any more? I don't mind moving. I could look at places with you. It's something we could do together . . .?' She realized she was gabbling and, strangely, half-adopting an idea she hadn't thought through. She hadn't written a list of pros and cons or thought about which bit of 'not London' would be bearable to live in. And schools – what about schools? And work? She could move her office easily enough. Clients weren't remotely interested in where their accountant operated from, so long as they got the adding up right. Perhaps it would be a good idea. A village perhaps; nothing too remote or too tiny, because she'd want a few neighbours, but a proper, perfect little community with a school and a pub and a shop. In seconds, she had them all in a rose-covered former vicarage, planting out bean seedlings and playing with the . . . dog. Dog? Where had that come from? She didn't even like dogs. They smelled and they bit. No, she didn't want a dog. They'd get a cat. And maybe a pony, one day.

He was filling the kettle at the sink and he laughed, 'Oh that! I was just idly looking for somewhere to rent down near Cove Manor for Thea's wedding. It seemed like a good compromise, somehow. We'd get to be just us on our own for Christmas like you wanted but Thea also gets us to be there for her wedding. What do you think?'

Oh, he looked so pleased with himself but Emily felt only a plummeting disappointment that was surprisingly physical. She could sense her face and body getting hot and anger was making her hands shake. Her breasts tingled with the familiar prickling sensation and she felt milk seep from them. Right on cue, from upstairs she could hear the little bleaty cry of Ned waking.

'I . . . I don't know. Well, I *do* know, but nobody cares what I think. I'll go and feed the baby. I can't, I just *can't* think about bloody Christmas right now. I can't think about anything at all.'

Thea had also woken early in the morning, slid quietly out of bed so as not to disturb the still-sleeping Sean and slid her feet into the sheepskin slippers she kept at the house – the mornings were now too cold for bare feet. Christmas soon, she thought. Wedding soon. They must add up the numbers and order some champagne while there was still the chance of pre-season bargains. She must . . . find a dress. A new dress. Nothing like the old dress; not even close to the one that had been so pearly-tulle beautiful, that had had her name attached to it, hand-embroidered on a little silk tag, but which, in the end, had never left the shop. Right now wasn't the time to think about that. Sean was nothing like Rich; he may be laid-back and casual to a near-fault, but he'd never let her down the way Rich had.

Woody miaowed around her feet and threaded himself through her legs. 'You'll trip me up, you mad cat,' she said to him, stroking his plush little brown ears. 'And then I won't be able to get your breakfast because I'll be lying on the floor with bones broken.' Woody purred and narrowed his squinty blue eyes at her, clearly not caring. 'OK, what is it today? Chicken flavour or fish?' She opened the old larder cupboard and pulled out the basket where Sean kept Woody's stash of food. Something glinted at her and she reached inside and from under the catfood sachets pulled out a silver bracelet studded with little red stones. 'Isn't this pretty?' she said to the cat, showing it to him before placing the bracelet on the worktop. She'd ask Sean about it later as someone must be missing it. Probably, she decided, it belonged to Maria, who ran most of the domestic side of the Cove Manor rental business; she organized cleaning and also occasional cooking for those clients who preferred to go for the luxury of a partly catered option. She was often in and out of the stables here, talking to Sean and calling in to feed the cat if he was away. She kept some of the manor recipes here too and had spent many an hour over the past year discussing with Sean and Thea possible meal options for the clients.

Thea put Woody's food bowl on the floor and he tucked in greedily, making little grunting noises as he ate. As she watched him she idly picked up the bracelet again, turning it over and round and deciding, on second thoughts, that it didn't look much like something Maria would wear. She was a big jolly sort and her jewellery tended to be big and jolly too: brightly coloured wide wooden bangles; hand-crafted necklaces with large multi-coloured beads. This was delicate, fine and slender and she could see it was hallmarked but not engraved. Maria's daughter Daisy's, possibly? She sometimes came along in the school holidays and at weekends to help out for pocket money. She was a quiet girl, blushing at the slightest thing. The previous

Christmas, Thea had accidentally caught sight of Daisy and Elmo kissing in the games room, table-tennis bats abandoned in favour of making the most of a piece from the massive clump of mistletoe that Sean had cut down from a tree in the nearby wood. They'd looked teenage-awkward but keen and she'd swiftly put herself out of viewing range so as not to embarrass the pair. Possibly Daisy had glimpsed Thea as she passed the door. It would explain why she never seemed to look Thea in the eye without going bright pink.

It was still dark outside but the kind of fuzzy dark that looks as if it's trying to rub itself out. Thea tried the bracelet on   it was a bit big for her and as Daisy was a skinny little teenager it was no surprise that it must have fallen off. She'd ask Sean about it later. It needed to find its owner.

FOURTEEN

'Sam sent a text. He says Emily won't go out of the house. He doesn't know what to do with her,' Anna told Mike as they drove towards the south coast. Online, Anna had seen a gloriously positioned beachfront house near Marazion and had arranged for a viewing. 'It's got to be worth a look, at least,' she'd said, flicking through photos on her iPad. 'And there's a building that's described as a studio so maybe it's one of those serendipitous things that is "meant".' Erring on the side of not getting over-excited by the prospect, Mike had said, 'Or it could be a fancy word for a shed,' slightly annoying Anna in the process.

'Well, Emily will have to get over that one,' Mike said, looking for the right exit at a complicated Penzance roundabout. 'She'll have full-on agoraphobia at this rate.'

'Hmm, well, that's about as much use as saying *pull yourself together*. I don't think it's something you just snap out of,' Anna told him. Sometimes, just sometimes, she remembered what it was about Mike that had made her go off the year before and be adventurous with someone else. He could be a bit damn set in his thoughts, so – and she recalled a phrase Thea sometimes used – so *last century*.

'It'll be hormones. She'll be fine once they settle.'

Mike still didn't sound worried enough, in Anna's opinion. 'Typical man,' she said. 'Always blaming our woman-equipment. It couldn't just be that she's actually right to feel worried? Some of the world out there is pretty horrid, don't you think?'

Mike slowed as they approached the village and peered around him. 'Down this lane here, I think. And there's parking. And no, I wouldn't say Emily exactly lives in a hotbed of civil disarray, not by any means. She's in one of the smart suburbs. One that's always described as "leafy". Honestly, sometimes I can't help thinking that girl doesn't know she's born.'

'Well, there is that. She could do with a bit of blessing-counting, but she could also get some medical help. Sam says she won't.'

'She needs something to look forward to. There's Thea's wedding. Can't she try and be positive about that?'

'You tell her then. Sam says she won't even discuss anything beyond whatever day they're currently on. We should go home as soon as we've seen Thea and Sean, help out a bit more with the children. You see, that's why I have qualms about moving so far away from them all. Where will we be when they need us?'

Mike stopped the car in a pull-in area alongside what looked like a fairly standard but large-scale Victorian cottage facing the sandy beach. To the side of it, there was a long detached building that looked like a garage but was presumably the studio, and there was plenty of space to park, which was at a premium in any Cornish village. 'I don't know, Anna, but at least with a bit of distance, they get time to sort things out for themselves without us charging in all the time like the cavalry. Anyway, this is it. What do you think?'

Before Anna could reply to any of what he'd said, the front door opened and a woman with carefully piled-up hair and scarlet lipstick was facing them. She wasn't smiling. 'You've a London registered car, I see.'

'Er, oh, have we? Does it matter?' Mike said, looking puzzled. Anna almost giggled: Mike almost certainly hadn't a clue about his car registration number. She re-membered, when they'd been pulled up by the police once for having a dodgy brake light, and Mike hadn't even been able to remember what make the car was, let alone the number.

'You have. You're from up-country,' the woman accused him. She seemed reluctant to let them in. Anna felt a bit cross. It couldn't be their appearance: West Cornwall had plenty of men of Mike's age with grey hair and a Willie Nelson-style bandana, not to mention women with boat-like purple shoes and colourful multi-layered clothes. The area was rammed with pension-age hippies.

'We've come to see the house. We do have an appointment,' Mike said. 'Or have we got the wrong place? Are you Mrs Carter?'

'Yes, it's for sale. But not to second-homers.' She still wasn't about to open the door any further, Anna could see. They'd apparently failed whatever test there was by having the wrong car. She felt quite annoyed. If this house was for local residents only, then why had it been advertised to all and sundry on a national website?

'OK,' Anna said. 'Well, we aren't looking for a second home, just a regular one. But we're sorry to have wasted your time.' She turned to go, feeling horribly unwelcome.

'Oh well, now you're here . . .' Mrs Carter said, opening the door another few inches, '. . . you might as well come in and have a look.'

'Thank you,' Mike said, treating her to an undeserved broad smile as they went inside.

The first thing that took Anna's breath away was the view. The front might have looked fairly traditional with big sash windows but the inside had been transformed. The entire back wall of the house, opening off from the kitchen and a large family room, consisted of folding glass doors leading to a broad stone terrace with steps to a small grassy garden with deep flower beds on each side. Beyond was the beach, the sea and the great rocky rising of St Michael's Mount.

'Oh, wow,' Anna said.

'Everyone says that.' The owner stood with her arms folded, glaring at the view. 'I suppose you'll want to see the rest of it.'

'That's the idea,' Mike said. 'If that's all right with you.' Anna gave him a nudge. She liked what she'd seen so far and didn't want to lose what slim chance an applicant from the wrong side of the Tamar River could possibly have of being in with a shout at buying this. Apart from the big family kitchen at the back, there were two other rooms at the front, both beautifully and freshly painted the colour of clotted cream, each with a new-looking wood-burner and plenty of deep, built-in shelf space. Anna felt pleased about that – she was willing to have a cull of her massive book collection but it would still leave a lot that needed accommodating.

Upstairs were three bedrooms each with its own bathroom, all simply furnished, painted in gentle seaside shades of white and palest greeny-blue and looking, Anna thought, like something utterly gorgeous from *Livingetc* magazine. She loved everything about the place, even how someone had thought it a good idea to paint exposed ceiling beams in a soft grey. In fact she felt heart-tremblingly excited about this house in a way she would never have thought likely. It wasn't *so* different in age or style from their own house, but lacked all the worn-out and crumbling bits that were about to become an endless money-pit if they stayed in it. The thought of a low-maintenance home, of being able to run the heating without expecting the boiler to go into a terminal sulk, was strangely exhilarating. Below, she could see from the main bedroom window, alongside the lawn, flourished huge clumps of agapanthus. At the far end was a group of echiums, half-grown to only about three feet now but next summer they would send great bolts of flower spikes over ten feet in the air. She wanted, more than anything, to be here to see them when they did. It was like falling in love. It was more intense than the crazy zinging she'd felt when she'd first got together with Alec the year before. It was better than that, in fact – this time she knew it wasn't going to be cut through with a huge dose of guilt and regret.

'Has it been on the market long?' Mike asked.

'If you're thinking of offering less than the asking price, don't even bother. This one will go in no time,' the woman said. 'It's not been on long but I've had quite a lot of interest.'

'It's beautiful,' Anna said. 'Just gorgeous and it has a great vibe to it. I mean look, it's a few days off November and it's still sun-warmed and glorious.'

Mrs Carter's face finally cracked into a smile. '"Great vibe"? My husband used to say that. He's gone now,

175

though, so I don't suppose I'll hear it much again. You just reminded me there for a second.'

Anna said, 'Oh, I'm so sorry,' and reached out to put a sympathetic hand on her but the woman moved back, holding gold-nailed hands up as if to fend her off. She came out with a vibrant cackle.

'Oh, he's not *dead*. Far bloody from it. He's living it up in Sennen with a nineteen-year-old waitress. *And* her mother. Good luck to the three of them, is what I say. He's fifty-six, the gullible sod. He buggered off without a backward glance just because some kid wiggled her skinny arse at him. Even gave up his beloved pottery. That's not a garage out there, it's, or it *was*, his studio. He had this idea he'd be the next Bernard Leach, bless his delusional ego. But in the end he could never turn a jug handle that didn't look like a dead bird perched on a tree trunk. I sold the kiln.' She turned away to the fridge and opened the door, taking out an opened bottle of white wine. 'Drink?' she offered.

'Er, no thanks,' Anna said, wondering what comment would be appropriate about the runaway husband.

'I suppose you think it's *too early*,' Mrs Carter said, 'and you're right. But in my case, it's too late, if you get my drift. I'm off out of this godawful place and I'm going to the big city.'

'Ah, off up to London then?' Mike said.

'No I am not. I wouldn't go there if you paid me. Truro, here I come.' She took a large gulp of wine.

Anna glanced at Mike and then quickly looked away again as she could see he was trying not to laugh and she knew it would be catching.

'You promise this won't be just for weekends and you can have the place. Asking price that is, no messing about. I put everything into getting it just right and I don't want it sat empty for forty weeks of the year. Got all the ideas from *Elle Decoration*. But local slate and everything and craftsmen from the area. Got to be loyal to your neighbourhood.' She waved her arm to encompass the maple kitchen units, the granite worktops, the dark walnut floor of old wide planks. 'It was our bolt-hole,' she went on, her voice sad and low. 'But then the bastard went and bolted.'

'I found this in the cat-food basket.' Thea handed the silver bracelet over to Sean. They were having breakfast of coffee and croissants outside on the terrace. It was a bit too cold really: it seemed mad to be eating outside while wearing Uggs and a sheepskin jacket but the sunshine on the terrace overlooking the beach was not to be wasted.

Sean took the bracelet and had a close look at it, frowning. 'I've seen it before but . . .' Then he smiled and said, 'Oh, yes. It's OK, I know whose it is.' He put it on the table and took a sip of coffee.

'And? Hey, you can't leave it in the air like that. I'm a woman, I need to know. Details, please!'

'Er . . .' he began, looking a bit shifty.

Thea's heart thumped. She'd been anticipating some local friend, possibly Sarah, but she felt a sudden small chill that wasn't about the weather. 'Who is she?'

'Hey, no one! It's all fine.' He squeezed her hand, laughing. 'It's just Katinka's. She visited for a day or two. No biggie. Must have fed Woody and dropped it in the basket. I'll post it back to her.'

'She's not local then?'

'Hell no. American, west coast. It was a fleeting visit during the Newquay surf comp, back in September. She's another surfer.'

'Right. Known her a long time then?'

'Oh yes. Years.'

'Was she a girlfriend?'

Sean shrugged. 'I suppose. Not for long, though, and all wiped out of the brain since I met you, obviously.'

'Did she stay here?' She didn't like to keep asking like this. It sounded both controlling and needy – something she'd never wanted to be again, ever. But the need to know was surely built into every woman when it came to the man you were about to promise the rest of your life to.

'She stayed one night. In the spare room. She and her friend. Don't you trust me, babe? You can, you know. I'm not a bastard.' He looked quite sad for a moment.

'I know. And of course I trust you. It's just that you

didn't mention her,' Thea said, still feeling a bit shaky. 'Pretty bracelet anyway.'

'I'll post it back. Katinka isn't an issue, I promise.'

'Oh it's fine. I just wondered whose it was, that's all. Now I know – sorry. It's just—'

'I'm not your last horrid fiancé,' he said, putting an arm round her. 'I'm a whole different bag of trouble.'

'I know, I know. Just, you know, now and then I can't believe everything's going so well.' She laughed. 'I've never been a luck-truster and so far I haven't been proved wrong.'

'Till me.'

'Yes, till you. And OK – I'm over that moment so after this croissant I must call Sarah and apologize for being such a pathetic wuss at supper the other night. She must think I'm the most useless bride-to-be. No sense or organization at all. No dress, even – that's unheard of!'

'Oh, she'll think it's just pre-wedding nervy stuff,' he said. 'And on which . . . are there things we're supposed to do? I know we've done all the registering with the relevant people and so on but it does all seem incredibly simple and uncomplicated compared with the usual Bridezilla sort of events.' He hesitated for a moment. 'I mean, that's fine by me – I just want to marry you and have a fun day doing it but if you wanted something more flash . . .'

'No, I really don't. Just you and me would be ideal if it really came down to it.'

'I didn't even get you an engagement ring,' he said, taking her left hand and stroking her fingers. 'I'm a hopeless lover, aren't I? I asked you to marry me, put some plaited bits of grass round your finger and that was it.'

Thea laughed. 'I've still got those bits of grass – they couldn't be more precious. They live in my knicker drawer. And I've had a fancy ring before – it didn't end well.' She'd been about to have a fancy wedding too. Glossy invitations had been ready to post, the church and the hotel reception booked. Rich had wanted the full Rolls-Royce and morning-suit event and she'd had to fight him on the details, arguing that it was all a bit too show-off and she'd rather chill it down. If anything, he'd been Bridegroomzilla. And then, suddenly, well, you couldn't have got feet much colder than his had become without having to chip ice off them. This time, though, this time would be different. It would be so much better: relaxed, casual, fun and somehow contained. It would be a celebration of Christmas with this funny little rural wedding thrown in.

'This is what you want too, isn't it?' she suddenly asked him. 'Is it just a bit too low-key even for you?'

'No! It's great! I love the Pentreath orangery and all I think we need to do is deck it with the traditional holly boughs, light candles and hope for a pretty frost beyond those windows as a backdrop. It'll be brilliant,

I think. I'm just a bit worried that you – being *girly* – might want more.'

'Cheek!' she said, laughing at him. 'No, I really don't. I want what we decided: the basics by way of a ceremony, a wedding breakfast that really *is* breakfast, on the beach if we can, and then later a lush Christmas dinner. No present lists because there isn't much domestically speaking that we haven't got between us, no show-off fleet of pointlessly posh cars, no—'

'No hats? My mother really will go mental. She's keen on dressing up.'

'Oh, hats if people want them. Who doesn't love a hat?'

'Then there's the other thing. We haven't really talked it through, have we?' He sounded hesitant. 'Like Sarah, I've been assuming you're happy to leave London and move down here next summer – but maybe that's a false assumption?'

Thea smiled. He really did look worried now. 'Don't be ridiculous. I really want to move down here as soon as I can! My job is only up there until July whereas your house is here and your job and that big wet thing out there that's probably more important to you than I am.' She pointed at the sea.

'Oh, Thea, nothing's more important than you are. But . . .'

'See? But.'

'The "but" is about running Cove Manor, not about

181

you and the sea!' he said, laughing at her. 'It would be hard to do it from London, but your family and friends – and your house – are all up there, so leaving will be a wrench for you. But you know I'd love more than anything for you to come and live with me full-time here.'

'I'm not so sure about the wrench thing. I can always go back and visit,' she said after a pause. 'But I don't want to be a stranger to Emily's children and to Elmo. I . . . I can easily rent my house out.'

'Or sell it?' he suggested.

Thea wasn't really surprised to find she hated that idea. The house represented an independence that had been hard-won. Being let down by someone she'd trusted had left her hugely reluctant to be reliant on anyone else, even the man she would go to the moon and back for if there was something there he needed. That house was her rock.

'I'm already looking for a job round here,' she told him. 'The house I can sort another time. And yes, of course I want to live with you full-time. Anything else is completely mad and not even thinkable, not long-term.'

He kissed her. 'Good. You have no idea how happy that makes me.'

'Me too. And it means I'll be on the premises to deal with any more of your ex-girlfriends who just happen to be passing!'

*

The decision seemed to have been made. Anna was light-headed with plans and excitement even though she knew that unless they sold the London house pretty damn fast there would be no chance of getting this one. The thought of *not* getting it was almost unbearable and she felt a ridiculous childlike anxiety at the possibility that this time next year she might not be the owner of this place. Heavens, it even had a studio. It was perfect. She could almost sense the tantrum she'd feel like having if they were gazumped. As they said goodbye to the owner (who was now on her second glass and had decided she *adored* Anna and Mike), she looked back at the building; she was already planning window boxes and a fresh coat of paint around the windows.

'I'm thinking a soft green, perhaps,' she said as she got into the car. 'Or maybe lavender. A mauvey-blue with window boxes full of dark lavender.'

'Getting a bit ahead of ourselves there, no?' Mike warned as he started the engine. 'Long way to go yet. But it's perfect, isn't it?' He turned to her and smiled, then reached across and hugged her. 'And we'll have lots of change to live on. Who knows, if we peg out reasonably soon there might even be a little bit left to leave the children. Though I'd rather not, obviously. If we don't get through it all, I'll probably think we've failed.'

'Are we being completely mad?' she asked as he drove towards Penzance. 'We are, aren't we? I spend longer in a shop changing room deciding on a dress than I have in that house but I know when something "fits". Will we be able to keep a base in London, realistically?'

'I don't know. Actually, I do know. Emily and Jimi both have houses – they can put us up. It's what people do.'

'Hmm . . . it's not the same, though, is it? Imposing. I don't want it to be all "Uh-oh, the olds are descending". We'll be "visitors". Visitors, fish and laundry, they can only hang about for three days without being thought a total pain.'

'Hey,' he said. 'So long as we bring Cornish champagne and a selection of pasties, I'm sure they'll be glad to have us. Now, let's go and find the agent and tell them we're making an offer before we talk ourselves out of it. Deal?'

'Deal.'

FIFTEEN

A little later, before Thea had a chance to call her, Sarah phoned from Pentreath Hall. 'We're having a work session today up at that school I run, Thea I thought you might like to come? We hold one every month and parents and children come up if they can and help out with a project. Today we're going to tidy out the polytunnels and put on new covers. I thought, after what you told me about feeling that children should be outside more, that you'd be interested to see how we run our operation. Or do you and Sean have plans for this morning?'

'No plans – Sean's got to talk to Maria about food for this week's clients. They're keen to be almost fully catered, so I'd love to come.'

'Great. I'll pick you up in an hour. I'm bringing the dog so you might need a peg for your nose. He's rolled in fox and I haven't had time to wash it off.'

'I'm sorry I got a bit emotional the other night,' Thea said to Sarah later in the car. She'd opened the window to offset the waft from Olly the wolfhound. 'It's not at all like me. I'm usually pretty stable.' She relaxed in her seat and put her hand through to the back to tickle the huge head of the dog that lay on the seat behind her. The car smelled strongly of him: damp, muggy – not an aroma you'd choose to share on a long journey; but it felt warm and sort of homey. When Benji had lived with Thea he'd always been confined to the boot and not allowed on the seats, especially after he'd been for a swim in the river, which he so loved to do while out on a walk. Yet the scent of him always permeated. Even now, after more than a year without him, there were times on a rainy day when she got in her car and had to look twice to make sure he wasn't in there. She had texted Rich to say yes she would dog-sit that weekend in early November, but told him it wasn't to be a regular thing. But it did cross her mind, now she was with Sarah and Olly, that if he *did* want a regular dog-sitter for Benji, she would almost be inclined to ask to keep him. A big dog like him would surely prefer living down here in Cornwall to hanging about in London, and he'd soon get used to having to keep on the right side of Woody, a cat that would never expect to take second place in his own home. Now that was a spontaneous train of thought that jolted her more than a bit – had she made at least half a decision?

Sarah laughed. 'Surely there isn't a bride on the planet who doesn't have a meltdown at some stage before the wedding? I do hope you make it up with your sister – I'm sure she'll come round to the idea when she's had time to think it through.'

'Hmm. I don't know. It seemed such a fun idea at the time – and surprisingly more practical than anyone would think in terms of who in the family can get here – but perhaps she's right and we're being horribly selfish getting married at Christmas. She's got her own ideas about how she wants to spend that time. I think Emily just wants to be at home with her own children, her own Christmas tree and her own turkey, and not have to whizz off to the far end of the country. I shouldn't expect them all to put their own plans on hold just to come and see Sean and me signing a register.'

'Oh, but it's more than that, isn't it? Your wedding is a major life event. It's to be celebrated. After all, in theory and in hope, you only do it once. And I tell you what: if Emily doesn't turn up, she'll hate herself for it later. Perhaps someone can give her a nudge about that.'

'Well, we'll see. Sometimes I think Sean and I should simply go ahead with it on our own, forget about inviting anyone at all and just have you and Paul as witnesses and a quick drink down the pub with who-ever's in there on the day. The way it's going at the moment, that would be a lot less hassle all round.'

'Oh, we can do better than that!' Sarah insisted. 'I think what you have planned, just family and a beach barbie breakfast, sounds absolutely lovely. And there's still a Christmas dinner thing for later so it wouldn't be so terrible for Emily, surely? After all, it's not as if she'll have to cook it or shop for it – who wants to do all that when they've got a tiny baby to take care of? I think your wedding sounds properly sort of home-grown without being twee. But – and I hope you don't mind me asking – did you deep down not actually quite like the idea of a fancier event?'

'Ugh, no!' Thea was vehement. 'I was supposed to have one of those before. I wasn't over-keen even then but it became something that gained its own momentum, like a big snowball. And then when it was all well under way he simply bailed. Moved out and did an absolute runner. In retrospect, as things turned out I'm massively glad that he did but at the time, all I could think about was how much I'd invested – time and effort-wise – into the day itself. I think I'd forgotten that it was supposed to be about *lerve*. This time, I'm not making the same mistake. This time it's the other way round.'

Thea wasn't sure what it was about Sarah that made her offload everything like this. She seemed to exude a calm optimism, a certainty that everything would come right in the end and that there was really nothing to fret about. By the time Sarah turned the car up a narrow lane and through a gateway into a small field, Thea was feeling properly relaxed for the first time in ages.

Physical distance from home, from the tensions of both work and family was finally making the worries slip away.

Sarah parked alongside several other equally muddy and hedge-scratched cars.

'The school is through there.' She pointed to a five-bar gate as they got out of the car and Olly was attached to his lead. The gate was hung with strings of conkers, pine cones, twigs and dry coppery leaves. Pieces of grey-cream sheep's wool were intertwined. 'The children made them,' Sarah explained as Thea admired them. 'They collected what was lying around our little woodland area and made "autumn". Then we hung them on the gate to welcome the season in. Soon we'll take them down and put up a new set of winter strings to take us through to December and January.'

'What a lovely idea,' Thea said as they unlatched the gate and went through. 'It's like a nature table but with a message. And . . . oh, wow!' As the hedge-lined path opened out into a little enclosed meadow edged with low woodland, Thea stopped in her tracks. 'Yurts! Oh, how fabulous! Are these your classrooms? I mean I knew you had a school but other than describing it as "small and wacky", Sean didn't tell me any more about it. It's gorgeous!'

'Welcome to the Meadow School,' Sarah said. 'And yes, two yurts, one for the tiniest children and one for the older group, though of course they are free to come and go between the two, depending on what activity is on. And they do a lot together anyway, especially when it comes to planting and harvesting.' She indicated two other buildings and a shelter, open at the front and with its roof supported by branched tree trunks. 'There's a kitchen – the children help prepare the food – and that shelter over there is our outdoor classroom, which gets more use in summer than the yurts do.'

There was a garden area, divided into small plots, and a pair of polytunnels, both – at the moment – lacking their plastic coverings.

'Do you grow the school food?' Thea asked. How different this was from the stark playground at the school where she worked, enclosed by a wire fence and with only a few shrubs and a couple of trees. Over in the far corner was a big climbing frame with swing ropes on it, ladders and a slide, all looking rustic and hand-made. Two small boys were shinning up a tree alongside and swinging off a rope on to a soft bed of bark below.

'As much as we can, yes. Obviously there's not a lot going on now and I think the children are a bit fed up with the endless spinach. Honestly, that stuff never knows when enough is enough, does it?'

Thea didn't know. She'd never grown more than a box of salad leaves at home and at school the food arrived in a van and disappeared into the kitchen area without a child ever seeing what happened to it between field, freezer and plate. How lucky these children were here.

This, she felt certain, was what early education should be about.

'Right – I see more people are arriving,' Sarah said. 'Shall we start with a cup of tea?'

'Sounds good. Where's the kettle? I'll do it, shall I, while you talk to the parents?'

Sarah laughed, 'A kettle! Oh, bless your sweet urban soul, Thea – we don't have a kettle. We only have enough electricity for very occasional minor use.' She pointed to a whirring little windmill up on a pole. It was a long way from the scale of those on a wind farm. 'I can run a few lights in the depths of winter but we mostly don't need to. We just finish school earlier instead. For tea and the school hot drinks, we light a fire, boil water. Primitive but effective.'

Thea and Sarah fetched wood from a heap behind the yurt and took it to the middle of the little meadow where a circle of stones marked the edges of a shallow fire pit. Sarah set up a metal tripod and hung what looked like a small cauldron over the flames.

'Er, I hate to say this . . .' Thea said, feeling puzzled as she watched small children chasing each other around, 'but – health and safety? Is this even allowed?'

'Course it is! We do have to make the usual full risk assessments, same as any other school,' Sarah said breezily. 'And the children are never near the fire un-supervised, just as the fire itself is never unsupervised, but at the same time they completely understand the rule about not setting foot across the stones. We don't have many rules: just ones about not being unkind to each other or to their surroundings and this one about the fire. If they're not overloaded with complicated instructions I find they don't have any problem with boundaries.'

As the morning progressed Thea wore herself out digging over the beds inside the polytunnels, chatting to parents and children and helping manoeuvre the new covers into place. She couldn't help contrasting it with her job in a regular school. The age range at this one only went from nursery age to eight years but, from what she could see of the kids, they looked lithe and ruddy-faced, well used to the outdoor life. The parents were generally an arty, creative bunch who were keen to have what one of them called an 'organic' approach to their children's education. Small children worked alongside her, even the littlest of them digging over the earth and pulling out weeds. Playing in the meadow, they swung upside down from low trees in the little area of woodland and nobody told them off or shouted 'Be careful!' at them. Later in the morning, before they stopped for lunch, Sarah gathered the children round the fire and they sang a song about the colours of autumn, waving sticks with streamers of fabric and ribbon in colours of rust and yellows and deep greens that they'd made during the last week of school before half-term. Thea was enchanted by it all.

When the time came to leave, she was almost as in love with the school as with Sean.

'So that's like a Forest School set-up, really, isn't it?' she said as Sarah drove her back to the stables.

'Sort of, but full-time, not just for visits. I taught for several years in regular primary education and all the time I was kind of adding up what I felt was missing, what wasn't possible to achieve given the constant SATs and the old national curriculum and one day I thought, you know, if I don't put this together now, this vision, then I never will. I started with one yurt and ten pupils and their brilliant onside parents and it went on from there. You like it?'

'Like it? It's fabulous. I'm all envy and admiration.'

'Not too hippie for you?'

Thea laughed. "Too hippie? You haven't met my parents! They're here on Saturday. I'll introduce you. They used to be so hippie that they grew ganja in the garden, in among the lupins. They don't now,' she added quickly, 'not since they graduated to good wine.'

'I can't leave Emily on her own for long but I need some help here.' Sam, in the back bar of the Fox and Duck near his home, got the drinks in for himself, Jimi and Charlotte and sat down with them at a corner table. 'Couldn't Rosie come?' he said to Jimi.

'No, she's taken Elmo to some music rehearsal for a Christmas show. She sends apologies.'

193

'No worries. You can pass on the info later.'

'I wondered what the SOS call was all about. Is Emily still Dagenham?' Jimi asked, sipping his beer.

'Dagenham?' Sam said.

'If you're on the District Line, it's near to Barking, sweetie,' Charlotte explained. 'It means: Is she still loopy?' She made a circular gesture with her finger up by her head.

'She's way past Barking. She's almost West Ham,' Sam said with a sad smile. 'No, seriously, she barely even gets dressed. Milly and Alfie have started avoiding her. If they want anything, it's always me they come to at the moment. They're in and out of the office every five minutes. It's hard to get any work done but what can I do? I'll be glad when they're back at school next week.'

'Oh, poor Emily. She needs a lot of TLC,' Charlotte said, taking a sip of wine. 'Is this a large?' she asked Sam. 'It looks a bit of a stingy measure.'

'You can always have another,' Jimi reassured her. 'I don't think they'll run out and I'm on the next round.'

'Phew,' Charlotte said. 'I'll be able to pay my way again soon but for now I'll have to owe you guys.'

'Aha – so you got the job you went for,' Sam said. 'What is it, a panto in the West End?'

'Er, not exactly. But it is showbiz and it's seasonal so I'm happy enough.'

'A Christmas show?' Jimi said. 'We'll have to get a party together and all come and see you. Emily might be up for that, Sam, if we get the tickets, drive her there and just damn well force her out for a couple of hours as a done deal. She'll be OK with all of us, won't she?'

'I don't know. I suppose if we all go, Mum and Dad as well, then she'll have plenty of back-up in case Ned cries. Or I could stay behind and take care of him.'

'Well . . .' Charlotte was looking hesitant. 'Sorry, but it's not really an actual show that you can kind of *go* to. And besides, it's, er, miles away. Take the children to see a local one. It'll be much better value.'

'How far away?' Jimi asked. 'Because I don't mind travelling. And you're looking a bit shifty if you don't mind me saying.' He gave her a nudge. 'Is it a naughty show? Bit of burlesque? Would Elmo be old enough for it?'

'Burlesque?' Charlotte spluttered. 'Burlesque girls these days are all thin pale wobbly things with little bubbly hints of the cellulite to come. They don't let the properly endowed near a stage any more.' She thrust her considerable frontage forward. Sam looked down at his beer. Jimi didn't. 'So trust me, Jim-Bob, your boy's actually way too old for what I'll be doing,' she said. 'But enough about me and my job, let's go back to Emily. My suggestion, for what it's worth, is to get her thinking about Christmas and start making all these plans she seemed to want. She likes to be well ahead and have everything planned to the nth degree, doesn't she? That's what I gathered from Thea last year. If she's going to refuse to go to Sean and Thea's wedding then she'd better damn well come up with the alternative at home.'

'But that's the thing,' Sam said. 'Milly and Alfie made lists of presents they'd like Santa to bring and she wasn't even interested in that. She just said, "Show them to Daddy," and waved them away. It's not like her. By now she's usually checking the tree lights and—'

'Really? *This* early?' Jimi said. 'But it's not even November till tomorrow. Blimey, you do like to be ahead of the game *chez vous*, don't you? Rosie and I are completely last-minute by comparison. I'm always the one out on Christmas Eve buying spare light bulbs and emergency batteries.'

'Well, you know Emily,' Sam said, shrugging. 'Or at least, we did.'

'And this isn't early,' Charlotte said. 'Maybe she needs a visit to the Selfridges' Christmas department. It's been open since July – I'm surprised she wasn't there at the door on day one. What you need to do,' she continued, 'is make it all so easy for her to get to the wedding and to *enjoy* it that she'll simply give in. I mean, think about it – if she's really feeling too washed-out and depressed to get it together here, then simply being put in a car and driven to a Christmas where she doesn't have to do anything at all except lie on a sofa like she is doing now will end up being a top option. But it's got to be no effort. For one thing, last year, because you were going away and you never usually do, you had to lug nearly all the children's presents down to Cornwall in the car – and she told me about the big flap organizing their bikes. What are you getting them this time?'

'I hadn't thought,' Sam told her. 'You see, that's usually her department. She decides exactly what is to be bought and I order it and I'm the one who is at home for the deliveries while she is – or was – at work. Same with the food. She's got a file for that. And Delia, of course. Smith, that is. The Christmas food bible,' he added, as Charlotte looked blank.

'Well, it's not her department this year, is it, because she's not as with us as she normally is. I think you should get Alfie and Milly a Wendy house for the garden. A proper big one.'

Jimi laughed. 'Yep. Great idea. And that'll need a trailer to get to Cornwall.'

'No, that's my point, idiot. You don't take it. You only take small presents, easily transportable ones that don't take up half the car. The Wendy house, you get someone to build it for you while you're away, then they've got this big thing to look forward to when you get back. I know a bloke. All I'd need is the key to your side gate.'

'Emily would go nuts.'

'But she already has. Have you got a better idea?'

Jimi and Sam looked at each other and together said, 'No.'

'Right, that's settled. And I've got a couple of weeks before my shifts . . . sorry, the *show* gets under way so I'm going to drag Emily out to get something fancy to wear, whether she likes it or not. But before that, Sam, I'm going to come round and babysit when you've made an appointment to see her GP. She can't go on like this. Agreed?'

'Yes, miss,' Sam said.

'Jimi?'

'Fine by me. You seem to have it all sorted.'

'Good. OK, Jimi, another glass of this vino for me, I think. A large one, please.'

SIXTEEN

November

'No trick-or-treaters last night then,' Thea said as she sat on the sand dune with Sean in the morning, drinking tea. The sand was probably dewy-damp but she didn't care because the day was bright and sunny: the sort you couldn't waste by staying indoors even at 9 a.m. with the air sharp and breezy with autumn chill. She had her sheepskin coat on and wrist warmers and was as cosy as she could be. Sean had been in the sea and she'd walked along the beach with Woody the cat at her heels, watching him and a couple of other keen surfers. Sean on a surfboard was in a class way above everyone else out there and she loved to see him snaking the board across the waves. It was obvious that the others took the lead from him, watching for the waves he went for and chasing after him seconds later.

'No. Most of the village families go on a mass outing

to Mullion and the kids do a sugar-grab all round the town while their parents are in the pub. It kind of works. Here, it's a bit limited. Cornish children have to be willing to travel for maximum fun.'

'At home,' she told him, 'Halloween is all about making sure you've got a huge supply of sweets in the house otherwise you get major egg-splatters over the front door and flour all down the path. They don't hold back. And then when you *do* give them the sweets the posh mums who are hovering at your gate in case you're a molesting monster glare at you and swoop to take them off the children "for later" because they feel guilty about them getting all that sugar. It's a middle-class minefield out there. No wonder Emily is so para-noid. I hope I wouldn't get like that.'

Thea thought about her sister for a moment, won-dering how she was. She hoped she was all right, that she was simmering down a bit and had recovered from the buggy-mugging. Jimi had phoned and asked when Thea was coming home, suggesting she go round to Emily's and simply make her spend time together in the same room, forcing her to have the contact she was so determinedly avoiding. Thea had sent her a friendly text early in the morning as a sort of lead-in, asking if she was OK and how was Ned, but so far there'd been no reply. She was missing out on this baby's early weeks and she felt sad about that. When she got home, she'd volunteer to take Milly and Alfie out for a day, give Emily some space. What new mother wouldn't jump at that?

'I was never allowed to go trick-or-treating,' Sean told her as he rubbed his hair dry with a towel. 'My mum said it would summon up the devil and the devil should be left in peace or it was asking for trouble. Those Catholic roots again. She always claimed to be a non-believer but you should have seen her with the Hail Marys the time we were on a rough crossing to Ireland.'

'I'm a bit the same as your mum but with planes,' Thea told him. 'I'll go on them if I must but there has to be something massively tempting at the other end to lure me on board.'

'You got as far as the Caribbean, you told me. With your ex? You must have thought that was worth it.' He gave her a bit of a teasing sideways smile.

Thea wasn't sure what he was getting at. Did he sound a bit jealous? 'Well yes, of course I did – at the time I was really excited about going. After all, it's not a usual destination for an underpaid primary-school teacher. But it was a lot less fun than I'd hoped it would be. It was very beautiful and all that but Rich found fault with absolutely everything: the service, the food, the room, because he'd assumed the hotel would be some kind of flashy show-off place and it was actually quite laid-back. His complaining made me feel tense the whole time and as if I should keep apologizing to everyone. I should have known I could never stick with someone who was rude to waiters. Why did you mention it? Did you want *us* to go there?' she asked.

'Ha, funny! If I were thinking about us having some sort of honeymoon, it wouldn't be to any place that was in the worn footsteps of your ex! I think that might not be the best start, do you? But otherwise I don't mind going anywhere if it's with you.'

'You're being all cheesy again,' she said, laughing and going to hug him. 'What I really don't mind is *not* going anywhere, but not going there with you. If you see what I mean.'

'I do see. I think. But . . . just now you said "at home". When you're back there at your house, do you refer to this place as home?' Sean asked her. 'I really want you to think of it that way round.' He kissed her neck gently.

'I will. I mostly do. I suppose it's because I still work up in London and my family are there. And that house – well, I bought it and made it my nest. Everything that's in it was chosen and put together by me, so yes, of course it's home. Think about it the other way round, do you ever call my house "home"?'

'Well . . . no. But also yes. I'm sorry – maybe I shouldn't have mentioned it. I just really, really can't wait for you to come and live with me here. It feels all empty when you leave. Even Woody goes into a sulk and sleeps on your side of the bed, all stretched out, as if he's hinting at what's missing.'

'He's probably just enjoying the extra space,' she said. 'But honestly, I feel empty when I leave here too. The minute I get to the A30 and head east I just want to turn round and come back.'

'So why not do it soon?' Sean said, smiling at her. 'Please? Don't wait till next summer. Quit the job, bring all your stuff, chuck out most of my tat. Combine the best of it and make *this* your nest, or rather *our* nest. Do whatever you need to do to it. Paint it the same colours that you've got in your gaff if you like.'

Thea looked out at the glittering sea with its heavy autumnal breakers hurling themselves at the shore, at the broad deserted beach with only three people and a dog on it. The wet sand shimmered in the sun. She thought about Sarah's Meadow School and the collection of warm-hearted and friendly parents and children there, and compared them with the school-gate mummies at home who slid into the classroom at every possible moment to try and discover why each of their little geniuses wasn't being *stretched*, as if children were bits of elastic. Why did she keep running away back to the grey city? What was there? Oh yes, her family and other friends – and her pupils, of course. And yet – what kind of a marriage would it be if they were so ludicrously separate?

'Of course I will, though I can't just walk out of the job,' she said suddenly. 'I'd be mad not to want to move here as soon as possible, wouldn't I? It's crazy to go on like this, living half-separately. Even Helena Bonham-Carter and Tim Burton only stayed as far apart as living next door to each other.'

'Didn't they split up?'

'Oh, right – yes, they did. OK, not a great example. I'm sure there are others but I don't want us to be them.'

Sean wrapped his damp neoprene-clad arms round her. 'At bloody last,' he said. 'I know it'll be a wrench with you having a close family, but no one in the UK is *that* far away. And even your parents are selling up and going off wandering.'

'I know,' she said. 'Cornwall isn't New Zealand, though there are summer weekends in the traffic when it feels as if it's taking just as long to get here as it would to get there. But I have to find a job. And decide what to do about the house. And get Emily to come for the wedding. And find a dress. And make lists. The wedding is the easy bit.'

'Hey,' he said, kissing her. 'You've just made a list right there. One thing at a time. It'll all work out, as the Tom Petty song goes.'

In Mousehole, the little hotel where Mike and Anna had spent the night had a Christmas Day menu up on the board and the gallery next door was selling Christmas cards designed by local artists along with hand-made tree decorations and Santa-themed bunting. The village Christmas lights were already up (had been for a couple of weeks, according to the landlord) and during the evening, as soon as it got dark, there had been people out on the street switching various displays on and off and checking them over ready for the great switch-on later in the month. Mike and Anna had sat in the bar drinking mulled wine, eating fish and chips and watching groups of children and adults in Halloween costumes and fierce make-up parade through the little town carrying lamps. The landlord had told them proudly about how people came from all over the country and beyond for Mousehole's famous Christmas lights.

'First of November and Christmas is all on the go. I don't know whether to find it depressing or what,' Anna said, picking up a pack of cards as they wandered round the gallery that morning. They depicted a harbour scene with Santa bringing sacks of presents on a fishing boat. 'I like these,' she said to Mike, 'but I can't quite bring myself to buy them. I don't want to be one of those people.'

'You could always buy them, hide them in a drawer and forget you've bought them till nearer the time,' he advised. 'Like Rosie did that time she went to the Matisse exhibition in August and bought a hundred cards then lost them somewhere in the house. She ended up buying emergency cheap ones at the last minute.'

'I know. And then she found the lovely Matisse ones

a week after Christmas. That's the way it goes. I expect she'll send them out this year instead.'

'Does that make her even more "one of those people"? Having had the cards since the Christmas before?'

Anna laughed. 'What, Rosie? The vaguest, scattiest woman on the planet? I don't think so, do you? Unless you count someone who drops her son off for his school ski trip at five in the morning on the day *before* he's supposed to go as a person who simply likes to get ahead. Poor Elmo. When he got back and I asked him how the trip was, all he did was grumble that he'd had to get up before dawn for two mornings in a row. I never did find out how the snowboarding went, bless him.'

'Fair comment. What I do need to know is about when we have lunch today with Thea and Sean. Do we tell them about that house we want to buy? Or do we wait and tell the whole family in one shebang once we're back home?'

'Play it by ear, I think,' Anna said as she paid for the cards and several beautifully painted tree baubles, 'and mind the step . . .' she called as he left the shop to collect the car.

'What was that?' Mike turned and, almost as if she'd set the whole thing in motion by warning him, he missed his footing and fell crashing to the pavement.

'Oh bloody hell!' Anna and the shopkeeper rushed to him.

'Are you all right? Which bit hurts?' Anna could feel her own heart thumping and hoped his was still doing the same. Mike had his eyes open but didn't seem to be focused on anything, like an over-dramatized TV corpse. People were collecting around him and she wanted to tell them to go away, stop blocking the air, even though she knew they were only being helpful and there was no shortage of fresh salt-scented air.

'Shall I get an ambulance?' the girl from the shop asked. 'Is he alive?'

'I'm alive. I think.' Mike started to sit up and put out his hand to Anna. 'Give us a paw. I can get up OK, but not from *here*, if you see what I mean.'

'Oh dear,' a concerned voice came through the group. 'Has someone had a fall?'

Anna and a pony-tailed, athletic young girl who'd been jogging hauled Mike to his feet. 'No, I have *not* had a sodding fall,' Mike announced, sounding grouchy, which was a relief to Anna. It was a sure sign of him being his normal self. 'I fell over. "Having a fall" is what *old* people do.'

'Well, quite. That's what I said,' said the voice, adding a smug sniff.

'Never mind that,' Anna said, conscious that Mike was leaning on her shoulder, 'have you hurt anything?'

'I appear to have damaged my ankle,' he said, grimacing. 'In fact it fucking well hurts.' He tried putting it to the pavement but went pale as he tried to put weight on it.

'Oh hell. I hope it isn't broken. Wait there, I'll get the car. We'll go to A & E and see if it needs an X-ray.'

As Anna drove the car back from the harbour-front car park she could see Mike sitting on a chair outside the gallery, adjusting his bandana. The girl from the shop was sitting on the step beside him. He looked slumped and in pain and she felt a sudden fear of a future of possible illness, pain, decreasing mobility. It was all very well him insisting that 'old' was other people, and to be fair he was younger than most of his old rock-star heroes. They were still leaping about onstage with a healthy gusto that their early lifestyles probably gave them no right to expect. But it wasn't something you could deny for ever. Were they mad to be contemplating a three-hundred-mile move to an area they had little experience of? Probably. But for now, as she pulled up outside the gallery, the one consoling thought was that in the event of various worst-case scenarios, the house at Marazion had a staircase plenty wide enough for a stairlift.

'Are you speaking to me yet? I promise I won't make you go out again.' Charlotte's head, encased in a huge furry hat, appeared round the back door. Emily was absorbed in looking at rural houses on Rightmove on her iPad at the kitchen table. The sight of Charlotte in her hat and her leopard-print boots made her jump.

'Bloody hell, Charlotte, did you have to creep up on me like that?'

'I wasn't creeping. And your doorbell's bust. Me and the postman were standing there like lemons. Here you are.' She came in and sat down opposite Emily and handed over a small heap of envelopes and one large, stiff one.

'Thanks. And yes, of course I'm speaking to you,' Emily told her, shutting down her iPad. 'But next time I look like I need my hair sorting, I'll make my own decision about what to do, thank you.'

'I was right though, you did look a fright.' Charlotte got up and switched on the kettle. 'And you don't look a lot better now, to be honest. Your skin's all sallow from lack of fresh air. But hey, if you're not going anywhere, then who's looking at you?'

Emily laughed and quite surprised herself. It was a sound she hadn't heard for a while. 'You don't have any kind of filter, do you, Charlotte? You think it, you come right out with it. Nothing in between. I don't know whether to hate you for it or admire you.'

'Go for admire,' Charlotte told her, searching in the cupboard for biscuits, 'because when I like something I always say so; I don't hold back on the love.' She pulled out a pack of organic plain oaty biscuits and made a face. 'Is this all you've got? Biscuits are for *pleasure*, not worthiness. Dear Lord.' She shook her head and sat down again, wafting a mixture of old perfume, ordinary soap and something of her own body at the same time. Emily quite liked it but found it disturbing. It was almost as if she was scenting Charlotte's physical core, perhaps even a powerful hint of libido. She'd bet it drove men crazy and was glad Sam was out at the park with the children. Poor Sam had been deprived of sex for months. Emily couldn't seem to get round to it and realized that now she had Ned to cuddle in bed at night, she'd completely lost any urge to do more than feed him and sleep as much as she could. Sam hadn't complained once. Was he just a saint or should she worry about that? Even if she did, at the moment there wasn't anything she was prepared to do to change things. The thought was too exhausting.

'Come on,' Charlotte said as soon as she'd had a few sips of her tea and pulled a face after dunking a biscuit. 'Get your coat. We're going shopping.'

Emily held on to the table edges. 'I can't,' she muttered, 'I can't. And just now you said you wouldn't make me.'

Charlotte laughed. 'Oh yes you can. And this time you won't be on your own, I'll be with you. We're only going to your posh supermarket, nowhere scary, and I won't leave you for a second, I promise. But your cupboards and your fridge are shockingly low on supplies and, well, suppose there's a sudden uprising? A riot or a . . . I don't know, a massive Noah-style flood? What will you do without enough teabags and milk and biscuits? *Real* biscuits, not these horrible things. They won't comfort you when your feet are soaking and the crazed rampage hurtle up the streets protesting about lack of chocolate digestives.'

Emily laughed again. 'Charlotte, you are mad, you realize that? But . . . OK. If you promise not to vanish up the washing powder aisle while I'm looking at teabags, then maybe we could go. I don't think Sam's bought anything for supper yet.' She flicked quickly through the mail and took the stiff envelope to the drawer where the tea towels were and slid it inside.

'So you can surprise him,' Charlotte said. 'He'll like that. They do.' She crammed her hat back on her head and picked up her bag. 'Get your coat and the car seat and we'll load that baby in.'

It took a while. Charlotte had got hot and steamy in her coat and hat before Emily had manoeuvred Ned into his little panda suit, brushed her hair and got herself into a coat, scarf and gloves. She took the car seat with Ned strapped into it and the blanket Charlotte had knitted and hesitated by the front door.

Charlotte shoved her way past and opened the door and Emily shrank back from the blast of cold air.

'It smells of smoke,' she complained, putting a hand over Ned's sleeping face.

'Always does in November. Bonfire night later this week, don't forget.'

Emily had forgotten. The weeks had turned into one long blur of baby-care, of feeding and fretting and being out of control of her life. She had been putting it down to missing the routine and order of her work life. When she went back to that, all would be well again. It really would. It wasn't as if there was anything wrong with her. Not at all.

Charlotte's car smelled of her but more strongly and with a mild overlay of cigarettes. Again, as she strapped Ned into place, Emily wondered if this was such a good idea, if breathing in this air would be good for him or give him . . . oh, she didn't know, a taste for weird scents? Too much exposure to an unfresh world? If she could keep him snuggled to her till he was twenty-one she probably would. Of course even she knew she was in danger of being smotheringly over-protective. But those boys at the mall had taken more than the buggy. They'd taken all her sense of having a safe place in the world.

'So come on, big or medium trolley?' Once they arrived, Charlotte wasn't having any dithering. 'Let's make it a big one and I'll get all my stuff too while I'm here. I don't often get to park in the parent-and-child section so I'll make the most of it.'

With Ned safely in his sling and bouncing gently against her breasts, Emily allowed Charlotte to walk her slowly round Waitrose. She felt strongly as if she were a member of the party of elderly ladies she sometimes saw in the big Marks and Spencer, having a day out from the local care home with assistants guiding them through their choices, sorting their money and credit cards, tenderly suggesting that a pack of three Brazilian-cut knickers probably wasn't what they'd meant to choose. She breathed evenly and calmly and kept her eyes focused only straight ahead or on the products she wanted, but even so, a certain unusual feature of the decor still got through her mental screen.

'Oh God, it's everywhere,' she exclaimed as she tried to find some plain white napkins. There was nothing but scarlet and green packs of paper tablecloths, napkins with stars and mistletoe and holly amid all sorts of seasonally themed tableware. 'Christmas. Isn't it ages away? Where did it creep up from?'

'It's been creeping up since August, love,' Charlotte said, reaching for a bumper pack of mince pies. 'You've been a bit . . . distracted, that's all. Now, if you've got everything, let's go back to yours and road-test these pies. I'm starving.'

'I must get home and make lists,' Emily said. 'I haven't done anything for Christmas. Nothing. I'm supposed to be the one who does this stuff. I want to be calm and everything to be nice.'

Charlotte took over wheeling the trolley as Emily was heading too fast towards the door and looked likely to forget about the checkout. 'It's OK, Em, just slow down. See, nice and calm. And as for somewhere nice and calm for Christmas, I think I know just the place. And all you'll need for that is a little something from the doctor and a lovely new dress. Trust me.'

'Can I? Really trust you?' Emily looked in the trolley and saw Charlotte's bags containing chocolate, ready-meals, biscuits and gin, but alongside was everything Emily had hastily scrawled on a list in the car on the way, neatly packed. There were ingredients for entire meals, plenty of fresh fruit and vegetables, treats for the children, nappies for Ned, wine for Sam. She didn't really remember how it had all got in the trolley. So if she wasn't the one who'd sorted it, then yes, she thought, perhaps she could trust Charlotte.

SEVENTEEN

It was now going to be lunch for six of them as Thea saw Paul and Sarah visiting the renting guests at Cove Manor during the morning and invited them along too.

'Ooh – yes please! I met your parents briefly last Christmas when you were staying here in all that snow and it would be great to see them again. We can do wedding-chat,' Sarah said.

But when they all arrived at Porthleven harbour, Thea was shocked to see Mike on crutches. After briefly reintroducing Paul and Sarah to her parents, she asked, 'Bloody hell, Dad, what have you done? Did you—'

'Don't say "have a fall", whatever you do,' Anna warned her in a loud whisper.

'I wasn't going to – I know what he'd say,' Thea whispered back.

'When you've kindly stopped discussing me . . . I tripped on a step that wasn't where a step should be. An American would probably sue.'

'It was a perfectly normal doorstep in a shop doorway. I don't know where else steps should be,' Anna said, rolling her eyes.

'Anyway, it's only a sprain and it's not broken,' Mike said to Thea as he hobbled awkwardly on the crutches for the few steps from the car park to the restaurant. 'We went to a very friendly A & E department where one of the nurses asked if I was Willie Nelson. I was sorry to disappoint her but I did take a bit of offence. I mean, OK, the guy's a genius and I admire him to bits but he's got a good few years on me.'

'This from a man who is always saying age is just a number,' Anna said. 'Vanity will out.'

'A sprain is almost as bad as a break though, isn't it?' Thea said as their party was shown to a table by a huge window overlooking the harbour. The tide was starting to come in and boats lounged on their sides on the mud, stirring as the water shifted them and reminding her of tired old seals flopped on a beach. 'And just as painful. I remember doing mine in netball at school. It hurt so much I was nearly sick.'

'You playing netball, in one of those teeny pleated skirts – now that I'd love to see,' Sean murmured in her ear, rubbing a hand against her bum. She gave him a hard nudge in the ribs and laughed.

'Yes, but not for as long,' Mike told her. 'And it doesn't involve pins and surgery or weeks in plaster. I can almost put my foot down already but I'd rather not. It should be fine in a few days.'

'You're not as—'

'Do *not* say "as young as you used to be", Thea. I expect better from you.'

'No, I wouldn't say that but—'

'But nothing. Really. End of, as Elmo would say,' he told her. 'Shall we order drinks? The one upside to being totally lame is that Anna now has to do all the driving. I fancy drinking a lot of something white, dry and disgracefully expensive.'

'Steady,' Anna said. 'We don't need to go mad.'

'Well, we're celebrating,' Mike argued, 'so let's have something deliciously fizzy to start with.'

'You can't start celebrating a wedding too early,' Sarah said. 'I can't tell you how thrilled we are that our first wedding at the hall is going to be Sean and Thea's. I'm so looking forward to it.'

'Ah yes, the wedding, that as well. Actually, mostly that. Definitely,' Mike said as the champagne arrived. The waiter poured it and Anna raised her glass.

'To Sean and Thea,' she said. 'And may it all go as smoothly as these things can. No snow, no storms and tempests and no—'

'Cold feet,' Mike finished for her. There was a silence. 'What? What did I say? I was only joking.'

'Not *that* funny,' Anna said, glaring at him.

'No really, it is,' Thea said, laughing. 'After all, why *not* say it?'

'Any cold feet won't be mine,' Sean said. 'Though I'll feel safer once Thea's excitedly trying not to tell me about the dress she's going to wear. There's last minute and there's panic stations. We haven't organized a single thing. But then we can't think of anything that really needs doing apart from making sure we've got enough sausages and buns for the breakfast. And drink, of course, but I'm ordering that through the Cove Manor suppliers.'

'I might not even wear a dress,' she teased.

'Even better,' he said, grinning at her.

'Bad man. I mean I might wear trousers, idiot!'

'Children, children!' Anna said. 'Seriously, Thea, do you really still have no idea what you're going to wear?'

'Sort of. I've got a favourite shop in mind. That's all I'm saying, apart from of course it won't be trousers. Oh, and I don't look good in white, especially in the middle of winter, so that's out too.'

'You'll need to take someone with you. Don't trust the shop assistants, they'll just want you to get the most expensive thing and then add a zillion hideous trimmings,' Sarah said. 'I nearly ended up with something strapless, gold-sequinned and with a twelve-foot train. I'd have looked like a drag queen having an off day.'

'Oh, don't!' Thea said. 'Maybe I'll just turn up in jeans and an old jumper. Strapless needs a woman who's a bit more . . . er, woman-shaped than me and

I'd be scared of it falling down. Plus it won't be the weather for it.'

'Also, it's rather tarty,' Paul said. 'If you don't mind me saying. And although I think there's an enormous amount to be said for a bit of the tarty on a bride, it doesn't look good with goosebumps. You'd freeze when you're doing photos outside.'

'How are you getting there? I suppose posh cars are out of the question on Christmas Day,' Anna said.

'Ugh, no, definitely not the Rolls-Royce option,' Thea said. 'I assume we'll just go in Sean's Land Rover. If he cleans it up a bit. Whatever I wear, I don't want mud all over it.'

'And flowers?'

'Ah. Not really a lot about at Christmas, is there? I hadn't really considered a bridal bouquet,' Thea said. 'Evergreens?'

Anna frowned. 'Well, I suppose flowers are not compulsory but it's quite nice to have something to do with your hands.'

'There'll be Christmas roses out – hellebores – but they tend to droop when picked,' Sarah said. 'But better yet, how about narcissi? I've got a friend with a flower farm on the Isles of Scilly. They're sending out hundreds of boxes of them every day by Christmas.'

'That sounds lovely,' Paul said, 'and we could get loads of them to mix in with the evergreens in the orangery. It would be very easy.'

Thea felt uncomfortable, having them all discuss the day. She still felt as if it was all a bit unreal. Too much detailed planning, she thought, and it might still all vanish into nothing like last time. She'd cross her fingers if it didn't make it impossible to carry on eating. She concentrated on her sea bass instead, letting them all talk around her.

'So long as there's mistletoe,' Sean said to her quietly, 'our lucky thing.'

She looked up at him and smiled. 'Exactly. You, me and the mistletoe. Everything else is superfluous really.'

'And I have a friend with a fabulous Moroccan tent that he said you can borrow for the wedding breakfast.' Sarah was on a roll now. 'He said he'll put it up on the beach below Cove Manor the night before so long as he's got some help from a few big strong blokes. He's one of the school dads, Thea – in fact I think you met him the other day. He's the one who built the climbing frame.'

'They're a fabulous lot, aren't they?' Thea said. 'I love the school, absolutely love it. It couldn't be more different from where I work. The head there even gets cross if a child has the wrong colour socks on. So much for personal expression.'

'So long as they're comfortable and safe in what they wear, we don't mind what it is,' Sarah said. 'You get the odd one turning up in a mermaid outfit or as

Superman but mostly they wear old clothes that can get filthy. All we insist on is that they have something waterproof. But it's not all rolling in the mud; we start the day quietly with a little yoga session.'

'Yoga? For tiny children?' Anna asked.

'Yes. It gets them breathing deeply and thoroughly, warms up their bodies and helps them to feel lithe and physically confident. And they have to concentrate quietly while they do it so that's helpful to put them into a learning mood.'

'Is that a Steiner thing?' Mike asked.

'No, it's a me-thing!' Sarah told him. 'I've taken elements from Steiner, Montessori and others and, like on *X Factor*, I've made it my own.'

'I'd want that for my own children if I had my time over again,' Anna said. 'I don't agree with hot-housing and endless testing. Nobody tests adults every couple of years – why do it to children?'

'We had tests every month at my primary school,' Mike told them. 'We had to sit in class in the positions we'd scored in the tests. So one month I might be near the front but a month or two later I'd be a couple of places back.'

'Oh God, that's awful,' Sean said. 'What about the children at the bottom of the class? They must know they're forever going to be *over there* in a corner at the back. How brutal is that? I wouldn't want it for our children, *at all*.'

There was a short silence and Thea realized they were all trying not to say something about whether the two of them would have babies, a silence thankfully interrupted by the waiter with the pudding menu. Sean squeezed her hand under the table and she squeezed his back. One day, she thought, perhaps they might have children enrolled at the Meadow School. Who knew?

'OK,' Mike said when the pudding arrived, 'there's one more thing we can celebrate.'

'Are you sure, Mike?' Anna said. 'It might still fall through.'

'What might?' Thea asked. 'What's happened?'

'Well, we've . . . er . . . made an offer on a house. And yes I know it's a bit mad but we liked it and wanted to bagsy it before someone else got in.'

'What? When? Where?' Thea was astounded. Her parents had lived in their London home for all her life-time and quite a bit more. How did you suddenly get to celebrate moving on quite so blithely?

'"What" is a house overlooking the sea. "When", yesterday morning, and the "where" bit is not far from here, near Penzance.'

'Down *here*? Wow.' Thea sipped her champagne and tried to absorb the news. 'But that has to need another question: why?'

Mike shrugged. 'It seemed like a good idea at the time. The others don't know yet so don't go phoning around, will you, Tee?'

'No. OK, no, I won't. I can imagine what Emily will say though. She'll have complete hysterics and say that it means she'll never, ever see you again or something.'

'No she won't,' Anna said. 'Because I want her to understand that it's to be a house for everyone. It'll be home for us when we're not out and about, because that's what we're going to be doing, but it's also a holiday place for the rest of you. And it's easily rentable as a last resort if we need to. If I were the sort of person who says it ticks all the boxes, then I'd say exactly that.'

Outside the restaurant, not much later, Sean and Thea went and sat on a bench overlooking the harbour. It was cold and Thea pulled her scarf up tight around her face. Now the tide was up, over by the harbour entrance a pair of young-teen boys in wetsuits and neoprene hoods were jumping off the steps and into the water, whooping and shouting as they splashed in.

'Are they crazy?' she asked. 'What is it about you lot that you want to leap into freezing-cold water in November?'

'Habit? Sheer love of the stuff? This is nothing – in the summer there are dozens of kids jumping in. It's a regular after-school thing. If we . . .' He stopped.

'Go on, *if we* what?'

'If we have kids, I was going to say. But I won't because I don't want to presume.'

'To presume I want them or that we'll be able to?'

He smiled at her. 'I suppose I don't want to jinx the chances by mentioning it.'

'A bit like the wedding,' she said. 'Not being over-organized just in case.'

'That's the kind of thing.'

'OK then, let's just leave it as a kind of "enough said" for now, shall we?'

'And see what happens?'

'Exactly.'

Emily exercised a massive amount of self-control and managed to wait till the evening when Milly and Alfie were asleep and Sam was out in the office writing his column. She took the envelope from under its nest of tea towels in the dresser drawer. She hid it beneath her jumper and quickly skipped up the stairs, treading as lightly and silently as she could, as if being found out would be the most disastrous thing ever. Perhaps it would be; for now, with nobody knowing, she could keep her little fantasy going, with no one finding a list of reasons to put her off and tell her it was all a silly nonsense. And those would be the words that were most likely to be used. Sam would say it kindly but slowly and precisely as if she were the same age as Milly and asking for the moon on a stick. Her parents would come up with reasons why it was crazy; they'd be practical and use words like 'unsettling' and 'on a whim', which, coming from a couple whose plans were to flog the family home and just *drift*, would be a bit much.

Once safely in her bed, Emily opened the envelope. Of course she'd already seen the house on the internet and looked at the photos, over and over again. She'd seen the little orchard, the sun-flooded terrace with its pots of lavender and the rose arch leading to the broad lawn and then the vegetable garden. Oh, but to touch the glossy photos was so much more sensuous. She stroked her fingers over each one as if she could make the scenes come alive, people the rooms with her family, see Alfie riding his trike on the terrace and watch Milly fishing for frogspawn in the duck pond with the little net she'd used in the rock pools down at Cove Manor last Christmas. The pond would need a fence; that much she'd insist on. A child could drown in inches of water; you heard horror stories.

The house itself was a cottage at its core – at least to look at – but with its loft converted to one long room and bathroom. There were extensions housing a gorgeous family kitchen and utility areas and it didn't have the low ceilings that she'd always assumed came with that kind of territory. There would be one more bedroom than this current house had but it was the location (as Phil and Kirstie always said) that clinched it. It was centrally placed in a little Wiltshire town, one that had a weekly market, a beautiful old high road, a choice (not a big choice admittedly) of schools. A community. Sam would point out that nowhere was crime-free and he'd be right but they'd be able to breathe good fresh air, keep chickens, maybe ducks for that pond. She'd seen Indian Runners on *Countryfile* and loved the graceful upright way they ran, all swirling along together like a white-feathered ballet.

'What's that you've got?'

Emily jumped, abruptly evicted from her reverie by Sam. 'Oh – er, just something that came in the post.'

'Can I see?' Sam sat down on the bed beside her and took the brochure. 'Wow, you get a lot for your money once you go beyond the M25. Always amazes me why it's not the other way round.' He flicked through the pages. 'So this just casually flopped through the letter box then?' he asked. 'Or . . . ?'

Emily looked over to where Ned, for once in his crib, was starting to stir. 'Or,' she admitted. 'I know, I know. It was just a thought.'

'It's not a bad thought. I wish you'd shared it with me earlier.'

'Really? Don't you think it's a mad one?'

He shrugged. 'No, not really. It's just too far for commuting, but then I don't commute. You do though.'

'But I *am* the office. It can come with me.'

'You've thought this through.' He looked at the photos again. 'It's big enough for weekend visitors. You do know we'd be spending half the time running a sort of bed and breakfast for mates but without the income?

Still, they'd bring stuff. Bottles of wine, swanky cheeses that they think we can't get, prosciutto and fancy veg from Borough Market that's three times the price it should be.' He laughed. 'No, I don't think it's a crazy idea at all. But . . . can it wait till after Christmas? Can we get your sister's wedding out of the way first?'

'It might have gone by then,' Emily pointed out. 'I want to have Christmas here, like we agreed, but we could just maybe drive down and have a look.'

'Possibly, but I'd have thought it pretty unlikely by this stage. If it's not under offer by now, I doubt it'll be flying off the market before Christmas. People don't want the hassle of moving at this point, do they? I certainly don't. Why not give them a call and see what the score is? We'd also need to know what we'd get for this one, though I've a pretty good idea. I think the answer would be "way too much for a glorified end-of-terrace".'

Emily smiled. 'Location though, you see. Our house would sell in a heartbeat, Christmas or not. If we had an open day there'd be queues. There always are round here.'

'I'm happy for us to go and look at the cottage,' Sam told her, sounding serious, 'but not yet; only if it's still on the market later. We could call now and let them know you're interested, but not go till we're on the way to Thea's wedding. That would work, wouldn't it?'

Emily said nothing. There wasn't anything she could say – she'd set herself up for being trapped in that particular corner. She stroked the glossy picture of the stone front of the house and imagined it was like an advent calendar with tantalizing little windows that she couldn't yet open. How far was Wiltshire? Surely she didn't have to go all the way on to Cornwall as part of the deal?

'Nice try, Sam, but you're not getting round me that way. I really, really don't want to spend Christmas in Cornwall and you promised we wouldn't have to. I'm just too . . . not ready. Too . . . scared.'

EIGHTEEN

So what use was that? And he called himself a doctor. Emily, furious, stamped down the steps of the group practice and out into the cold, cuddling Ned in his sling closer to her and pulling his woolly hat further down so it covered the back of his soft little neck. How dare the weather be so damn cold, she thought as she looped her scarf across him for extra warmth. She blamed the season: hated it. Tiny babies needed to be warm, for heaven's sake, not have evil winter inflicting its worst on them. It felt almost cold enough for snow and that was one thing she, baby Ned and everyone in the world could sodding well do without. Everything felt so very much against her. There was Sam trying to blackmail her into going to Cornwall, Thea so selfishly getting married on bloody Christmas Day of all bastard days, and now her GP – a man she'd known since long before Milly was born, a man she'd counted on to be on her side in all things 'health' – was telling her that she was *perfectly well*. How dare he? She strode across the road at the junction before the green man showed, annoying a woman waiting with two small children who was loudly instructing them in the fine art of road safety, and she barged in through the door of the pharmacy to get some cream for Ned's nappy rash. There was a queue at the counter for prescriptions and after she'd found the cream on the shelf, she stood tapping her fingers furiously on the glass counter-top, glaring at those who held their precious little prescription slips.

Why couldn't she have one? She'd looked up on the internet exactly what was safe to take when you were still breastfeeding and had found what she thought would work. It would only be a short course, a few little pills to tide her over, to help her be more bearable to live with so that Sam wouldn't actually run right out of patience and start to hate her. She wouldn't blame him if (when?) he did. With her GP's back-up she could have shown Sam that she'd been right all the time – she really wasn't well enough to carry on as normal. Not well enough to travel all those miles away at bloody *Christmas*, to risk leaving the safety and comfort of her own *home* just to please *other people*. But no. To be fair, Dr Mackenzie hadn't laughed at her, hadn't dismissed her totally. He'd gone through the motions – but then he did that for everyone, even those who'd come in with an immovable splinter. He took her blood pressure, asked her about Ned, admired him even. He asked how the feeding was going and if she was attending the baby clinic and still checking in now and then with the health visitor. She'd tried, truly she had, to get some help, and she answered all his questions like the good mother she was. In exchange all she required was a touch of medication that even Sam thought she needed.

'Go and see the doc, please, Emily. I'll drive you there if you can't face walking round the corner,' he'd said when she'd flopped at the kitchen table that morning in her dressing gown and with unbrushed hair, too spaced out to deal with Alfie's spilled Coco Pops. She'd simply stared at the mess as if that would make it clear itself up. Milly hadn't helped, though she'd tried to, grabbing a roll of kitchen paper and using it to blot the liquid without actually tearing any sheets off so that the whole roll was instantly sodden from outside to centre and no use for anything except for being shoved straight into the recycling.

'They're back at school tomorrow,' Sam said. 'Maybe if you start taking something – something mild and safe – from today and getting a bit of peace when they're out of the house, you'll get back to normal.'

'I *am* normal,' she'd told him. 'This is *my* normal. And it's Monday, why aren't they back at school today?'

'Christ on a bike, Em, don't you ever look at the calendar? They've got an inset day. Some of the teachers are off. That's why Thea's still down at Sean's, though I guess she'll have to drive back today.'

'Will she?' Emily asked wearily. 'I don't know why she doesn't just stay down there. Or he could come up here. Then they could get married in Richmond or something. Much more—'

'Leave it, Emily. It's their choice. They aren't going to change it just because you say you can't be arsed to go there, join in and enjoy yourself.'

But Emily didn't even have any choice over her own health, it seemed. She paid for the cream and slammed out of the shop, wanting to kick the prescription-holders. What secret code had they uttered that had worked its magic on whichever doctor *they* had seen? Should she have seen a different one? But it had been hard enough to get an appointment with Dr Mac. It could be halfway into next year before she got another one, the way the complicated bookings system worked.

It was all about cutbacks, that must be it. Nobody got what they needed (apart from that shopful, all smugly lined up) if there was the slightest chance of a cash saving being made. What was it he'd said? Oh yes, 'conservative management'. For a moment she'd assumed he'd been talking about government policy regarding the NHS but then quickly realized he was talking about treatment for post-natal depression. 'Avoid caffeine and alcohol,' he'd told her. Well, yes, she was doing that already, apart from the odd cup of tea. Did he really think she was the sort of mother who breastfed while bingeing on booze and triple espressos?

Exercise. He said exercise. 'Walking is good.' He meant she should go out and push a pram round the park and get talking to all the other knackered, pissed-off new mothers. Which was fine if you still *had* a pram and also fancied listening to strangers treating you to too much information about their perineal stitches. No thanks. It wasn't the weather for walking anyway. It wasn't even easy to persuade Alfie and Milly to go to the swings or to wander down to the river and feed the ducks in November. They'd always hated having cold fingers and they got lazy in winter, reluctant to leave the nest, like hibernating squirrels.

But it was the other thing that most pissed her off. 'Don't isolate yourself,' he'd advised, with the kind of smile that used to go with an avuncular hand on the knee in the days before that sort of thing got you arrested. 'Keep up with friends and family,' he'd said, while already looking at his computer and Googling what to do about the nasty eye infection awaiting him on his next patient just the other side of the door. She'd vaguely mentioned Thea's wedding in Cornwall and how she didn't feel she should go and he'd beamed at her. 'Oh, but it'll be just the thing!' he'd said. 'Splendid event, just what you need to take you out of yourself.' She didn't think she'd mention this to Sam. No. That was the kind of thing that came under 'patient confidentiality'. Perhaps she should have told Dr Mac about her snow phobia. She could tell him how she'd felt when she'd watched Milly on her new bike, careering across the ice. How in the seconds before she'd reached her she'd pictured the child, who'd ended up tangled in the bike's frame, with her legs at the wrong angles, bones sticking through her skin, maybe an artery ripped. And no way of getting her to any help or hospital. Even now, she felt sick at the thought. She walked a bit faster as she neared home. Perhaps she'd try and make another appointment for next week after all. But with one of the other doctors.

All the best things are over far too soon, Thea thought as she drove out of the village on her way back to London. The Polo chugged up the hill away from Cove Manor as if it too was reluctant to leave. She stopped at the top of the rise, pulled over into a gateway and took a last long look back at the bay. The day was bright and sunny and the bare hawthorn branches were stark and dark against the pale blue sky. Far below, the wet beach shimmered and the waves were cresting with white. Sean had said there would be rain later and a high wind, possibly quite a storm, but for now it looked benevolent and beautiful, the kind of scene that graces TV holiday shows and has people rushing to book cottages for the summer ahead.

Thea pulled away from the roadside after a few

lingering moments and began the long haul to London, mentally checking in her head that she'd got everything. It was easy to forget things now she kept quite a few clothes here at the stables and on the last visit she'd had to go back after a couple of miles for her most comfortable boots that she liked to wear at work.

She thought about the Meadow School as she joined the traffic moving slowly towards Truro. How much more fun it would be to work there than under Melanie's iron reign. Thea did her best to bypass the rigid reading schemes, preferring to get children enthusiastic about books by reading them stories where the language had an entrancing rhythm and flow, but Melanie had this idea that all books should be age-labelled and reading outside a prescribed range was not encouraged. If she came in to Thea's class during the designated Literacy Hour and found the children acting out the stories that Thea read to them she often disapproved. She had once told Thea that she should be far more formal in her approach. Thea had children in her class who were almost ready for *War and Peace* and others who were finding it hard to grasp the basics of three-letter words, so she was firmly on the side of flexibility. She wondered how Melanie would react to Sarah's free-range method of teaching the smallest children letters: taking them outside to walk the shape of, say, a W; forming the large letter on the ground out of shells or stones; maybe collecting from the hedgerows and the

JUDY ASTLEY

field small items that began with that letter; making up alliterative rhymes. She could just see Melanie's face if she saw Thea had her class out in the playground, making letters out of sticks and leaves instead of painstakingly forming them with stubby pencils on paper or tracing them on dots in workbooks.

She'd already gone past the Falmouth turning before she realized that one essential – her bag containing the school marking she'd been doing this week – was still on the desk in the stables sitting room. For a few moments she contemplated continuing the journey without it. Was having Sean post it to her an option? But no – that wouldn't work. She'd need it from the first day back – tomorrow – as it contained all the books in which the children were writing stories based on the theme of autumn. She'd asked them to collect as many different fallen leaves and fruit as they could find over this half-term week to write about them, so they would need their books straight away.

There was no choice but to turn round and go back. In spite of this adding a good hour to what was already going to be a long journey in slow London-bound post-holiday traffic, she couldn't help feeling a small thrill at the idea of just a few more moments with Sean. It had been a horrible wrench leaving him earlier and she'd felt quite tearful as she kissed him goodbye.

'You soppy thing,' he said to her, mopping her damp eyes with a tissue.

'Sorry. I'm an idiot. It's just been such a lovely week.'

'It has,' he said, hugging her tightly. 'But I'll see you in a couple of weeks and then it'll be no time till Christmas and our mad little wedding. I can't wait.'

'Me neither. And it *is* a bit mad, isn't it?'

'Tell me truly,' he then asked. 'Is it a bit *too* informal and casual for you? Are you sure you don't want hundreds of guests and a sit-down meal and a marquee and—'

'And a diamond tiara and a twenty-strong team of bridesmaids? No I don't! Don't even think about it! We've talked about this. Just us and a few family members will be perfect. All I hope is that your mother is onside about it.'

'I'll find out next week when I go up to see her. She's keen to come to it, and she's bringing my sister Patti. But if you hear someone tutting all through the ceremony, asking me why I couldn't have got Father Dooley to officiate, and then demanding to know why there isn't a five-tier cake covered in iced roses and with a plastic bride and groom on the top, then that'll be her.'

'Oh God, I'm sorry. Not a good start, is it, getting on the wrong side of my mother-in-law?'

'Oh, she'll be fine. She likes you. Who wouldn't? And so long as she gets to try on every hat in John Lewis so she can get the one that's guaranteed to be the biggest at the gig, I think she'll be as happy as a clam.'

It was disappointing, as Thea arrived back at the stables, not to see Sean's Land Rover there. As she climbed out of the car, Woody the cat came running up, miaowing, and he let her pick him up. With him snuggling and purring against her, she went to open the door but was surprised to find it wasn't locked. That wasn't like Sean. Although he'd agree with most of the village that crime wasn't an issue in the area and that there hadn't been a burglary for years, he wasn't likely to take pointless risks and leave computers and his precious surfboard collection vulnerable to that rare passing chancer.

'Sean? Are you here?' Thea called as she went inside, in case he'd moved the Land Rover somewhere else and was actually on the premises. The coffee mug she'd used that morning was still in the sink. Maria's cookbooks were heaped on the kitchen table. The washing machine was whirring in the utility area.

Thea found the bag she needed, put it by the door ready to take with her, and then went into their bedroom. She could smell her Clarins shower gel and she sat on the bed and breathed in the scent. She almost felt like getting back into bed and waiting there for him, as a surprise. A tap ran in the bathroom – so he *was* there after all.

'Sean?' she called, thinking it was probably not a great idea to give him the huge shock of coming out and seeing her there with no warning.

'Hey, who's that?' The voice wasn't Sean's and Thea stared at the bathroom door as it opened. A girl came out, a towel wrapped round her tall slim body and another one turbaned on her hair. Thea took in the smooth silky tanned skin, cheekbones as angular as Kate Moss's and arms with the kind of defined slender muscles that only serious fitness commitment could provide.

'Oh my *Gaahd*!' The voice was American and squealy. 'You, like, *so* scared me! I was expecting Sean!'

'That makes two of us,' Thea said, her heart thumping. 'Who are you?'

'I could ask you the same. In fact I will. Who the hell are you?'

'I'm Sean's girlfriend. I'm Thea. And' – she looked at the girl's feet – 'those are my slippers you're wearing.'

'Really?' The girl looked down as if her footwear was a complete mystery to her. 'It's so lucky they fit!' she said. 'They're toasty warm.'

'Aren't you going to take them off?' Thea said. 'Or do you usually just take other people's stuff to wear?'

The girl shrugged and pulled the towel off her hair. A cascade of wet blond hair fell below her shoulders. Thea felt a bit sick. What was going on here?

'So you're the new girlfriend,' the girl said, running her fingers through her hair. The ends curled into little tendrils.

'Not so new,' Thea told her, looking around the

room. Where were the girl's clothes? Was she intending to pad around all day in the towel? And where the hell was Sean? 'It's been nearly a year,' she went on.

'That's pretty new!' the girl said, laughing. 'You're really kinda cute,' she added. 'I like your hair.'

'Thank you. So where is Sean?' The tall, elegant girl had used the 'cute' word. The instinctive suspicion escalated to dislike.

'Oh, he went to see someone called Paul. I think he said Paul? Back soon, he said, and then he's going to take me to lunch at the pub. I was just taking a shower . . .'

'I know. That was my shower gel you used.'

The girl laughed. 'Really?' she said again. 'Hey, but no worries, I do have my own clothes. You don't have to look so paranoid. Do you mind if I go put them on?'

'Feel free,' Thea said, half-expecting her to open a drawer and take out Thea's own underwear and spare jeans.

'OK. Give me a sec, be right back.' The girl pulled the towel tighter round her body and padded out of the room, still in Thea's sheepskin slippers. Drops of water glistened on her shoulders and dripped a trail from her hair as she went, passing the kitchen and entering the second bedroom.

Thea went into the sitting room, closing the bedroom door firmly behind her. She felt shaky and a bit sick. This girl seemed perfectly at home here. She appeared entirely confident of her right to be on the premises and certainly knew her way around, barely a couple of hours since Thea herself had got out of Sean's bed.

Thea went into the kitchen and switched the kettle on, rinsed out the mug she'd used only that morning and plonked a teabag in it. She didn't feel like offering to make one for this interloper. In fact, she felt far more like grabbing her by her long swishy curls and hurling her out of the door and into the cold, preferably still wearing only the towel. Where the hell was Sean? She'd love to hear what his explanation was. Woody sat on the bench by the table, watching Thea and blinking his blue eyes slowly. She stroked his ears, gaining some small comfort from the softness of his fur and the way he so lovingly pushed his pointy little face against her hand.

'So . . .' The girl came back into the room, her hair brushed and even blonder as it dried. She was wearing skinny jeans and a pale blue chunky soft sweater with a drapey neck. She looked fresh, pretty, appealing. 'Sean told me you're supposed to be getting married.'

The kettle boiled and Thea poured water into her mug. The girl eyed it but said nothing. 'Shall I make you one?' Thea heard herself say just as she cursed her own good manners.

'No thanks. I don't do caffeine.'

'What do you mean, "supposed to be"?' Thea asked. 'It's next month.'

The girl laughed. 'Yeah. Sure.'

'Well yes. *Sure,*' Thea replied. She went to the fridge to get milk. Inside were two new bottles of champagne and a duty-free bag containing a bottle of vodka that hadn't been there earlier that morning. 'Yours?' Thea pointed to them.

'Yeah. Gotta thank your host, haven't you?'

'You're staying here then?'

'Hey, lighten up, honey. Could you *be* more hostile?' The perfect all-American teeth were still showing but no longer even pretending to be part of a smile.

'Yes, I probably could. I don't even know your name. Sean never said anything about a friend staying. And that bedroom where your clothes were, it's got its own bathroom.'

'Yes, but it doesn't have your shower gel.' The girl grinned as she sat down on the bench alongside the cat and he moved out of the way, twitching his tail. 'It was a last-minute call,' she said. 'It's what we do – a surf thing. We crash on each other's sofas, worldwide. Sorry if it upset you. Sean knew you wouldn't be here, so I guess there was no point in mentioning me. I'm just passing through. It's no biggie. I think he might have wanted us to like each other but I guess it's not the best start. Sorry about the house-shoes. I'll put them back in the room, shall I?'

'Just give them to me, I'll put them back.' Thea sipped her tea. It was still too hot and she scalded the end of her tongue. 'Where are you passing through to?' she asked.

'South Africa. I've got a comp there.'

'Comp? A competition?'

'Sure. I'm a surfer. I know Sean from when he was on the world circuit. We go back a *looonng* way. Has he never mentioned me? I'm Katinka. I'm surprised he hasn't.'

'No, never . . . except . . .' Thea went to the window ledge and picked up the bracelet. 'Oh yes, he did once, last week. I think this is yours. You must have left it last time you were "passing through".'

'Hey! That's great! Thank you *so* much – I thought I'd never see it again. It has great sentimental meaning to me.' She slid it on to her wrist and looked at it, stroking her fingers over the smooth scarlet stones set into the silver. 'It was actually a present from Sean on my wedding day,' she said, looking up at Thea.

'Oh right – so he was a guest at your wedding?' Thea felt some of the horror lift slightly.

'Hell no, sweetie, Sean was the *groom*.'

NINETEEN

The book group would never be the same again. Anna had missed the email while she was away because it had gone into her junk mail folder and she simply hadn't thought to check it till she was home and back on her computer rather than just the phone. The message that Miriam had died had come from Alec. He'd written it from a different email address from the one he'd used to contact her back when they were having their . . . What should she call it? It *was* an affair: almost anyone would call it that, but as Anna and Mike had been going through a phase of 'extra-marital exploration', as Charlotte had once put it, with a view to the possibility of a totally amicable divorce, it hadn't had the sneaky intensity, the lying, the guilt and the sense of cheating that is usually associated with the word. All the same, seeing Alec's name confined to junk mail seemed sadly symbolic now, as if their former relationship itself had become a matter of garbage, fit only to be thrown away.

So Miriam had gone. Big, clumsy, flamboyant

Miriam would never again spill red wine on someone's new pale sofa while declaring that *Vanity Fair*'s Becky Sharp was the first example of a truly liberated woman in fiction. Anna remembered not quite agreeing with her on this (citing the Wife of Bath and Shakespeare's version of Cleopatra), though seconding Miriam's notion that Becky's quest for a rich and comfortable life was organized entirely on her own terms. Others, she recalled, had shouted them down, arguing that she'd merely prostituted herself by marrying for money and position and not for love. That particular book group meeting had been here in this house, Anna remembered now as she was about to leave for Miriam's funeral. Miriam had flailed an arm and sent a vase of tulips flying from the table beside her chair. Anna had been finding teeny shards of the vase's glass for months after that and had had to ban Alfie and Milly from running around barefooted in the sitting room.

'Charlotte's here. She's waiting outside in the car,' Mike called up the stairs as Anna was putting on some lipstick. 'She says hurry up or you won't get good seats.'

'Not sure getting a good seat is what you go to a funeral for,' Anna grumped as she came down the stairs. 'But it's OK, I'm ready.'

'Are you sure you don't want me to come too?' Mike asked as he gave her a goodbye hug. 'I could fling a decent coat on and a black bandana.'

'No, it's fine. And anyway, you still need to rest that foot. Also, she was my friend: you didn't know her. And she hated black.'

'I know Alec though.' He hesitated for a moment. 'But . . . not that well. Only that week last Christmas.'

'Thanks for not saying, "Not as well as you do though,"' Anna said as she opened the door. 'I know you were dying to.'

He did a mock-innocent look. '*Moi?* Would I?'

'Probably. Oh God . . .' She looked down the path towards the old green Mini where Charlotte waited, revving the engine to hurry her.

'God what?'

'I'm going to the funeral of my ex-lover's mother with my husband's ex-mistress who is also the ex-girlfriend of my ex-lover. It's practically *The Jeremy Kyle Show* on a plate.'

Mike laughed. 'We're too old for our so-hectic love lives to be of any interest to the entire country, thank the Lord.'

'You're right. The bare facts would only summon up a collective "Ugh, yuck" from the nation.'

'And hey, all that was way back. We've moved on and all is well. Apart from for poor Miriam, of course. Have a good time,' Mike said, kissing her briefly and waving to Charlotte. 'Or as good a time as can be had at these things.'

'Thanks. I don't know what time I'll be back. I probably won't be out long. I'll go back after for a polite drink but leave pretty soon.'

Charlotte was wearing a scarlet satin coat under which was a bright emerald dress that had ridden up her thighs and showed a froth of lace-edged shocking pink net petticoat and red fishnet tights. 'Alec said no black,' she said as Anna climbed into the car. 'But I hope he'll make an exception for these boots.'

'I know. That's why I've chosen purple.'

'It's quite subtle though,' Charlotte said as she took a turning on to the main road. 'Can't you jazz it up a bit?'

'I've got this with me.' Anna pulled a pink and scarlet scarf out of her bag. 'I think I'm waiting to see if everyone's gone with the dress code or reverted to standard funeral issue. I'm trying to be flexible.'

'Me, I never bother. They'll have to take me as I am,' Charlotte said. 'I liked old Miriam; she and I understood each other. She'd have made a great mother-in-law and I'm sorry things didn't work out with me and Alec, but only for that reason. She approved of me and that's not something I can say about most of the mothers of men I've dated. We once had sex at her house in the spare room when we thought she was out but it turned out she was in her bedroom having a nap the whole time. We only knew she was there because after we'd finished she shouted "Bravo" and "Encore" through the wall.'

'Oh, hell's teeth, how embarrassing!'

'I didn't mind but Alec was mortified.'

'Yes, he would be. He was funny about . . .'

'. . . about sex, yes. Rather, er . . .'

'Furtive?' Anna supplied, wondering why on earth she was having this conversation with Charlotte of all people.

'Furtive! Yes, that's the word. He only really liked it when he felt he shouldn't be doing it. No wonder his marriage broke up.'

Miriam believed in colour and fun but she didn't believe in God or the afterlife. The funeral party assembled outside Mortlake Crematorium were a cheerful-looking crowd in bright jolly colours, chatting and laughing as if they were at a party. Anna felt horribly sad though – was this how things were going to be in the future? Many a visit to this venue or others like it with everyone trying to pretend that never seeing a friend again was no big deal? And one day it would be either her or Mike arriving in a box. They hadn't discussed it properly, had no real idea how they wanted their own departures to be. She could guess what Mike would say: that he didn't care as he wouldn't be there, but perhaps they should discuss the options some time. A green burial or a simple cremation? All she knew was that with luck they had a good few healthy years left in them. She prayed she'd outlive her children. Mike's sprained ankle had shaken her, though. It showed how easily things could change from pretty much perfect health to loss of mobility in a few brief seconds. She tried to reason that the same could have happened at any age and that it was, as it turned out, no big deal. But it was different now they were older. Ten years ago, tripping on a step wouldn't have given her any pause for thought. Now, she couldn't help running a worst-case scenario at any tiny mishap.

Charlotte parked the Mini and she and Anna walked towards the front entrance where everyone was waiting in the chill damp air for the arrival of the coffin. Alec detached himself from the group and walked towards them. He – ignoring Miriam's instructions – was wearing a formal dark suit with a white shirt and a grey tie. In the background lurked a woman who Anna assumed was his ex-wife, holding the hands of two children who looked under twelve and very solemn. Those three were also in neat tidy dark clothes, the children's hair brushed to a shimmer. The former Mrs Alec stood a little apart from the motley crowd of Miriam's noisy friends and was frowning as Alec talked to Anna and Charlotte. Anna wondered if she'd put her foot down about suitable funeral attire for the deceased's closest relatives.

'Thanks so much for coming,' he said to them, hanging back a few seconds before kissing them each on one cheek. Anna guessed he'd been debating which one to greet first and decided he'd opt for her on grounds of seniority.

'Our pleasure, sweetie.' Charlotte beamed at him. 'Well, not pleasure exactly, but you know what I mean. I'm so sorry about your mum. She was great fun.'

'She was. She'd always said she wanted one of her poems to be read at her funeral.' He grinned. 'I had quite a time finding one that was suitable so I gave up and just picked my favourite. Luckily I'm not the one who has to read it out. Oh . . .' He looked up past the two of them. 'She's here. She always said she'd hate a parade of cars trailing after the hearse so that's why we all had to meet here. If she'd had her way she'd have been brought here in the back of Sandy the fishmonger's van but Sandy had a row with the undertaker about it and that plan came to nothing.' He went back to meet the undertakers and Anna and Charlotte went inside the chapel to take their seats.

Anna felt moved to see that Miriam's coffin was draped in a multi-coloured patchwork quilt that she remembered hanging over the back of Miriam's sofa. 'I'm mending it,' Miriam had explained, and had pointed to the needle and thread that was poked into it, waiting to cobble together some of the unravelled seams joining the hexagons. It had been there the next time she'd gone to Miriam's too, and the time after that, and now Anna felt certain that if she went and looked closely, the needle and thread would still be there, waiting to be used. She just hoped, as the coffin was slowly paraded down the aisle, that it wouldn't stab one of the undertakers as he slid it on to the plinth. She also rather hoped someone would remove it before Miriam went into the flames – a lot of work had gone into it and Miriam would hate all that effort to go up, literally, in smoke.

Someone had to say it, Anna thought later with a deep sigh once they were in Miriam's house for the wake: 'She had a good innings.' To Anna's surprise, given Miriam's self-confessed atheism, she'd requested a vicar conduct the ceremony and there'd been hymns, 'Fight the Good Fight' and 'Eternal Father, Strong to Save'. The vicar had said Miriam loved a good lusty session of hymn-singing, even if she didn't believe in the message. He was the one who mentioned her having the innings, as if she were an England batsman scoring her last winning run.

'Someone always says that,' Charlotte said, downing half a glass of red wine in one go. 'It would disappoint Miriam. She never liked a cliché,' she told the vicar firmly.

He put his hand out. 'Cecil Horley,' he said, taking her hand and giving it a thorough pumping, 'and yes I know it's a poncy name but I think my parents were hoping for a foppish actor.'

'They weren't far off,' Charlotte said. Anna laughed, embarrassed by her bluntness and the simple truth of it: he was wearing a traditional dog collar but with a yellow and grey striped waistcoat over a pink shirt. A lilac silk scarf hung from his neck.

'Thank you,' he said, bowing slightly.

'You did well to read that poem,' Anna said, glad that he seemed to understand Charlotte. 'I first heard it early last year. She recited it at a book launch and I think she shocked a few people.'

Cecil laughed. 'It takes a lot to shock me. You'd be surprised what vicars get told.'

Anna looked at Charlotte. Her eyes were gleaming and she slyly reached sideways to where someone had left an open bottle of red wine and topped up both her glass and Cecil's. 'Really?' she said to him. 'Do tell me.'

Anna wandered off in search of something to absorb the wine. Miriam's poem had been a pretty terrible one in which she compared a slug to a penis. There'd been a nervous outbreak of tittering as the poem was read at the crematorium but that soon turned to unbridled proper laughter. All Miriam's poems had been fairly awful but they were exuberant and wordy and fun, which was a lot more than could be said for those of many people. As she had told Cecil, Anna had first heard that particular gem at Miriam's book launch where she'd met Alec for the first time. They'd gone to a bar afterwards for chips and champagne and thus had started a lovely, sexy interlude that had made her feel so exhilarated and joyful and a good thirty years younger. Would she ever feel like that again? Or would she – one day – come to terms with the knowledge that youthful passion being a part of her life had gone for ever?

'Is this all OK, do you think?' There was Alec, beside her now, 'Would Mum approve?'

'I think so,' Anna told him, fighting a sudden urge to put her arms round him, to be close to his warm strong body. 'You've done her proud and she'd love it. Everyone's having a splendid time.'

'Except her,' he said, looking sad. 'It's all very well, all this . . . I don't know . . . determined jollity, but she's gone and I'll miss her. The children no longer have their gran and she won't see them grow up. She'll mind that, wherever she is now. She'll mind missing this. She always loved a party.'

'That's the thing, isn't it, with funerals,' she said. 'It's the best party you ever have and you're the one who misses it.'

Alec nodded and then looked down at the floor for a few moments. 'Come with me, Anna?' And he took her hand and led her through the kitchen and out to the conservatory where Miriam's hardy annual seedlings were leaning towards the light and looking a bit dry. Anna had decided she would water them before she left but after that she hoped someone would take care of them. Miriam treasured her bright summer flowers. These seedlings of cornflowers and calendula and tobacco flowers would have been sown in autumn so they'd flower as early as possible next summer. Miriam would have sown more outside next year once the earth warmed up but these would go in early and, in the late spring, give her that first taste of colour that she so loved.

'Will someone take care of these?' Anna asked Alec.

'What, the seedlings? I suppose so,' he said.

'Once they've got another couple of leaves they should be out in the greenhouse really. It's going to be too warm in here for them.' She wondered what he'd brought her out here to say, away from the noise of the party. She felt she was putting off an awkward moment; she was slightly nervous about what he might say to her. Funerals did that, she knew. People would take the opportunity to reveal secrets, confess things better left unsaid.

'It was sudden,' he said, opening the door and letting some cool air into the overheated house. Behind her, Anna could hear the laughter levels rising as the guests drank more. They were becoming rowdy and raucous. A proper wake, she thought. Near-riotousness compensating for the sense of loss and of life's ending. Partying as denial. 'She fell and had a stroke, apparently; or the other way round. Wouldn't have known anything about it anyway, they tell me, though I'm never sure how they can be so certain.'

'Well, that's got to be a blessing, hasn't it? Who wouldn't want to go like that?'

He grinned. 'Mum wouldn't. She hated not knowing everything that was going on. She liked you.'

'Thanks. I liked her. I hear she liked Charlotte too.'

He blushed, which Anna found a touch too boyish, reminding her of their age gap. 'She did. But it was never going to work. Suki – my ex – wants to give us another go, she says. But . . .'

I bet she does, Anna thought but didn't say, now having, through her own property dealings, a very good idea of the value of a four-bedroom house with conservatory bang in the middle of prestigious Chiswick. Suki had been the one to leave the marriage, taking the children to the far end of the country and barely letting Alec see them except strictly on her terms.

'But I won't go back to her. I couldn't, not after . . .' Anna expected him to say almost any name, most likely Charlotte, but he finished: '. . . you.'

She took a deep breath. 'Alec . . .' she began. 'It could only . . .'

'I know, I know, only be a short-term thing. I guess it sorted a few things out for you, home-wise, but for me, well, it spoiled me for your regular girlfriend type.' He laughed. 'But who knows what's out there? I hear Sean and Thea are getting married. Good for them and I'm glad it worked out.'

'You'll be OK,' Anna said with more conviction than she really felt. 'You've at least got plenty of time on your side. And actually, I'd better go now. I'll see if I can find Charlotte but I expect she'll need to leave her car here.'

'That's fine. If she gives me the keys I can put it on the driveway when people have gone home.'

'Thanks. There's no way she could drive. I think she only brought the car because she was being kind to me, giving me a lift. And . . . thanks, Alec, for today. And . . .' She couldn't really continue, not without getting tearful.

'It's OK. I know,' he said, putting his arms round her and hugging her close. She had a feeling that this wasn't just a goodbye for the day but a more permanent one. There was probably no reason for them to meet again now and she-and-Alec would fade away into a simple memory that would make her smile when (and if) she reached properly old years.

Anna went in search of Charlotte but couldn't find her among the crowd in the sitting room. Thinking that she might as well go to the loo before she left to catch a bus home, Anna went up the stairs. A shadowy figure crossed the landing from a bathroom to a bedroom and, as the door opened, Anna caught sight of Charlotte's bright green dress in a crumpled heap on the floor. Next to it was a lilac puddle of vicar Cecil's silk scarf. Miriam, Anna thought as she shut the bathroom door, would definitely approve.

TWENTY

'Thea, my darling. I can explain.' Thea heard Sean's words on her voicemail and immediately switched it off. *I can explain* was, in her opinion, one of those phrases that no one should ever trust. It was a weaselish little term that meant the person doing the explaining already knew there was a problem with what they were about to explain – and had known for some good long time.

Thea had arrived home from Cornwall well into darkness, weary and depressed. She went straight to bed without bothering to unpack and had a horrible restless night in which she flipped and flapped about, got the duvet tangled and woke up hot and miserable and wishing she had to be anywhere but at the school that day. Furious, hurt and all jangled inside, she showered and washed her hair and spiked it up for maximum Melanie-annoyance. If the head teacher picked on her for 'unprofessional' appearance, she'd give her both barrels. Just let her try. As she drove to school in the slow-moving rush-hour traffic and the still half-dark of that winter morning, Thea was well aware that this attitude was bordering on the childish but she wasn't in any mood to care. If she couldn't punch that smug Katinka in those perfect all-American teeth, hard, then she'd take on anyone else who was unlucky enough to be in the firing line.

She was disappointed to find that Jenny wasn't in school that day. She was the one person she'd have told about Sean. Jenny would have somehow put an optimistic spin on it, might even come up with some reason why Sean hadn't bothered to mention that he'd had (possibly still had) a wife, but it turned out that she'd been in France with her son's school trip and they'd been delayed returning on their ferry by the stormy sea that Sean had predicted. Melanie was fuming, stalking round the staffroom and loudly complaining about the cost of supply teachers and general lack of organization.

Thea's early-morning spirit of anger and rebellion subsided into a pit of gloomy depression and she kept out of the head's way, going quickly to her classroom to deal with the inevitable stream of parents with questions about costumes for the nativity play, reasons why their infant couldn't play outside at lunchtime and a mother who wanted to be given – in advance each Monday – a list of the week's school lunches so she could work her way through it to see whether she felt it was a suitable diet for her picky-eater child. 'They can't run on empty,' she whined. 'And he can't eat a thing if there's something green on the plate. Green terrifies him. He can't even look at it.' Thea answered all the queries, even the last one (pointing out as kindly as possible that the child was quite happy to eat peas and when he'd finished his own he didn't hesitate to nick them from the next child's plate), with dogged patience and tact. Yet all the time she felt that she was playing a role to keep herself sane and busy so she wouldn't have to think about Sean and that brash and beautiful Katinka. She *couldn't* think about them, not at work, not if she didn't want to end up in a corner, sobbing. But . . . there was surely no way he could have *not* known Katinka was going to stay with him? 'Just passing' would surely have meant at least a phone call, at the very latest the day before? Thea had been gone from the stables for no more than an hour, in which time the girl had had time to get into the house, undress and take a shower. What else had she had time to do, and with Sean? Thea's insides contracted painfully as she tried not to think about it.

As soon as school was over for the day, she drove home, unpacked the clothes from the week before, shoved a lot of them in the washing machine and then went and lay in a hot steamy bath for a while. She felt numb inside and still hadn't spoken to Sean. There were over twenty missed calls on her phone, all from him, and a long list of text messages. *For fuck's sake talk to me, Thea,* was the last one, showing he was running out of patience – and who could blame him? A man wanting to make his excuses wouldn't want them to be kept waiting. Holes in the arguments might present themselves. She was longing to talk to him, desperate to hear something that would stop her thinking the worst but she didn't trust herself not simply to burst into tears the moment she heard his voice.

When the house phone rang she didn't answer but the voicemail told her it was Anna.

'Can you come over for supper, Tee? I know it's short notice and you might be busy but I want to talk to you about this house. We're going to need to get rid of a lot of stuff so it's less cluttered and easier to sell and I want you to come and decide if there's anything you'd like. Jimi and Rosie are coming over too. I've asked Emily as well but she says she "just can't". She still seems to be in a silly sulk. I hope she comes out of it soon – it's very tedious.'

Thea wasn't keen to go but her mother sounded a bit despairing. They weren't going to get through the evening without mentioning the wedding and she'd have to tell them it might not be on. Or it might. If she didn't talk to Sean she'd never know. OK, so it had to be done. She sent a text to Anna to say that she'd be there later and then, taking a few deep breaths first, dialled the number of the stables. She didn't want to call Sean's mobile as the signal down at Cove Manor wasn't reliable and if they were going to have a proper in-depth discussion about issues of honesty and whether this little matter of the unmentioned marriage to Katinka was a deal-breaker or not, then she didn't want them also to be dealing with crackling down the line and the chance of being cut off.

She was trembling as she heard his phone ring. She pictured him either in the kitchen or in the bedroom where the second handset was kept. She hoped he'd grab it at first ring but it rang five times before it was picked up and a voice that was girly, American and definitely not Sean's said, 'Hiiiii!' with an upbeat cheerleader over-brightness that made Thea want to throw her own phone out of the window. So Katinka was still there. Terrific. Without speaking, Thea switched off her phone.

'But it's a school night and we haven't got a babysitter,' Emily was saying to Sam.

'If you'd said earlier that your folks had invited us out, we could probably have got someone,' Sam replied, 'and we can take Ned with us anyway – it's only to your parents', not some fancy dinner party.'

'I know, but . . .'

'You don't want to go because Thea will be there. That's the bottom line, isn't it? You still haven't spoken to her.'

Emily shrugged. 'No. And I feel bad about that but

I've not been, you know, that well, have I? I mean, obviously she's my sister and I've got to face her some time but I don't think I can face going over the whole thing again. I don't want her to hate me for not wanting to spend Christmas in Cornwall but I still think it was unreasonable of her to expect me to. She knew from the start how I feel about it.'

'I think we all know how *you* feel, Em,' Sam said, sighing. 'You never stop telling us. Look, I'll babysit. You go on your own. Well, you and Ned. Or leave me a couple of bottles and I'll have him.'

'Bottles? What, of formula?' Emily said. 'No way! I don't even have any!'

'Oh, for heaven's sake, Em, it's not as if I'm suggesting poison for him. I just thought you might like an evening out without having a baby glued to your front.'

Emily stared at him. 'It's called "contact parenting". It's not "glue". I'm just doing the best I can for *our* baby. Is that so bad? Is there *anything* I can get right for you these days?'

'Of course you can. You're doing a terrific job with Ned.'

'Don't patronize me.' She was almost growling.

'I'm not.' Sam frowned. 'But, of course, you being in this crazy bubble, it doesn't cross your self-obsessed mind that I might quite like doing a bit of contact parenting myself. I hardly get near the baby. You're like a mother wolf with him. Oh God, Emily, don't go and fucking *cry*.'

Emily pulled off a piece of kitchen paper and mopped her eyes. 'If I go tonight, will you come with me down to Wiltshire to look at that house?'

'Of course I will,' he said, hugging her.

Emily beamed at him. 'That's all I ask. Thank you. I'll go and shower and put something nice on.'

'Good,' he said. 'See? Not too hard, was it?'

Thea decided she wouldn't say anything over supper about the Sean thing. She would leave the problem at home, grit her teeth and answer any questions about the dress she hadn't bought, the flowers she hadn't yet ordered, the barbecues they'd need for the beach breakfast that they hadn't yet sorted out. It was only one evening. How hard could it be? And also, she hung on to the tiny hope that while she didn't listen to Sean and his explanation, perhaps all might still be well. Once she'd heard what he had to say, the excuses as to why he'd somehow omitted to tell her such an important thing, she wouldn't have any choice but to make up her mind about what she wanted to do. That's if she had the choice. Perhaps, like Rich the year before, he'd simply gone off her and Katinka had moved in seamlessly and for good before Thea's side of the bed was even cool.

Just as she was leaving the house her phone rang yet

again. She almost ignored it, assuming it was Sean, but the ID showed up as Rich.

'Hello,' she said, while delving in her bag to find her keys.

'Hi. How are you?'

Thea waited a second, hardly trusting herself to speak. 'I'm fine,' she said at last. 'Couldn't be . . . er . . . Yes, fine. And you?'

'Also fine. Well, still camping in a mate's flat and it's not ideal for me or for Benji. I'm sorry to ask, but do you think you could have him for a bit longer than just next weekend? It's just, I'm trying to find somewhere to rent and it's not easy taking him to view places. A couple of them rejected me on the spot just for having him with me. You won't believe how many landlords stipulate "no pets" as if a lazy poodle like him was no different from a snarling Staffie.'

'OK,' Thea said. 'That's not a problem but you do know I can't take him to work? He'll be on his own in the daytime so I can't do that for more than a couple of days. It's not fair to him – and not to me either if he gets bored and starts chewing furniture. I know he's a great one for putting in a good day's sleep but it's still not ideal.'

'That's OK – I can pick him up on Tuesday, early evening, after you get back from school. I do appreciate this, Thea. You've no idea how much.'

Well, at least one man in the world appreciated her,

she thought as she left the house and went to the car, even if it happened to be the one out of the planet's entire population that she absolutely didn't want.

Jimi was lurking by the front door when Thea arrived at her parents' house. He had a final puff on the cigarette that he thought nobody knew he was smoking and went to open her car door for her.

'Hello, you,' he said, hugging her. 'Come to divvy up the parental spoils like the rest of us?'

Thea laughed. 'I'm not so sure about that. You know how tiny my house is – I haven't got space for anything else.'

'There's always room for a painting or two,' Anna said as she opened the door and ushered them both in. 'And maybe the odd bedside cupboard or something? I think we'll have more luck with the selling if we had about half the contents. It's only now, when I look at the place with the eyes of a pretend buyer, that I can see how much more space there'd be and how much more attractive too. Belinda our agent said that potential buyers don't have that much imagination. I think that's estate-agent-speak for "get rid of half your garbage and it might look a quarter-way decent".'

In the kitchen, Emily was sitting at the table, feeding Ned. Thea was a bit taken aback, not really having expected to see her. Well, at least here was one person who would be delighted if the wedding didn't go ahead.

That sour thought didn't help her state of mind and she tried hard to put thoughts of Sean and Katinka out of her head, at least for the next couple of hours.

'Hello, Thea.' Emily smiled at her. Thea thought she looked nervous, possibly thinking there'd be a no-speaking situation.

'Hi, Emily. How's the baby? He looks much bigger already.'

'Well, you haven't seen him for a few weeks, have you?' Rosie chipped in. Thea and Emily looked at each other.

'Now, girls, play nicely,' Mike said, handing a glass of Coke to Emily and some wine to Thea. Thea didn't really want it but was pleased to have something to hold. It gave her a bit of much-needed stability.

'Sorry. Did I say something?' Rosie said, blushing. 'I tend to.'

'You do,' Jimi said fondly. 'But we'd expect nothing less.'

'Thank you,' she said to him, 'I think . . .'

'OK, everybody, find a chair and we'll eat first and maybe you can give us an idea about things you might want to take from here. Or would it be a good idea to do that first?'

'No, let's eat. I'm starving,' Emily said, putting Ned back in his sling.

'Good plan,' Anna said. 'And if we talk about it we can start to whittle down who wants what. You might have favourite pieces that you want to mention.' She went to the oven and opened the door. 'It's just a lamb tagine with couscous and a big salad.'

Thea relaxed into her chair, breathing in the comforting aroma of home-cooked food made with love and half a lifetime of experience. What she'd give to know that some day she and Sean too would be welcoming their own grown-up children to a home like this. She looked across the table at Emily, who was gently stroking the soft, suedey head of the baby. Thea wasn't going to cry, she was determined about that, but it was quite hard trying not to. If she lost Sean, she'd be losing not just the man she really, really loved but all the years of a possible family life together.

'I still wish you weren't selling up,' Emily said as they began to eat. 'But . . . I can understand that you might want to move away from London. I've . . . er . . . been thinking about it too as it happens.'

'Really?' Jimi said. 'Where are you thinking of going? I always had you down as the ultimate outer-London mum.'

'Not sure but, you know, out. I want my children to be raised in a proper community. I'd like a small country town or a big village where people look out for each other and I can feel they're safe.'

'Don't you feel safe here? You live in one of the bits of London that everyone envies,' Jimi said. 'What could be better?'

'She wants to pull up a drawbridge. I know the feeling,' Anna said.

'Drawbridge? What do you mean?' Emily asked.

'I mean that you want a proper edge to your tiny town, the equivalent of a moat. Some definite place where the houses stop and the countryside begins and there's a road sign with the place name on. Everyone inside it is supposed to feel they belong.'

'That's it!' Emily said. 'I want to be inside and feeling secure, not here where everything's blurry. I feel sort of lost in London now. I think it's since Ned.'

'It's not Ned, it's the mugging,' Mike said. 'You do know it can happen anywhere? And that when you move to this haven you'll still be getting in the car to go to a city for some shopping and still be joining the crowds for the odd day at Ikea? It'll all just be further away, that's all.'

'Thanks for your support, Dad,' Emily said, looking disappointed. 'I was hoping you'd understand. After all, you're moving out as well.'

'Hmm. Well, sort of. I'd like us to keep a little toe-hold in the area. It might be too big and "blurry" for you but it's where a lot of our friends are.'

'The ones who aren't dropping off the perch, that is,' Anna said.

'But, Emily' – Jimi had a mischievous look on his face and was enjoying niggling his sister – 'aren't you currently one of those Queen Bee yummy mummies that occupy most of the coffee shops? What will you do out in the sticks without Starbucks?'

'Jimi!' Anna said sharply. 'When has Emily ever been like that? She's got an important career under way. Just because a woman has a baby it doesn't mean she turns into a coffee-house . . . blob.'

'They're not blobs either,' Thea said. 'Just women doing a different job from the one they get paid for, and mostly temporarily.'

'Childcare – still mostly considered a women's issue. Western feminism won't make any advances till that little issue's dealt with.'

They all turned to look at Rosie.

'What?' she said. 'It's obvious, isn't it? I mean, Sam and Emily have got it right because Sam mostly does the childcare but he can't while Em's feeding Ned. Hence that forever inequality. Also, Emily, just about every little town in the country has a Starbucks so you won't miss out.'

Mike laughed. 'But you can't change physiology. Men can't feed babies.'

'I wouldn't want them to even if they could,' Emily said.

'Me neither,' Rosie agreed. 'Can you imagine how much they'd whinge about it? Too uncomfortable, too *difficult*, too time-consuming . . . all that.'

'We are here, you know,' Jimi said. 'Mike and I are in the room.'

'You've got all this to come, Thea,' Rosie said, giving her a nudge.

That was too much for Thea and the tears she'd been holding back for the whole day spilled out at last.

'Oh God, you poor darling!' Anna said, putting an arm round her. 'What is it now? Has something happened? You and Sean looked so very happy when we saw you last weekend.'

'I hope the wedding's not off. I've bought a hat,' Rosie said, laughing nervously as everyone looked at her again. 'It's me, isn't it? I've said something again.'

'No, it's not you.' Thea managed to get the words out between sobs.

'It's me then,' Emily said glumly. 'I knew it bloody would be. I shouldn't have come.'

Thea got up from the table and went to get a glass of water. 'I don't know what's happening. There's . . . there's been a bit of a hitch. I don't want to talk about it.'

She saw Rosie, Anna and Emily look at each other. She almost smiled: they looked disappointed at her refusal to talk and she didn't blame them. If she were in their shoes she'd be dying to know what was going on and be thoroughly miffed to have to deal with the tears but not get the information. All the same, until she'd spoken to Sean she wasn't going to say anything. Coming out with all that had happened and the thing about bloody Katinka might make them all hate him.

Even now, she definitely didn't want that.

'I suppose if there's a big hitch it's a good thing you haven't bought a dress yet then,' Rosie said. 'Not like last time.'

'Rosie!' Jimi said. 'For goodness' sake, operate your off switch, if you've got one.'

Thea couldn't help but laugh then. 'Oh, Rosie! I'm still hoping it won't be a waste of your hat.'

Thea didn't want to look at emails before bed. She was certain there'd be something from Sean and she didn't want to feel any worse than she already did. It wasn't that she thought he'd end their relationship via email – no one but the most heartless bastard would do such a thing and Sean could never be described as heartless. But she didn't want to know any details about Katinka, about her sudden reappearance in his life, not before she tried to sleep anyway. Her imagination was capable of filling in any gaps all by itself. How, for instance, could anyone claim they were 'just passing' when they were on their way to South Africa? By what stretch of a crazy travel itinerary was south-west Cornwall on the way?

Thea went to the drawer where she'd kept the little plaited grass ring that Sean had placed on her finger back in August. What a beautiful, sunny day full of hope and love and happiness that had been. She moved underwear out of the way, pushing aside silky knickers and her favourite bras, looking for the pink envelope she kept the ring in. Maybe just holding it for a few minutes would help her feel a bit more positive. The envelope was right at the back, not at the side of the drawer where she'd thought she'd put it. She pulled it out, opened it and looked inside. The grass ring had gone. Only a few tiny grains of seed were left in the envelope's corner. How could that have happened? She took everything out of the drawer, carefully, one item at a time, and shook it over the bed in the hope it had somehow escaped. Nothing. Then she closed the envelope and opened it again, like a magician re-conjuring a missing dove from a hat. Still nothing. Somehow, and so sadly, the little plaited ring had simply vanished.

TWENTY-ONE

It was going to be a task and a half, clearing the house. Anna, opening the cupboard under the stairs and casting an eye over the sundry contents, almost wished everything the space contained was staying put when she considered the forty-plus years' worth of possessions that had found their way on to the premises and refused to leave again even after they'd long become redundant. Still, the clear-out had to be done one day and it would, she thought grimly, save the children a job after she and Mike had died.

The other night, colour-coded stickers had been applied by Jimi, Emily and Thea to various pieces of furniture, paintings and ornaments that they were going to take, but Anna felt that in some cases they'd claimed them out of a desire to be helpful with the clearing rather than because these were items they really wanted. And truly, it wasn't really *that* helpful unless they actually came and took their choices away.

She pulled out a set of golf clubs that had belonged

to Mike's late brother and hauled them to the front door. She couldn't even remember why they'd got them: Mike detested golf. He considered it tedious and pointless. Would a charity shop want them? She hoped so. Or Gumtree; perhaps that would be even better because whoever wanted them would have to come and get them. That was probably the way forward. Or a yard sale might be an idea . . . She could do that at the weekend and put a note on the wall inviting people to come in and help themselves. A giveaway would be better than a sale really, especially with Christmas coming up. Who had spare cash for what was essentially junk at this time of the year? She could put a tin out for donations and give the resulting cash to a charity. Miriam's funeral had had a collection for the NSPCC so she'd go for that one.

The golf clubs were joined by two of Jimi's old cricket bats, an ancient suitcase, an unravelling wicker picnic basket (for the tip, that one) and an ironing board that she'd meant to throw out a good ten years back. There were coats that hadn't been worn for years, rotting wellington boots and two pairs of white ice skates (Emily and Thea's) from the long-ago days before the rink at Richmond closed. She put them all together with the golf clubs, fetched a broom and dustpan and gave the cupboard a thorough sweeping. Then the phone rang. It was Belinda on the line asking if it was OK to bring a family for a viewing that afternoon. Anna agreed and then looked at the clutter that now graced the hallway. It couldn't stay there; it represented exactly how *not* to welcome in people who were being invited to spend nearly three million pounds on a house. So she gathered everything up again and stuffed it back in the cupboard, albeit in a far more orderly fashion than it had been loaded in before. Oh well, she thought, it was a start. But she knew it wasn't, not really.

Thea didn't intend to avoid Sean. It had been two days and she knew she had to talk to him and to hear what he had to say. She felt stronger by the next morning, although still deeply sad about the grass ring. It going missing felt like an omen although she fervently hoped it wasn't. She reminded herself, now she was feeling a bit calmer, that Sean hadn't exactly told her any lies, but could she trust the rest of her life to a man who was, as politicians liked to put it, 'economical with the truth'? After the disaster that had been Rich, was she really so wrong to expect all-out honesty and genuine commitment?

The school day was hectic. There was a rumour in the staffroom about a possible Ofsted inspection and after an intense session of numeracy that wore both her and the children out, her class was summoned to the school hall for a long rehearsal for the nativity play. Melanie was keen that the lines should be in rhyming couplets and she'd got the year six teacher

– who fancied himself as a poet – to write a kind of chorus that all those who didn't have main roles would recite together. The first run-through was a disaster. Thea could sense Melanie trying not to stamp her foot with impatience as the children read the lines with maddening slowness and with no expression at all. Thea wasn't surprised: some of them were only five.

'They'll be OK once they've learned what it's all about and they've had plenty of practice,' Thea tried to reassure her. 'Half of them aren't nearly up to the necessary reading standard for this yet so it'll take some time.' Privately, she thought they needed a far simpler script. What on earth did they understand about un-explained words like 'Hosanna' and 'Cherubim'? She would give her own class a talk about it all but she felt a lingering sadness for her own discarded project about the changing of the seasons. From the thunderous look on Melanie's face she wondered if she too was regretting being so dismissive. Having the children dress up as the Green Man or dancing around the stage pretending to be sunlight triumphing over darkness would have been a doddle compared to this. They'd have loved it.

The signs of Christmas were coming out into the streets now. On the drive home, Thea could see that Christmas trees supplied by the council had, that day, been put up in the high street, leaning at ninety degrees over the shops. Their lights weren't yet attached but it would only be a couple of weeks till they flashlit her way home each night. As she parked outside her house, she noticed Mr and Mrs Over-the-Road had put a pair of wire-framed deer in their front garden, one each side of the path. They were unevenly lit and one gave the impression in the dark of only having three legs and one antler. The sight gave Thea an added moment of depression. She was so near to her wedding day. That's if it was going to happen at all. As she locked the car, June's door opened and she crossed the road clutching a large white parcel, a massive bouquet that was almost as big as she was. With her light grey hair, beige mac and the package, she looked peculiarly ghostly, lit palely from behind by those deer. She seemed to have something important to say.

'Thea? These are for you.' She held out the flowers and pushed them into Thea's arms. Thea, already carrying her bag and the car keys, almost dropped them. They were ridiculously heavy – and vast. She wasn't sure she had any vases big enough to accommodate them, unless she opted for the bright blue bucket she used when she was washing the kitchen floor.

'They came this morning. On a van,' June said, her eyes gleaming. 'I think they're from your young man.'

Thea's spirits lifted massively. Sean. Wow, this was some gesture. She thanked June, clutched the bouquet to her and went into the house. The flowers were huge white Madonna lilies, which surprised her a bit. For one thing they were madly out of season (which Sean wouldn't normally approve of) and must have cost a fortune. Also, Sean didn't like lilies so it must have been the florist's choice. He knew their pollen was deeply poisonous to cats and had once said he'd never buy them as he didn't want to encourage the trade.

Thea put the bouquet on the kitchen table and looked for a card, which was nestled among the blooms in a small blue envelope. The edges were a bit scuffed and she guessed June had already had a quick read. She hoped the message wasn't too intimate – how embarrassing that would be, to have had her neighbour read something deeply personal, possibly a bit suggestive. June would forever after be giving her little meaningful looks and as for Robbie, he'd up the level of his customary near-leering to a whole new realm. He was bad enough at the best of times: only that summer he'd told her she was 'a fine figure of a lass' when she was on her way out in a short tea dress. Thea read the card twice in the feeble hope that she wasn't seeing the right message:

With massive thanks in advance from the two of us. With all love and a big woof. Rich and Benji.

Could she be more disappointed? Flowers from her ex and his dog. Oh, the joy. The surge of love for Sean and the whizz of adrenaline dissipated fast and she sat down heavily in the chair and put her head in her hands. The phone rang and, despondent, she picked it up.

'Thea. At last.'

'Hello, Sean.'

'So, er . . . how are you?' He sounded nervous, she thought. She probably did too. Her entire future could hang on this conversation.

'I'm . . . OK.'

'No, you're not.'

'No – that's true. Did you expect me to be?'

'Because Katinka was there? Well – I suppose it must have been a bit of a surprise. She said you went off in a big hurry and . . .' he laughed for a second then stopped as abruptly '. . . she said you were "steaming mad".'

'You could say that. Why didn't you say she was coming? And how *not* steaming mad do you expect me to be when I find her coming out of *our* bathroom dressed in nothing but a towel?'

'Ha. Yes, well, I don't know why she used that one.'

'For my shower gel apparently. Was that before or after she also got into the bed I'd only just left with the boyfriend I'd only just—'

'Hey? No! How could you say that?'

Thea hadn't meant to go that far but she was just so upset, she couldn't stop herself.

'I have *not* slept with Katinka!' Sean sounded quite angry now.

'Never? *Really?*'

There was a second of silence. 'We went out together for maybe three months about seven years ago when I was still competing and she was a newbie. I mean, come on, Thea, you and me, we're not teenagers, we've both got a past.'

'Is she still there?'

'No. She left this morning. I dropped her at Redruth station and she was heading for Heathrow. I don't expect to see her again any time soon. She was just passing through on her way, you know. Honestly, it was no big deal. You don't have to pull this big jealous number, really you don't. There's no reason.'

'She told me the "just passing" thing too. But tell me, Sean, how is our part of Cornwall on the route to anywhere? You live miles from anywhere that's remotely between the USA and South Africa. You're one hell of a detour for someone who's just an old friend.'

Sean sighed. 'It's not a detour from Newquay. She'd been to a meeting with the British Surf people there, about next year's Boardmasters contest. She's going to be the poster girl representing America. It's a business, Thea. You might think surfing is just a hobby but it's been my working life and now it's hers.'

That gave Thea a jolt. Was she being ridiculous? She now felt more than a little foolish. All the same, he must have known she was in the area.

'Not the first time she's stayed then?' she persisted, wishing she could stop. She felt she might be on a self-destruct mission but all the things she wanted to ask, wanted to know, had to be said or there was no moving forward.

'You have to trust me, you know.' Sean sounded more soothing now. 'Nothing's going on, I promise. I love you. It's you I love and it's you I want to marry.'

'I'm glad,' she said. 'But . . . can I just ask, when were you going to tell me you were married to Katinka?'

'I didn't need to, for heaven's sake,' he said, his voice turning dull and cross. 'Because I'm not.'

Emily was feeling unusually cheerful and was on the floor in the sitting room, helping Milly and Alfie to put their Lego safari park together. Ned was, for once, up in his crib and she was starting to feel just slightly closer to her normal self rather than like a scared animal that only wants to huddle in a safe corner from where she can keep an eye on all the threats around her.

'I want the lions over *here*,' Alfie decreed, picking up pieces of fence and slotting them together.

'They don't need a fence,' Milly told him, doing her grand big-sister voice. 'They are *free-range* lions.'

'But they'll eat the camels,' he protested.

'They might not,' Emily told him, soothing. 'They might be calm, nice lions. And besides, they might already be full of dinner.'

'They're not,' Milly said, an impish gleam in her eyes. 'They're *hungry* lions and *fierce*.'

'Let's put the camels inside the fence then. So the lions can't get to them.'

'And the elephants. And the tiger,' Alfie said, picking up the plastic animals and lining them up in twos, ark-fashion, if mismatched for partners.

Emily, her back aching, got up and sat on the sofa, watching her children absorbed in their playing. If they had that house in Wiltshire they'd have a lovely big play area just off the kitchen, she thought. She would get window seats made, padded on the top with gorgeous fabric but with pull-out storage for their toys. She'd seen it on one of those makeover programmes and thought it a great idea.

'Sam?' She went into the kitchen and found him chopping an onion for a chilli sauce. 'Sam, can we go and look at the Wiltshire house this weekend?'

'*This* weekend? Er . . . no, I don't think so. I've got to put together the old annual "My Favourite Christmas Reading" piece for the colour supp. I should have done it last week but it fell off the list.'

'But you said . . .'

'Said what?' He was smiling at her. She thought he looked a bit sly, as if he knew something she didn't. For a crazy moment it crossed her mind he'd had a secret lottery win and already bought it for her. How glorious that would be. She could see herself, seconds from now, throwing her arms round him, giddy with delight and then running to tell the children. Ridiculous, really, but that was what thinking too fast did.

'You promised that we could go and look at it. If I

went to Mum and Dad's for supper last night, you said that was the deal.'

'Ah yes, that. I did promise and I'll keep the promise. But the old deal also holds. I'm willing to go and look at the place just as I said – but on the way to Thea's wedding. Christmas in Cornwall.'

Emily was overcome once more by the old heart-sink feeling of weightless, numb inability to move. She had no power, not over her body or, it seemed, over anything else.

'But that's not what you said,' she finally managed to blurt. 'Snow. I was so scared.' She was rambling. 'I want to be here this time.'

He stopped chopping and put the knife down and looked at her properly, his eyes gazing hard into hers. 'I said we'd go and see the house. I didn't say when. I think you'll find *that's* the deal. And it's the one I'm sticking to. There won't be snow in Cornwall this Christmas. You can look at all the weather stats you like but I bet you any money you won't find two of them in a row that were either white or where anyone was snowed in. And if you miss that wedding, Emily, there'll be a hell of a lot of people who won't forget it in a hurry. And at the front of that queue' – he picked up the knife again and made a start on the parsley – 'there'll be me.'

TWENTY-TWO

The loss of the grass ring was still getting Thea down a couple of days later. What with that and Emily still showing no signs of abandoning her boycott of this wedding and then the stupid Katinka thing that had so deeply unsettled her, Thea was finding her mood as low and gloomy as the cold dark days of November. She felt too pessimistic even to think about finding a dress to be married in, somehow convinced that this, too, would go wrong and that she'd buy a gorgeous outfit and then spill beetroot juice or something equally staining on it the night before the wedding. And Sean still hadn't told her anything about what had happened with Katinka, other than to keep insisting that there was absolutely nothing in what she'd said about him being her bridegroom.

'She's probably still got a thing for you,' Thea told him. 'Maybe she was warning me off.'

Sean laughed. 'I doubt it – she went off with someone way further up the world rankings than I was. She loves a winner, that one. But, really, Thea, it's horrible trying to talk to each other from this ridiculous distance. We need to talk properly, see each other's faces, touch each other. I want to kiss you, reassure you, convince you all is fine, but I can't get to you for ages. We've got a production company coming to check out the manor for an advert and then I've got the weekend up north with my mother and sister. It's ten years since my dad died and they want to go and dance on his grave or something.'

'You are joking, aren't you?' Thea said, picturing the three of them holding hands and cavorting round a big white cross. In the background she also imagined God, looming and white-winged and bearded, standing with his arms folded in disapproval and a huge frown on his face.

'Of course I'm joking! You see? That's the problem with being apart. You'd have known I wasn't serious if we weren't doing this by phone,' Sean said, laughing at her. 'Though I have to say Mum hasn't ever forgiven him for smoking himself into an early grave. No, she wants to do a grave-tidying session and plant some bulbs for spring. It's a bit late but I've got her some fancy local daffodils from one of the farms here and they come up later in the north anyway. She'll like them, even if he wouldn't.'

'Wow, who doesn't like daffodils?'

'My pa. He was more of a lupin man. But seriously, Thea, we do need to see each other. I don't want this stupid Katinka thing, or rather this *non*-thing, to hang over us. I can tell you all about it and even get you to laugh about it along with me but I'd rather do it face to face. All I can promise is that it's not a big deal.'

'How can marrying someone *not* be a big deal?' she asked. 'Or do you feel that way about us too?' She could have bitten her tongue off for saying that. She could hear her mother warning her in her head, 'Do you want to push him away? No? Well stop shoving then.'

'Of bloody course I don't feel that way about us! Christ on a bike, will you listen to yourself? I'm here wondering if it's you who's having second thoughts. It sure as hell isn't me.'

'No, of course I'm not. It's just that I've been let down before and . . .'

'And you don't want it to happen again. I get that, trust me I do. But I can't believe you'd think I'd set out to hurt you.'

'No, I don't think that,' Thea said. 'I think I just panic about stuff, especially at the moment. It's just so frustrating – Emily still won't even talk about coming down for the wedding. I can't find a job in Cornwall near enough to be worth applying for and—'

'And have you bought the dress?'

'Er . . . no.'

'You see? If anyone should be feeling insecure here, don't you think it might be me? Get the dress. Please, babe. Just get the dress.'

*

Emily kept looking out into the garden to keep an eye on the weather. She didn't trust it. It was only ten thirty in the morning and it seemed to be getting darker already, which wasn't right. The forecast had said there might be 'light snow showers' in west London and she needed to watch to make sure it didn't get out of control. Snow was dangerous, frightening. Even in fairy tales she'd hated it. It had killed the Little Match Girl and smothered the Babes in the Wood.

She was constantly checking the weather app on her phone, hating the little snow symbol that came up for that day. She willed it to change. Flicking through to see what the weather was to be like in Cornwall, all she found was rain and a temperature five degrees higher than here, which was annoying and unfair. Wasn't it usually colder down there? It certainly was in summer. She moved a chair close to the window and sat down, tucking her feet under her and holding Ned close. He was such a good baby, calm and happy, and she loved him to be right there, always so close against her. When he looked up at her and treated her to a huge smile she felt great waves of pleasure as they connected.

The fat flakes of snow started falling at midday. Emily was on her computer, ordering Christmas presents online, and she watched the snow and tried to think of it as something to enjoy. But she knew the streets in London would get slick and icy; the snow would pile up at the sides of the roads and get brown and filthy. People would break limbs on it. Everything normal would come to a halt: bus routes, trains, *life*. At least country snow was prettier. She tried to think how it would be in her little Wiltshire town. It wouldn't have that cut-off terror that she'd felt in Cornwall the Christmas before. For one thing there would be neighbours. There would be a shop within walking distance and a station not far away if the roads were bad. But also . . . it would be her new nest and she'd be OK about being cosily holed up in it for a few days. All would be well. And the house was still on the market – the vendors didn't want to go anywhere right now. She was in with a chance.

Rich dropped off the dog at Thea's house on Saturday morning rather than Friday. She still didn't want him in the house, invading her territory, but she thanked him for the flowers and promised to walk Benji far and often and take good care of him.

'I know you will,' Rich said, smiling at her. He had his head slightly on one side like someone who'd been told it was how you act 'fondness'. She felt awkward about that and was a bit abrupt with him. Even though it was the weekend he was wearing a suit and tie and looked uncomfortably formal. Thea could see he'd had his hair recently cut; it was far too tidy, too short. He looked a lot like a small boy about to be sent off to prep school. The contrast with Sean couldn't be greater. Sean's hair was never short, never tidy, never less than pretty much out of control, flopping over his eyes in tendrils that he'd push out of the way but only bothered to trim when they got in his eyes while he was in the sea. He'd asked her if she'd like him all tidy for the wedding but the idea had horrified her. 'God no! It's you I want to marry, you and the whole way you are. Not all gussied up like a shop-window dummy!'

'Old jeans then? Two-day stubble?'

'Er, well, you don't need to go *that* far down the laid-back road, but yes, more that than George Clooney boring, please!'

'One thing,' he'd said. 'Let me know what colour you're going to wear.'

'Are we having matching outfits? Please tell me no. We'd look like the twin children of a madwoman.'

'No, but I thought maybe even a slob like me could do a bit of colour co-ordination. It was Sarah's idea. She says it looks good in the photos.'

'Oh, right. In that case, I'll let you know, as soon as I do,' she promised him. There were only a few weeks to go, she realized, feeling a quick flood of nerves, so she would have to have a look online before she went out and find the kind of dress she'd love. If she simply hit the shops, especially now when they were crazy with Christmas shoppers, she would panic and come home with nothing and know that it was all her own fault for leaving it so late. She phoned Anna and asked to go round so they could have a look together, see what kind of thing would work. She had a vague idea of what she'd like but could do with back-up. And if a girl couldn't get her mum onside for a wedding frock then what were mothers for?

'Oh, about time! What sort of style do you like?' Anna asked. 'You're not a frills type, that I do know.' They sat at the kitchen table, flicking through images on Thea's iPad. Thea had taken Benji with her and he dozed under the table. The day outside was grey and damp but the snow that had fallen the day before and so excited Thea's class – to the point where they could barely concentrate for jumping up and down – had melted and gone.

'It's easier to say what I don't like, really,' Thea said, 'which I know isn't helpful but at least rules a lot out.'

Mike made tea for them and then retired to his hut to sort out his paints and to throw out everything that he no longer used. 'That last lot of people who came round to look at the house want to come again,' he told Thea on his way out. 'They're bringing their teenagers, apparently. Our agent Belinda says she's sure they're about to make an offer.'

'I hope so,' Thea said, 'and it'll be lovely for me and Sean to have you down in Cornwall, but the others will miss you. I know we all live our own lives but this has always been a sort of base.'

Mike laughed. 'Well, first, we're planning to be in Nashville for a while. And then Anna has always wanted to go to India. I told her she should have done the hippie trail at nineteen like everyone else but she missed out. So that's a possibility. We might rent somewhere up here still. But it'll have to be cheap. I don't want to waste money on something that will be empty half the time. It'll take a while to find something we could buy instead.'

Thea considered for a moment. 'You could always stay with me,' she said. 'The spare room is small but it's doable.'

'You know that could be a brilliant solution. But are you really keeping your house on?' Anna asked gently, 'Aren't you going to move to Cornwall and live with Sean . . . you know . . .'

'Properly?' Thea suggested.

'Yes. It's the usual thing, you know. Man/woman/married – they tend to share premises.'

'If I can get a job, yes, that's the plan. But at the moment they're hard to come by down there so I can't leave mine yet. But ideally, yes, of course. As soon as possible.'

Thea went back to the images of models in wedding dresses online. There were thousands of them and she hated almost all of them. 'OK, this is what I don't want: no crinolines, no plunging necklines, nothing long and trailing, nothing that's white.'

'Not a wedding dress then,' her mother said, laughing. 'You'll want something you don't freeze in, for a start. How about velvet?' The doorbell rang and she got up to answer it, leaving Thea to consider velvet.

'Here we are, another voice for some input,' Anna said, bringing Charlotte through to the kitchen. 'Or did you come to see Mike?'

'Anyone really. I was just passing.'

Thea thought briefly of Katinka and the 'just passing' thing. She really must get that girl out of her head. Easier said, till she saw Sean again. As he'd told her, everything that needed to be said was communicated so much better when you were actually together.

Charlotte kissed Thea hello and glanced at the computer. 'Oooh, frocks! Is this your wedding dress? You're cutting it a bit fine, aren't you? The rate you were going – or rather *weren't* – I thought you'd end up getting married in your bra and knickers. I don't suppose Sean would mind that but it's not the usual thing. What held you up? Weren't you sure or something?'

'Charlotte!' Anna said. 'Of course she's sure! There just hasn't been—'

'Don't say "time", Mum. There has been, really. I didn't want to jinx anything by getting too far ahead. Not after last time.' She had a quick flashback to the cream dress hanging in the shop, the assistant unpinning her name tag from the bag and saying how sorry she was and wasn't it lucky they hadn't started on the alterations. 'Lucky' was hardly what Thea would have called it at the time.

Charlotte sat down beside her and patted her hand. 'That was then. This is now. Your other one was a twat; this one's a gem. I knew you two were perfect from day one.'

'I wish I had,' Thea said, laughing. 'I thought he was gay and shacked up with Paul. And then because of even more crossed wires he thought I was gay too. So we were both idiots.'

'All will be well. The mistletoe brought you together last year. You've got to trust that stuff. It's magic.'

'Charlotte, please will you come to the wedding?' Thea suddenly asked. 'I'd so love you to.'

'Ooh – really? I'd love to but . . . hmm . . . I'm working till Christmas Eve so it might be tricky. I'll see what I can do.' She laughed. 'It would be such fun and I didn't have other plans. Nothing set in stone anyway.'

'When does your show start?' Anna asked her. 'And where is it?'

Charlotte blushed a bit. 'The job starts next week. And it's, er . . . not too far away, thank goodness. Seasonal work pays jack shit so if you can keep travel costs out of the mix it does help. Now, let's look at *frocks*. There's nothing better on a freezing horrible day. But first, go and stand over there, Thea, and take your big jumper off.'

Surprised, Thea did as she was told. Charlotte and

Anna gazed at her and Charlotte narrowed her eyes and pulled odd calculating faces as if measuring something.

'What are you doing?' Anna asked.

'Eyeing up her lovely little body,' Charlotte said with a grin. 'No wonder Sean calls you Elf. You'd look rubbish in most of these,' she added, indicating the screen full of gowns, and startling Thea slightly. 'They're proper big-girl dresses. You'd look like a kid dressing up from Mummy's wardrobe. You need something smaller scale without being ditsy.'

'That sounds about right but how can you be sure?' Anna asked.

'Years in showbiz. I can tell when a costume will work on an actor. And when it doesn't, they get the role all wrong. *Flapper*,' she suddenly said. 'But not a hundred per cent because that would be just fancy dress.'

'Flapper? Like a twenties type of dress, do you think?' Anna said, looking Thea up and down. 'That could be pretty.'

'I don't mean the full swirling pearls and headband kind of thing,' Charlotte said. 'Just the basic shape. I've got an idea . . . Shove over,' she said to Anna, taking over the iPad. 'Let me just look, though I could' – she glanced at the fridge – 'use a bit of lubrication to help me think.'

'White or red?' Thea asked.

'I think white today please, seeing as we're talking weddings.'

Thea poured her a large glass and came and sat beside her. Beneath the table, the dog woofed gently in his sleep. Thea looked down at him and saw Charlotte had taken her shoes off and was resting her feet on his body. He didn't seem to mind.

'Please may I look?' Thea said, seeing Charlotte checking through one website. 'Maybe something will leap out at me, so to speak.'

It felt as if she didn't choose the dress, more that it chose her. There were many that were black or white, drop-waisted, embroidered, some way too sparkly and others with a mass of fringing but suddenly there was 'the one'. Not at all garish, a colour between a deep cream and the shade of the lightest Scottish sandy hair, not far from Benji's apricot shade; a simple couple of layers of tulle with the top one swirled with embroidered beads. The hemline was pointy, just above mid-calf length. 'That's it,' Thea said, pointing to it. 'It's perfect. I'll need something on top of it because it's sleeveless, maybe a little jacket, but I *love* the dress.'

She looked at Anna, whose eyes had suddenly filled with tears. 'Oh, Mum, don't go all soppy on me, please! I probably can't afford this anyway, it's just a thought.'

'It will look so pretty. Just wonderful, and you mustn't worry about the cost,' Anna said, sniffling into a tissue.

'Oh, you can afford it,' Charlotte insisted. 'I picked

this company on purpose. They make theatre costumes and look – here are the prices. They did a load for the last *Great Gatsby* film. There's a branch in Soho. See? Sorted. Shall we go and get it?'

'What, now?'

'Why not now?' Charlotte said. 'When better?'

'Go on,' Anna said. 'I'll take care of the dog. I'll even give him a walk. You two go.'

'Right. I'll give Ronnie a call – he should be there till later today. If he's got your size I'll get him to keep it for us. And if he hasn't, then he can either order one in or we'll start all over again.' Charlotte was already picking out the number on her phone, squinting at the website.

Only an hour later, Charlotte and Thea were coming down the stairs of the tiny shop behind Carnaby Street, Thea holding tight to the bag containing the box with her wedding dress in it. It was perfect, just glorious, and if everything went to pieces between now and Christmas Day she'd bloody well set fire to it rather than return it and let anyone else have it.

'Don't tell your sister it was me who went with you,' Charlotte said. 'She'll wish it had been her.'

'She doesn't want to come to Cornwall, why would she want to buy the dress with me?'

'Oh, she'll be there on the day.'

'She's ordered a Christmas tree, a fancy bronze turkey and she's insisting they'll all be at home,' Thea told her. 'I don't see anything in there that says she'll come to the wedding. I wish she would but short of cancelling it, I don't know what more I can do. She associates that place with being trapped and scared and out of control. Nothing can persuade her it won't happen again.'

Charlotte smiled as they jostled their way through the pre-Christmas Saturday crowd on to Regent Street. 'Don't you worry about it. I think we all know deep down that she doesn't want *not* to be there. She's just still a bit baby-demented at the moment. You wait.'

It was a lucky chain-store moment, the sort that doesn't ever happen when you're looking for something specific. Top Shop, H&M, Zara: all of them have their affordable gems and one of them was in a window on a dummy. Strangely, one of its hands seemed to be in a beckoning position, calling to Thea.

'I like that . . .' Thea said, coming to a sudden stop and causing three women behind to crash into her, almost knocking her down.

'Oh gosh yes, I like it too,' Charlotte said. 'Come on.'

The jacket was fluffy fake fur, sleeves at what was called bracelet length but which went all the way down to Thea's wrists and the perfect shade of gingery cream to go with the dress. There was a queue for the changing room but Charlotte wasn't having that. Hollering 'Bride on a mission coming through!' she pulled Thea to the head of it and the gatekeeper girl showed her straight to the next free changing room.

'Come on, put the lot on. And now I'm glad it's only

me and not your family,' Charlotte said. 'Because they should be the ones being stunned by the surprise of what you're wearing and if they'd seen all this already the impact wouldn't be quite there.'

Thea changed into the dress then put the jacket on top. It was warm and snuggly and would be just right for a beachfront breakfast.

'Shoes?' she asked Charlotte.

'Boots. Long foxy boots, chunky heel, not too high,' she said, 'but for now, I'm knackered. Ah, and just one more thing,' she said as they walked through the shop. 'Look at this . . .' They were crossing the children's department which gleamed and glittered with Christmassy frocks for little girls. She pulled a cream dress from a rack. It had subtle sequin beading in the same colour as Thea's dress. 'I knew something would come to me,' she said, tapping the side of her skull. 'The thing to do is ask Milly to be your bridesmaid. A sly trick, I know, because what kind of parent would tell a child no she can't? But I'm pretty damn sure it'll work.'

'Hmm. Not sure about that. I think it would just infuriate Emily and make her even more determined. She'd say I was undermining her.'

'That's a point.' Charlotte was silent for a rare moment. 'OK, how about this then: ask Sam.'

'To be a bridesmaid? I'm not sure he'd look that good in drag.'

'No, you daft tart, ask him about Milly. Then he can sort out Emily. Somehow.'

As Thea paid for the little dress and the jacket, she hugged Charlotte. 'I don't think it's so much the mistletoe that's magic, you know, I think it just might be you.'

TWENTY-THREE

It was a long way from ideal, having the dog in residence, even for a few days. Benji was a quiet, patient sort, as so many really big dogs often are, but once he was out of the house he did enjoy a lot of exercise. Thea took him out twice a day, mostly in the dark, and spent many a nervy hour walking him across the green where the drunks lurked on benches even in the November cold, and sometimes through the park, which was closed to traffic at dusk and left to the shuffling deer and the dog-walkers and anyone else who liked to roam in the blackness.

Robbie and June Over-the-Road saw her coming back on the Tuesday night and Robbie grinned at her. 'We could walk them together. You and me in the park in the dark.' He leaned towards her, close enough for her to be repelled by the lingering smell of well-boiled cabbage. June tutted.

'He's going back to his owner in a couple of hours, Robbie,' Thea told him. 'He's not mine.'

'Oh, we know whose he is. He belongs to that nice young man that's moved out. Lovely manners,' June said. 'You could have done a lot worse than hang on to him.'

Thea was in no doubt that in June's eyes she'd failed to keep a seriously good catch. 'I'm about to do a lot better. I'm getting married on Christmas Day,' she told them.

'To that one with the hair?' June said, her mouth hanging open in horror. 'Oh, Thea! I hope you know what you're doing.' She shook her head. 'You young people. And Christmas Day! I didn't think you could. Isn't there enough going on at Christmas without the complication of a wedding? Which church will it be? And will there be carols?'

'It's not in a church and it'll be down in Cornwall, not round here. We're having the ceremony at a friend's house and yes, you can get married any day of the year if you can find someone who'll take it on.' Thea sensed she was disappointing her neighbours on all fronts here. 'We're having a simple low-key thing, with family and a barbecued breakfast on the beach.'

'Oh, my.' June was practically fanning her face with her hand at this. 'A beach! In December! Now that's not what I call a wedding party. What does your mother think? All mothers have big plans for their daughters' weddings – she'll have wanted you in a proper church and a sit-down do.'

'You don't know my mother,' Thea said, just

301

managing to keep her smile going. What was it with some people? But then she remembered that June and Robbie had got married in the 1950s when all was still a bit austere and any chance for a proper bit of showing off was hugely welcomed. If she and Sean had half as many years together as these two she'd feel they'd done very well.

'Anyway, Rich is coming to pick up the dog soon so I'd better get back,' she told them. 'Your deer look very festive,' she added, indicating the lit-up stags in their front garden. Robbie had adjusted the lights but one of them had only one functioning eye and looked as if it was winking. She felt horribly insincere but wanted to be kind to make up for the inner anger that they didn't even know she was feeling. How stupidly English that was, she thought as she led Benji to the front door, but they were kind and sweet neighbours and she'd miss them when – God willing she soon found a job – she moved to Cornwall.

Rich was bang on time as always. She remembered he'd had a thing about punctuality. He was never late for anything (he'd consider that not so much bad manners as a failure on his part) but also he'd never arrive a second too soon, sometimes insisting on waiting in the car if they were a few minutes early to see a film or for a table he'd booked. 'We'll only have to hang about,' he'd say if she suggested going in, never acknowledging that it made little difference: early was early, it didn't much matter where they spent the extra minutes. But hanging about in the car was fine by him as he was in charge of it; he preferred that to being at the whim of a waiter who might suggest the bar for a drink first or sitting in the cinema with the lights on, simply relaxing.

This time it really would have been rude not to invite him in. Thea opened the door and Benji woofed at Rich and bounced around a bit. Rich made the dog sit down, for fear of contact with the mud that was still wet on his fur from the walk.

'Sorry, should have mopped him down,' Thea said as Rich kept his distance. Benji looked a bit hurt, she thought, and well he might, but he must be used to Rich being so damn fastidious by now.

'Er . . . is that what you're wearing?' Rich said to her, indicating her jeans and big blue jumper and her Ugg boots.

'Sorry? Well, yes of course it is, what do you mean?' Thea looked down at herself, wondering if she'd accidentally put on something weird and hadn't noticed. She had got changed in a bit of a hurry after school.

'For dinner?' he said, following her into the sitting room.

'What dinner? I was only going to have some pasta and whatever I can find in the fridge,' she told him.

'But I'm taking you out!' he said. 'Didn't you see the message?'

'Er . . . no, I didn't. Sorry.' She picked up her phone and saw a text from him: *Dinner at Olivier's, as a thank you. 8 pm.*

He looked at his watch. 'Hurry up, sweetie, we don't want to be late.'

'But I haven't said I'll go. And you thanked me already, with the lilies, which was very kind of you.'

'Oh, but they were just flowers. I thought dinner, then we can chat.'

It was only when she was in his car and wearing a snug old green velvet dress, make-up and rather uncomfortable shoes that Thea remembered how persuasive Rich could be. She didn't particularly want to be here, doing this, and yet he'd convinced her, saying that she had to eat anyway, and they wouldn't be out late, that the restaurant wasn't far and wasn't it a lonely old life for the single in London? So she'd ended up caving in.

And it was good to be out, to be wined and dined and treated like someone special. It wasn't that Sean didn't do that – on the contrary, she always felt special with him – but the two of them didn't tend to blow the budget in places that had proper linen napkins and a wine waiter flaunting the bunch-of-grapes badge of a qualified sommelier.

They talked (or rather Rich did) about his job, about the poodles that his sister was still showing and breeding, about the flat he was now about to move into. It was only when they got to the coffee stage that she realized he hadn't asked a single thing about her. She didn't much mind: it had been a busy day at school, still endlessly rehearsing the nativity play and dealing with over-excited children geeing themselves up for Christmas. Only that afternoon she'd had to deal with the calamity of the oldest child in the class (all of seven years old) grandly informing the youngest few that Santa didn't exist and causing near-hysterics to most of the rest. So she didn't mind zoning out a bit while Rich went on and on about his own life.

'I've missed you, Thea.' She jolted back from thinking about how many sets of angel wings she'd need for the play as Rich put his hand over hers on the table.

'What are you doing?' she asked, wriggling her hand out from under his.

'I was thinking, maybe I was too hasty last year. I'd like us to try again.'

She laughed and then apologized, 'Sorry, Rich. But honestly, that was the last thing I was expecting.'

'Why? You must know I never stopped caring about you.'

'Well actually, no, I didn't know that. I thought you made it pretty clear at the time. You didn't want children or me, you wanted poodle puppies and your sister.' A passing waiter turned and gave them a look. She didn't blame him – it wasn't a statement he was likely to hear every day.

'A man can change his mind,' Rich said, going for her hand again.

'Rich, I'm getting married in six weeks.'

'I don't see a ring.'

'I don't need one.'

'He should have got you one. Only a cheapskate wouldn't,' he said, frowning at her left hand with its naked third finger. He smiled and reached into his inside pocket. 'So, Thea, how about you wear mine again? We could get back to how we were. Marry me instead.'

'Oh God, Rich, are you mad? Didn't you hear a word I said? It was over ages ago, you and me. I met someone else and I'm marrying him. Please don't do this. In fact . . .' She put her napkin on the table and picked up her bag. 'Please let's just get the bill and go home. Honestly, this conversation is crazy. And I'm paying my half.'

'Don't be silly, you don't need to do that.'

'No, please listen to me. I *do* need.'

He sighed and clicked his fingers at the waiter. Thea cringed inwardly, horrified. The bill arrived and she took a quick look then got out her wallet.

'I didn't have a pudding and you didn't have a starter but my steak was more than yours so . . .' He got out his phone and started doing calculations. If nothing else reminded her why she was so happy not to be with him any more, it was this. This and the finger-clicking.

'Look, just split the thing,' she said. 'There's no need for complex bistromatics.'

'If you insist. But I'm sure I owe you £3.67.'

'Have it on me,' she said, getting up from the table. 'I should get a cab back.'

'No, don't be silly, I'll take you.'

That 'silly' word again. How she hated it. She remembered he'd used it a lot, back in the day, thinking it suited her 'cuteness'.

The drive back was pretty much silent. Outside the house there was an awkward moment where Thea had to invite him in but make it clear that it was only to collect Benji.

'Your dog awaits,' she said as they went up the path. 'I'll just put his lead and his food bowls in a bag for you.'

Inside the house Rich shifted about looking embarrassed. 'There is just one more thing,' he said. 'It's about Benji. I'd like you to have him. Think of it as a wedding present.'

'But . . . I can't take him to work with me, Rich, any more than you can.'

'No, really, he likes being with you and my new job is going to involve travel.'

'You've thought this through, haven't you? This is really why you asked me out, isn't it? A home for the dog?'

'No, no, of course not! I hoped we could get back together, I really did. But I can see you need time to think about that.'

'No, I don't need time, sorry. I really don't.'

'Are you sure?' He came towards her, putting his arms round her and squeezing her too hard towards him. 'Why not let me take you to bed and remind you what we used to have, what we could still have?'

'Let go of me, Rich,' Thea said, struggling. He laughed and pulled even harder, pushing her towards the stairs. Benji started barking.

'Rich, just *fuck off*, will you? Get off me!' She kicked out and found a kneecap but all he did was wince. She shouted at him again, louder, and he pulled her up the first few stairs. 'You *bastard*, what the hell are you trying to do?' she shrieked at him. There was a noise by the front door, the sound of a key. She found a small reserve of strength and heaved Rich away from her, feeling the sleeve of her dress rip as he kept hold of her. The door opened and Sean came in.

'What the hell is going on? I could hear you out in the street. Are you OK?' he said.

'She kicked me,' Rich whined, rubbing his kneecap. 'I was only—'

'I know what you were "only", mate. And if her shoe had connected with what she should have been aiming at, you wouldn't be thinking of doing it again with anyone, ever. Now get *out*.' Sean got hold of Rich, bent his arm behind his back, hauled him through the front door and flung him to the ground. He landed on the puddled pavement and swore loudly. Across the road, a light showed in Robbie and June's bedroom and their faces could be seen, silhouetted against the light.

'I think we've given them something to talk about for a while,' he said to Thea as he came back into the house, closed the door and put his arms round her. 'Are you OK, babe? I take it that was your bastard ex. What the hell did he think he was doing?'

Thea gave a shaky laugh. 'Believe it or not, that was the follow-up to asking me to marry him.'

'Oh, nice. I presume you accepted his generous and honourable proposal?' he said, grinning as he led her to the sofa. They sat down, wrapped around each other. Her fast-beating heart gradually calmed down.

'You could tell, couldn't you?'

'Yep. It was all there in the body language.' He touched her ripped sleeve. 'Shame about the dress. I liked that one.'

'So did I but I never want to see it again now. It'll remind me.'

'Aw, forgive the dress. It's not its fault. Stay there a sec, I'll get us a drink.'

He came back with a couple of glasses of wine, and she asked him, 'So how come you're here? It's fabulous that you are but I thought you'd be back in Cornwall by now.'

'I couldn't leave the Katinka thing like that till the next time you came down. I just wanted to tell you what happened because I didn't want it festering. I thought I might as well come this way down from the north rather than the M5 and call in. Just as well I did, isn't it? You might have ended up dumping me for your so-charming ex.'

'Well, it would have evened up the previous-marriage score, I suppose, but honestly, there was never, ever any question of that. He only took me for dinner to thank me for having the dog over the weekend. Or at least, that's what I thought it was about. I hadn't a clue about the other thing. But . . . tell me about your wife number one.'

'OK, what happened was . . . we'd been in Santa Monica for a contest, a whole bunch of us. And our sponsors treated us – well, they called it a treat, it was totally not our thing – to a few days in Las Vegas.'

'All gambling and Elvis. Nice,' she said. 'Go on. Were you with Katinka at the time?'

'Yes, but it wasn't a big thing. We didn't get together that much. The women's circuit isn't always the same as the men's so we were mostly on separate continents. She was just back from Australia and I was about to go there so we only had those few days that time. But we all drank far too much and got talking about visas and the problems we sometimes had visiting various countries. Not everywhere thinks surfing counts as a proper competitive sport.'

'I don't see why not,' Thea said. 'It's got to take more skill than, say, throwing a hammer. And things like fast running are mostly a matter of luck and genes, surely?'

'Possibly, possibly. That and a lifetime of training,' he said, nodding. 'So Katinka said we should get married and then I would be able to get into America easily any time I wanted to.' He smiled, rather wanly. 'It seemed a good idea at the time.'

Thea laughed, mostly with relief. She'd imagined him madly in love with the girl, and later pining that they'd broken up, rethinking the whole thing just as Rich had.

'So we and our mates and our passports and however many dollars it takes went to one of those wedding chapels and did the deed.'

'Oh – so you *did* marry her!'

'Ah – well, yes and no. Mostly no. It turned out that the guy doing the so-called service was the cleaner seeing a handy chance to make a few crafty bucks while the real dude was out at lunch. Someone else who worked in the building saw what was going on and ripped up the papers before we even got out of the door. So it happened but it didn't happen. Never got the dollars back though. That's when I bought her the bracelet, for being kind enough to be willing to do that just for the sake of my visa status.'

'Sweet of her,' Thea said, feeling bad about too many things to list – she hadn't been nice to Katinka.

'So . . .' Sean kissed her neck. 'Can we go to bed now? Or have you still not forgiven me?'

'Forgiven *you*? Have you forgiven me for going out to dinner with my ex?'

'Oh yes, absolutely. It was worth it just to shove the bastard into the dirt. I'm afraid I *really* enjoyed that. Bad, isn't it?'

'He had it coming after mauling me like that.'

'Sure did. So – can we go up now?'

Thea stood up. 'Yes, but could you just let Benji out into the garden for his late-night pee? I hate to say it, but I think we've acquired a dog.'

'So long as he and Woody can find a way to cohabit, that's fine by me,' he said, stroking the dog's ears.

'And don't come up till I tell you. There's one thing I have to do first.'

'What? Have you got another total knob of an ex-lover up there that you need to hide in a cupboard?'

'No,' she told him, 'no lovers to hide. Just my wedding dress.'

TWENTY-FOUR

December

It was late at night and Emily was in the kitchen, wrapping presents at the table. They were the small ones for the children's stockings; she'd made sure that there was an equal balance between them so that there wouldn't be a five-in-the-morning outbreak of 'It's not fair' on Christmas Day. She loved doing this, loved assembling each child's collection of goodies and assigning them to the named bags so they could easily be loaded into the stockings late on Christmas Eve. It was something she and Sam always did together, working silently and swiftly in their bedroom before they crept back to hang them on the ends of the children's beds. Ned had a stocking too, of course. Anna had made it for him, as she had for the other two (and for Elmo back in his babyhood) out of scarlet felt with their names appliquéd on with Liberty prints, a different pattern for each child. Ned wouldn't have a clue what was going on but that didn't matter. She still knew he'd like his selection of baby toys – he'd taken to doing a lot of smiling and everything seemed to please him, especially his baby gym and things he could reach out and hit so they made sounds. She and Sam had bought him a beautiful Noah's Ark containing hand-painted wooden animals. It was one of those for ever toys, nothing plastic or tacky about it. And although she knew it would hurt just as much when she trod on one of the carelessly misplaced animals in bare feet, it wasn't something she'd then kick across the floor in painful fury. No, she'd pick it up and lovingly reunite it with its beautifully carved partner. In her head she projected years onwards: Ned giving it to his own children. Would she still be around to see that? She hoped so, God and good health willing.

The Christmas tree was up in the sitting room hung with her favourite silver and white colour theme. Usually, she and Sam did that together too but she'd ended up decorating it alone as Sam had taken the children to the park on the afternoon she'd scheduled that it should be done. Today. She liked lists. Life went with the right smoothness if you had a list and the tree had been on the list for today.

'You're much better at that kind of thing,' he'd said as he carried the boxes of decorations down from the loft for her. He hadn't even helped her with the lights – which were usually his department – simply plonking the boxes down and going to fetch the children's coats and gloves, barely saying a word. Without him, her heart hadn't really been in it but she'd got it finished and waited to switch the lights on till they all came home.

Milly and Alfie were gratifyingly impressed. 'Whee! Santa's coming soon!' Alfie bounced up and down clapping excitedly as Milly gave him a thoughtful look.

'That's right, he *is*,' Emily told him, giving Milly a warning look back. One more year, she wanted, one more year before Alfie too discovered that Santa wasn't a magical figure that actually existed but merely another childhood lie like the tooth fairy and the Easter bunny.

'Will we be getting Santa at that place with the beach and the snow?' Milly asked over tea.

Sam looked at Emily and said, 'Yes, will we?'

'Santa goes everywhere,' she replied carefully, not looking at Sam. 'He'll be at every house in the world.' She crossed her fingers against this blatant untruth.

'Yes, but will he be *there*. When we are,' Milly persisted.

'We'll be here, at home, silly!' Emily said. 'Santa's bringing your presents here this year. You know that.'

'Ohhhh.' Milly spread the word out for several syllables of disappointment. 'But Grandma and Grand-dad and everyone are going to that beach place. *I* want to go too. And I want to see the *bride*. Thea's being one.'

Emily heard Sam sigh. 'I know, darling. But this year

we're going to be in our own house. Mummy wasn't very happy there last year.'

'I was,' Alfie said. 'It was nice. I want to go *again*.'

Over his head, Sam mouthed, 'See?' at her. Emily's hands started to shake. She was doing the wrong thing and she knew it but there was something almost physical about her fear of going to Cove Manor again. She knew she had got everything out of perspective but it was no good telling her, as Sam had several times and her mother just once, that it was ridiculous. She tried to breathe her way through to acceptance but it just wasn't working. And it wasn't fair either – Rosie had a phobia about flying but nobody ever told *her* to get on a plane and simply get over it. No, all *their* holidays accommodated her fear. They went by sea or train.

'I tell you what, this week I'll take you to see Father Christmas at the garden centre,' Emily tried placating them. 'He'll give you a present and you can open it right there, not wait for the day. How about that?'

'Suppose so,' Milly said, reluctant to accept this as compensation. 'I hope it's a good present. I want a kitten.'

'Sorry, but Santa doesn't bring kittens,' Sam told her. 'He's not allowed to carry animals on the sleigh in case they fall off.' Milly pouted at him.

'There might be a kitten in the spring,' Emily heard herself saying, 'if you're good.'

'We're good!' Alfie said. 'We're really, really good! I want one like that cat down at the beach!'

'What did you go and say that for?' Sam asked as the children raced upstairs to get ready for bed. 'You can't bribe your way out of this one with a Siamese cat, Emily. I'm going to do some foot-stamping of my own right now. Thea asked me if Milly could be her brides-maid. I want to tell her yes, so I'm going to. Don't even think of arguing with me. It's happening, OK? Whether you come or not, the children and I are going to this wedding. Got it?'

Emily said nothing. She looked through the doorway at her Christmas tree that glittered and shone. The turkey would be arriving the day before Christmas Eve. She'd ordered everything they needed for a family Christmas in their own home, to be together, safe and warm and with the world's evils locked outside, and Sam was rejecting it. Silently, she left the table and went upstairs to bath the children. Then she would feed Ned and get into bed with him and cuddle him close. With her eyes closed and the promise of sleep, she didn't have to think about how much Sam was no longer even partly on her side.

It was the last day of term, the nativity play was over and Thea was thankful that none of the children from her class had fallen off the stage, wet their knickers, been sick or done anything else to incur the fury of

Melanie. Melanie herself didn't look too happy but as 'disapproving' was her default expression these days this didn't mean a lot.

As the parents, several of them mopping tears, filed out after the final strains of 'Away in a Manger' faded away, the deputy head approached Thea.

'I don't know if you'd heard,' he said, 'but I'll be leaving at the end of next term. You should go for my job – it's high time you were a deputy and you'd be terrific at it.'

'Hmm . . . Melanie and I don't see eye to eye. And also, I'm likely to be moving on myself soon. I'm looking for a job in Cornwall but there's a bit of a shortage.'

'Yes – those village schools, once someone's got a job there, they tend to stick with it. You can probably get supply jobs.'

'I might have to. I'll see what's going. And congratulations – I assume you're moving up the ladder yourself?'

'Yep. Head of a big primary out in Kent. We've been fancying a move away from London.'

Thea was clearing up the remains of the scattered costumes in her classroom when Melanie came in. 'I was looking for you,' she said, as if she'd looked everywhere but the place where she was most likely to find Thea. 'I wanted a word.'

'Really? OK . . .'

'I just wanted to say that, with Maurice leaving, you

might be thinking of applying for the deputy head-ship. And I'm sorry but I also wanted to warn you that I wouldn't be able to support the application.'

Thea was taken aback. 'May I ask why? I think I do a good job here and have been for the last three years. I'm committed to the children and they're all doing well.'

'It's a matter of school policy. I don't think you and I are on the same page regarding how the place should be run and I think you have . . . shall we say . . . rather *revolutionary* ideas about education.'

'Really? Good grief. I haven't been accused of that before. You make me sound like the Che Guevara of education!'

'I'm just trying to save you the effort of putting together an application, that's all. They can be very time-consuming,' Melanie said. 'As I said, I think you'd be marvellous in a different environment, working with something less structured. Just not one like this where we need to be results-based rather than experimenting with unorthodox techniques. We have to provide what the parents expect and this area has a very demanding demographic. You have woolly ideas about the children being "happy" and about all-inclusive projects. It's not really for us.'

'Well, that's telling me,' Thea said, then considered for a moment, 'OK, let me make your Christmas for you, Melanie. I'm giving in my notice, right now.' She turned to pick up the last of the broken angel wings and shoved them hard into the bin.

'Thank you,' Melanie said. 'You'll need to send it in writing through the usual channels.' She smiled. 'And I wish you a very happy Christmas. Are you doing anything special?'

Thea looked at her, hard. Surely Melanie knew? The staff had had a collection and bought her and Sean a stunning abstract-patterned ceramic bowl from a local gallery. Melanie's name had been on the card but it had possibly been signed by her PA.

'Yes, I'm getting married.'

'Oh yes, of course. I did know that. Well, good luck. I'll see you next term.' And she walked out of the class-room, leaving Thea to wonder if she'd actually been effectively fired. Either way, it didn't matter. She felt as if something that had been weighing a piece of her brain down had been shaken out. Her new work life, whatever it was to be, was under way.

Thea was packing. This was *it*. She really was going to be marrying Sean on Christmas Day. Apart from a little superstitious sadness about losing the plaited grass ring, everything seemed to be falling into place. Sean had taken Benji down to Cove Manor and reported back that after a day of hissing and lashing out from Woody in the battle for the fireside rug territory, the cat seemed to have accepted the dog. In turn, Benji recognized his place in the household hierarchy; he now backed away from the temptation of Woody's food bowl after the cat had whacked him hard on the nose for stealing Go-Cat.

Anna, on the other hand, had gone into panic mode. 'Wedding rings. Are you having rings?' she phoned to ask. 'You didn't say.'

'We are. We've each had something special made and we're keeping them secret from each other. I hope he likes what I've done.'

Later, Anna called again. 'Your dad says you won't want to be "given away" because you're not his chattel but don't you want him to walk you into the room? And where are you staying the night before? You can't be with Sean, it's unlucky.'

'Sean will staying at Pentreath Hall with Paul and Sarah and I'll be in the stables. If Charlotte comes, she can have the other bedroom. And if Dad wants to walk me into the orangery, that would be absolutely lovely. I was going to ask him anyway and I probably should have done before now.' She felt quite tearful at the thought and hoped that on the day she wouldn't end up with make-up trickling down her face. She probably would. All weddings she'd ever been to ended with the bride, groom and many of the congregation in tears.

'Right.' Anna sighed. 'So everything's organized? I feel I haven't had to do anything useful. But I have got the most glorious hat. It might even outdo Rosie's.'

JUDY ASTLEY

'All I need is for you to be there,' Thea said. 'And if you could help me put some orange and red streaks in my hair the night before, that would be brilliant.'

Anna cheered up. 'Ooh yes, I can do that. I'll bring disposable gloves. I don't want orange hands on the day. Now . . .' She went quiet for a few seconds. '. . . Have you heard anything from Emily?'

'Sam said he's got a plan. I've no idea what but I'm to say nothing to Emily. We've got to wait and see. Actually, I'm seeing her this afternoon. She wants me to go with her to take the children to visit Santa at the garden centre grotto near her. It's my last chance to persuade her to come.'

'Oh dear. I do hope it works out. If she doesn't come, you'll hardly notice among all the excitement and in the end it's you and Sean that count. But Emily, she'll regret it for ever.'

Thea was rather nervous about this outing with Emily. It had been Sam's idea. 'I'll get her to invite you out for lunch,' he'd said to Thea, 'to see if she can bring herself to apologize and salvage something of the sisterhood. Maybe she can be shamed into changing her mind. Something will work out, trust me.'

'OK, I'll go but I'm leaving the next morning so any salvaging will have to be fairly quick.'

It wasn't going to be lunch. Thea was quite glad as she'd slightly dreaded the prospect of sitting opposite Emily and finding something to talk about that wasn't

322

'the Situation'. She'd been prepared to describe her wedding dress, tell her about the cream lace-fronted boots she'd come across in a charity shop when taking a bag of clothes (including the green velvet dress with its mended sleeve) in to sell. She'd even imagined Emily telling her off for buying used boots (Emily wrinkling her nose and saying, 'Ugh, strangers' feet') but they'd been so gorgeous, barely worn and in her size, that she didn't see why on earth she should reject them. It felt as if she was giving them a new home, like a puppy. After all, as she'd have told Emily if they'd actually had the conversation, lots of people buy shoes that turn out to hurt a bit and only wear them that painful once.

The garden centre had been completely taken over by Christmas. If you wanted to buy anything that wasn't holly, mistletoe, a Christmas tree or a poinsettia plant then you'd be out of luck, plant-wise. Inside, a million Christmas decorations were arranged in colour-coordinated displays and boxes of crackers were stacked dozens high.

'Do you think they get the same tat out every year or do they ever actually sell out of things?' Emily asked Thea. 'It's only a few more days to go and there's a massive warehouse-worth still on offer.'

'No idea. But I suppose there's no "Best Before" on a box of crackers or shiny baubles so it wouldn't matter.'

'And who likes those poinsettias? There must be

miles of glasshouses somewhere, growing nothing
else,' Emily said. She looked mildly frightened. 'It's all
just so *much*.' She shuddered.

Milly and Alfie had run off and were clashing wind-
chimes behind the display of raffia reindeer. Emily and
Thea joined a slow queue for Santa's makeshift grotto,
a flimsy plastic construction meant to look like a snow-
capped cave, surrounded by fake fir trees and some
reindeer like the Over-the-Roads'. Lights flickered on
and off; some were broken so it was all a bit uncoordi-
nated. If anyone with migraine tendencies stayed there
long, it wouldn't end well.

'All this . . .' Emily said, waving her arm over the top
of Ned's sleeping head. 'All here and then instantly
gone. I can't bear it, this year. Usually I love it. I think it
was last year that spoiled it for me.'

Thea felt something of an ouch-moment. 'Now come
on, it wasn't all bad. Didn't you love finding out you
were pregnant? I so envied you.'

'No, I didn't. Not at the time. It was a huge and
horrible shock.' Then she gasped, 'Oh, Thea, I'm sorry.
I didn't mean that, especially as—'

'Yes. I know. Mine was due on Christmas Day. But
it wasn't to be and you live with what you get, in the
end. Actually' – she put her arm through Emily's – 'I
saw Rich recently and although I was devastated to
lose the baby at only twelve weeks, I'm so glad now
that I won't be having one of his. Not that I wouldn't

have loved it if it had worked out, obviously.'

'I rather liked him,' Emily said. 'At least he was . . .' she laughed ' . . . sensible. Sorry, but that's awful, isn't it? If the best you can say about a man is that he's "sensible" it's not a lot. Sean is so much more . . . you.'

'So come down to Cove Manor,' Thea asked, 'even on Christmas Eve, as last minute as you like. Please, Em?'

It was their turn next with Santa. Milly and Alfie came flying over and hurled themselves into the dimly lit cavern in front of Thea and Emily before Emily could answer the question. Thea cursed the timing as they bent to get in through the low curtained doorway.

'Ho ho ho, little boy and girl!' The ho-hos boomed out loud and clear but the voice wasn't a particularly deep one. Santa's face was mostly hidden behind plenty of beard and the hood came low over his eyes. Milly pulled back, clutching Thea's coat.

'Have you been good children?' Santa asked in time-honoured fashion.

'They've been as good as children their age can be,' Emily answered for them as they both seemed to have been struck unusually dumb.

'Then you deserve lovely, lovely presents. What would you like Father Christmas to bring on Christmas Day?'

Milly found her voice. 'A kitten.'

'I want to go to the beach place,' Alfie said.

'Oh, do you? I wonder if that might be possible or

not?' Santa looked up at Emily. Then: 'I heard something nice,' Santa's oddly pitched voice went on. 'I heard you, little girl, are going to be a bridesmaid.'

Milly stared, her eyes wide.

'What?' Emily said. 'I don't think so!'

'I want to be! Mummy, say I can be!'

Emily glared at Thea. 'Did you put him up to this? What the hell is going on?'

'Of course I didn't!'

Santa reached into a sack, first taking his black gloves off to rifle around among the packages.

'Santa's got nail varnish on!' Milly yelled. And Santa had. Thea could see several shades of pink, different on each fingernail. She knew someone who often did that . . .

'Santa's got *high heels* on as well,' Alfie said. Milly giggled and stepped further forward. Emily and Thea were just too slow to see what was coming. Milly hauled off the beard and Alfie pulled back the hood before either of the grown-ups could stop them. Santa flailed an arm and knocked over a big plaster elf, which clattered into the next one and sent them rolling through the fabric doorway and into the waiting queue. Children outside started wailing. There was a flash and a bang and the lights went out.

'It's Charlotte!' Milly shrieked, opening the curtain and telling the assembled line. 'Father Christmas is called *Charlotte*.'

'Oh God, what the fuck is going on? Why is every-thing always *you*?' Emily said, picking up the beard and shoving it hard at Charlotte, who was trying to pull the hood up again.

A couple of people who looked like management came hurtling in. 'What's going on? Where's your beard? God, I knew we were taking a risk with you . . .'

'I'll meet you in the coffee shop,' Charlotte said to Thea. 'I'm guessing this might be my last day.'

Thea got the teas, some apple juice and cupcakes and carried them to the table where a fuming Emily was waiting. Charlotte, still in her Santa coat and looking like she was heading for a fancy dress bash, came and sat with them.

'How could you?' Emily tore straight into Thea. 'You set this up and now look what you've done. She'll be all disappointed. She hasn't even got a dress, even if she *could* go to the wedding.'

'I didn't set up anything,' Thea insisted. 'I had no idea Charlotte was working here. Also, it was *your* idea to come here, not mine, remember?'

'Oh, and Milly has got a dress,' Charlotte said. 'Thea and I found just the thing, in case there was a change of mind at the last minute. Thea's got it at home. I'm sorry, I thought Sam would have had all this out with you by now.'

'Sam? He knows all this? He's been plotting with

you? He can't *do* that! It's never him who does the organizing because he's useless at it – it's *my* role. I've got all of Christmas planned for having it *here*. Just like he promised we could after last year. What can I do?'

Charlotte sipped her tea and then shrugged. 'It's simple. Unarrange it.'

TWENTY-FIVE

Most of Thea's party were now down in Cornwall, settled into Cove Manor ready for Christmas and the wedding, but the lack of Emily and her family was keenly felt. It was a bit of a 'Don't mention the war' situation. Somehow, however much anyone tried to avoid talking about her, her absence kept coming up in conversation.

'She can be a grumpy cow and likes everything so damn organized that you sometimes wonder if she's put up a going-to-the-loo rota in their house,' Jimi said over the first night's supper. Maria was cooking most of the food, as last year, and it was just as delicious this time round.

'It's because of her job,' Anna said. 'You can't have a flaky accountant. I'm not sure which way round it was, whether the job has made her this way or if she was always like that and fell into the perfect profession.'

'She always did her homework on time,' Thea said. 'And she had her school uniform all hung up and ready every Sunday evening, with her games kit folded up for Wednesdays well in advance. I remember once how she took her hockey kit to school on a day when it was going to be netball and she went into a total meltdown. She was sent to the sickroom to breathe into a paper bag.'

'Rather extreme, that,' Rosie said. 'I used to love it if I had the wrong kit and did it as often as I could get away with. That way you sometimes got out of games altogether.'

'Mum's like *so* lazy,' Elmo said, laughing. 'She even finds sport on telly tiring. I've seen her drift off to sleep watching Wimbledon.'

Thea looked at Elmo and grinned. So this was her lovely sixteen-year-old nephew, at last emerging from the sullen years and into the general melee of conversation. It was either the chrysalis moment or a certain spirit-lifting resulting from having been re-united with Maria's daughter Daisy on the beach that afternoon. From the stables terrace she'd seen the two of them walking along the beach together. They weren't holding hands but were doing that walking-too-close-together thing where they kept bumping into each other 'accidentally'. Oh, she remembered those lovely awkward first-date days. She looked across the table at Sean, who raised his wine glass to her and smiled.

'Shall we escape for a bit?' Sean murmured to her as they helped clear the table a little later. 'I've got something to show you.'

'Sounds promising . . .' she whispered. 'Yes, let's run away.'

'Great. Because tomorrow night my mother and sister will be here so we won't get a chance to be on our own.'

Back in the stables, Thea grabbed her sheepskin coat and her Uggs and the two of them went out and climbed into the Land Rover.

'So where are we going? Shall we go and steal some mistletoe again?'

Sean laughed. 'Paul's cut down so much of the stuff to decorate the orangery in honour of how we first got together that I doubt there's much left.'

'Oh, good. Because I have this feeling that going up a ladder in the dark two days before our wedding would be asking for disaster.'

'Yes – breaking my neck wouldn't be the best start, would it?'

'Exactly. I remember thinking that was what was going to happen last year when you were up there getting some for me and that big owl spooked you.'

'It was huge, at least the size of a pterodactyl, *two* pterodactyls even,' Sean told her. 'But then it's like all close encounters with birds. I had a wren in the kitchen a few weeks ago and when it was flapping about in a panic it seemed a lot bigger than when they're sitting on a wall being teeny and shouting at you. No, where we're going is to Sarah and Paul's. They want us to approve the decor. I wanted us to sneak out together, rather than have the others wanting to come. They can wait and be surprised on the day.'

Pentreath Hall was a lot warmer inside than on their last visit. Sarah and the wolfhound came to let them in and she ushered them into the kitchen where Paul was threading holly and ivy on to strings.

'Last one,' he said. 'The rest of it is up and we just wanted your approval. The boiler man did his magic thing so you should be warm enough in whatever gorgeously diaphanous gown you're planning to wear, Thea. Plus, just in case, we'll light the wood-burner in there so it's properly cosy. You can't have a cold wedding – I'm sure it would be a bad omen and we don't want any of *those*, thank you very much.'

Sarah handed round glasses of champagne, saying, 'Any excuse but also we're so excited at you two being the first of our weddings venture. Now come and see what's been happening in the orangery. I hope you like it.'

She flung open the double doors from the drawing room and they all went inside.

'Oh, wow!' Thea said, feeling her eyes beginning to brim. 'It's stunning!'

'We haven't done anything with the narcissi yet because they'd droop but they're arriving tomorrow. I'll make sure enough are sent over to you early enough to do your flowers, Thea. Are you having a headdress of any sort?'

'I think so. It depends if I can get something together with the real flowers. But I shouldn't say any
more because Sean's here. It won't be anything fussy,
anyway.'

'It's OK, I'm not listening,' he told them, putting his
fingers in his ears and humming.

The room looked beautiful. Great swags of mistletoe,
holly and ivy hung from the wall over where the
registrar's table was placed. More greenery spilled from
the two pairs of great urns that flanked the doors to the
terrace. A collection of jars and vases stood on a cloth
on top of a grand piano in the corner. The chairs had
been unstacked and were set out waiting for guests.

'I don't remember the piano being here,' Thea said.

'No, well, we thought we'd move it in here from the
drawing room. There's plenty of space for it and not
everyone wants music that's recorded. Actually' – she
looked at her watch – 'I've got mince pies in the oven,
I'll just go and check on them. You two stay here for a
few minutes and see if you can think of anything we
need to add. Come on, Paul,' she said, pulling him out
by his wrist.

'Ah, that's sweet, leaving us on our own,' Thea said,
recognizing a moment of serious tact.

'It's in case we want to do unseemly snogging,' Sean
said, pulling her close to him. 'I'm glad, because I do.
And also, part of why I wanted us to go out and be on
our own is that I've got something for you.'

'You have? What more could I possibly want? I'm getting you,' she said.

'Nicely put and almost as cheesy as when I proposed but I never did give you an engagement ring,' he said, searching in his jeans pocket.

'Well, you did. You gave me the plaited grass,' she said, suddenly feeling a tiny bit sad. 'But—'

'But someone stole it from your knicker drawer.'

She stepped back and looked at him. 'How did you know it was in there?'

'Because I gather – only from wide reading, you understand, nothing more – that a knicker drawer is where all women keep things that are a bit precious when there's nowhere else quite right to put them. Also you'd said it was there.'

'You've been rootling about in my underwear?' she accused him. 'But why?'

'Yes, and great fun it was too. But I had a good reason. I want you to have this.' He handed her a small painted box. She opened it. Nestling on a soft pad of tissue was a pendant, maybe an inch and a half long, on a golden chain.

'Have a close look,' he said, moving her under one of the lights.

She gasped, 'Oh – my goodness, it's the plaited grass. You have no idea how upset I was, thinking it had gone for good. I couldn't think how, as I was so sure I hadn't taken it out of its envelope. Oh, this is so beautiful.' She took it out and held it up. It seemed to be suspended in something, like aspic but solid. 'How did you do that?'

'Well, I didn't. But I know a man who does. A jeweller mate in St Ives. I gave it to him and he cast it in resin. It's backed with gold leaf but the effect is the grass suspended like in liquid. Those sparkly bits round it, they're grains of sand from that sand dune.'

'Oh, let me put it on!' she said, taking it out of the box.

'Well . . . if you like,' he said. 'But . . . I was hoping you could wait and wear it for the first time on the day. And I promise that if you keep it among your knickers I won't be stealing it back.'

'That's a deal,' she promised. 'Now, please can we have that unseemly snog? You can't believe how happy this has made me.'

'In that case I'll accept the snog as a thank you. After all, it's pretty much compulsory, seeing as we're surrounded by the biggest load of mistletoe you're ever likely to see outside the Nine Elms flower market.'

Christmas Eve. By the middle of the morning Emily was horribly unsettled and feeling almost ill with it. Ned was fretful and she knew this was her fault for being so stressed. He wasn't feeding happily, pulling away from her every few minutes and crying. She was passing her mood on to him. Milly was quiet, playing with her dolls' house, but Emily could see that she wasn't putting her heart into it as she normally did. She was simply moving one of the dolls in and out of the beds, unable to decide which one to let it sleep in.

'What do bridesmaids do?' she asked. 'Would I be a good one?'

'They carry flowers and walk with the bride.'

'And they wear a pretty dress,' Sam told her.

Emily glared at him. 'Don't,' she warned.

'Why not?'

'Because it's all too late. Christmas is under way; we've got everything organized here.'

He shrugged. 'If you say so.'

'We agreed a year ago,' she reminded him.

'So you keep saying.'

She heard him go upstairs and shut their bedroom door. Drawers were being opened and closed and then he went into the children's rooms and there was more clattering about. She was glad – the rooms needed a good tidying and he was nothing if not thorough at that. So it was quite a shock when he came downstairs carrying suitcases.

'I've packed for you too, if you want to change your mind,' he told her, going back up to collect more luggage.

'Are you mad?' she called up. 'It's way too late. We've got all the food and . . .' She dropped her voice to a whisper as he came back down the stairs. '. . . and the presents are all here, ready for under the tree.'

'No, they're not. They're in the car stashed in bin

bags. And I've given Steve the key to the back gate. He's promised to have the Wendy house up before we get back. Now, that blue dress you haven't worn yet – was I right to put it in?'

'No! You can't *do* this! I won't be bullied.'

'I'm not bullying you, I'm making a decision I should have made weeks ago. OK, Milly, Alfie, go up and have a last wee. We're going to a wedding.'

'To the beach place? Yay!' Alfie said, racing up the stairs.

'And I'll be a bridesmaid?' Milly was bouncing.

'You will!' Sam promised.

'It's three in the afternoon on Christmas Eve,' Emily protested. 'They'll be asleep for most of the journey and then you'll go and wake them at God knows what hour. What will they be like tomorrow?'

'Tomorrow? They'll be as happy as clams. Go and get in the car, Emily, you know you want to.'

Emily said nothing. The frozen feeling was on her again and she couldn't seem to move. Not that she wanted to get in the car anyway. She'd got a turkey she'd only just stuffed, red cabbage just out of the freezer, sprouts cleaned and prepared. The pudding (OK, ready-made, one of Heston's) was ready to cook.

Sam loaded the children into the car and strapped them in, adding at the last minute plenty of scarves and their furry boots. He came back in, breathing hard.

'Last chance, Emily, are you coming or are you

and Ned staying here for a lonely Christmas on your own?'

'I . . . I can't . . . It's all too *sudden* and not thought out . . .' Her brain couldn't deal with this. She hadn't made a list, or planned anything except what she'd expected to do tomorrow. From the kitchen she heard the first notes of 'Once in Royal David's City'. The carol service from King's College chapel was beginning. It was scrambling her brain and she couldn't work out whether to hear that or to listen to Sam.

'Right. Well, don't say I didn't try. Merry fucking Christmas to you.' Before she could take another breath Sam had gone. He slammed the door hard and before she could open it again she heard the car start up and the brakes squeal as he raced away from the roadside.

She must have sat on the sofa, leaning forward, listening, for close to an hour before she realized he was not coming back. The fact sank in, horribly, keenly and painfully as the last of the hymns from the service was begun. She caught the words, 'Hark! The herald angels sing' sung with full, glorious voices. She and Ned were on their own. She got up and switched off the radio and then the Christmas tree lights, feeling they were a kind of insult to her mood.

Emily was wrong but so was Sam. If he'd given her another ten minutes after the children and luggage were loaded, just to think it through, she might have been with him now. It was the immediacy of it that she couldn't cope with. A piece of conscience told her that wasn't entirely true. She'd had months to get her head round the idea of going to Thea's Cornish wedding but she'd stubbornly refused to consider it. This was the price.

And yet . . . Frantically she went on the internet and tried to buy a rail ticket. She could surely just make it if she left now. A train, then a taxi from Redruth. But on Christmas Eve there were no tickets to be had without reservations and no reservations still available.

She called a couple of car-hire companies but there was no joy there either. Even at Heathrow none were available and most of the offices had a jolly 'Closed for Christmas' message on their phones, wishing everyone compliments of the season but nothing to drive.

Eventually Emily gave up. It was past 6 p.m. and she sat on the sofa clutching Ned and sobbed her heart out for the loss of her Christmas, her family and the chance to be at her much-loved sister's wedding.

She had wept herself almost to sleep when the doorbell rang. Wearily she went to answer it, expecting lazy carol singers who hadn't even bothered to sing.

It was Charlotte. Her green Mini was parked by the gate and the passenger door was open.

'You,' Charlotte said, pulling Emily's arm and pointing towards the car. 'Get in.'

TWENTY-SIX

This time last year, Thea thought as she looked out of the window, all was white and snowy-stark out there in the garden and towards the beach. It had been so cold and there'd been so much deep snow that she and Sean had made a snow cat just above the sand and it had lasted till after Boxing Day when a thaw set in. Now it wasn't even frosty and without the false light that the snow gave, she could see only the outlines of the dunes and the shimmer of the sea beneath the moon. On the side of the first dune, just sheltered by the rise of the sand, she could see the top of the stunning Moroccan shelter that Sean had borrowed for the wedding breakfast. She'd watched it being put up the previous afternoon. It was lavishly embroidered with bright pinks and yellows, hung with bells and tassels, and today would be filled with the seats and fat, buttoned cushions that were waiting in the hallway in the manor across the path from the stables. The barbecue was already up too, waiting for Paul to cook the simple wedding breakfast (or more accurately, brunch) of sausage and onion and tomato rolls.

'It's hardly a steak dinner,' Sean's mother Susan had sniffed the evening before over supper. 'Didn't you want a nice sit-down do somewhere warm?'

'There'll be a "nice sit-down do" later in the afternoon. Proper Christmas dinner,' Sean had explained. 'We just wanted something different and fun.'

'It's different all right,' Susan had said. 'But then you always were a funny one.'

The one flaw in the perfect scene, Thea thought now as she went to let Benji out for a pee, was the lack of Emily.

'So what's up with this missing sister of yours then? Have you had a falling-out?' This had been another of Susan's blunt questions.

'I apologize for Mum,' Sean's sister Patti had said. 'She's not one to keep schtum. It's a northern thing.'

'A bit like me then,' Rosie told her.

Jimi nodded. 'Yep. Can't argue with that.'

'Is she a right mardy sort?' Susan went on. Sean winced.

'Not at all,' Anna said. 'It's just . . . a thing. To do with being snowed in last year. And other stuff. Also, she's just had a baby.'

Susan looked out of the window into the moonlit night. 'Well, she'd have to whistle for snow this year, I reckon. There's not even a frost out there. You could die of damp in this county, but not snow.'

Any hope that Thea had had that Emily would change her mind at the last minute vanished when Sam had arrived, halfway through the evening, carrying in both half-asleep children at the same time. Delightful as it had been to see them, she'd been almost floored by the disappointment of Emily not being with them. How could she do that? Simply not come with them? Anna and Thea and Patti helped bring in their luggage and then stacked their presents under the tree. Sam let the children hang their stockings up, even though they barely had any interest in anything but sleep by this point, and then he went off to bed, looking absolutely exhausted. What kind of massive row must there have been for Sam to storm out and take the children away over Christmas like this? And would it ever be reparable?

My wedding day, Thea thought now. She even whispered it out loud to make it even more real.

She reached across and switched on the bedside light. Her beautiful apricot dress hung from the wardrobe door along with the little jacket that went so perfectly. The cream charity shop boots were fun – slightly chunky lace-ups which would give a hint of punk and tone down the 'bridiness' of the rest of the outfit. She'd never been too much of a girly sort and would have felt too unlike herself in over-feminine footwear. She'd taken the original laces out of the boots and replaced them with long strips of narrow salmon lace that matched the dress. Charlotte's brilliant idea, as so many things were. She'd heard her come in the night before, very late, and go straight to her room. The very least she deserved, given that she and Emily and the children had almost (thank goodness, not quite, in the end) cost her her job, was a cup of tea in bed. Thea would give her more time to sleep and then take one to her before she started to get ready.

Thea went and ran the bath, pouring her favourite Clarins gel into it. As she lay among the suds she ran her hands over her flat stomach. Would she and Sean have children? She very much hoped so and it was what he wanted too. With luck, another pregnancy wouldn't end so sadly as her last one had. She made a little cross on her skin for luck, splashed about for a few more minutes and then climbed out of the water and put on her dressing gown and the sheepskin slippers that Katinka had so admired.

Charlotte was already in the kitchen, sipping tea. Thea, now in her old trackie bottoms and a jumper and Uggs, gave her a hug. 'Oh, Charlotte, I'm *so* glad you could make it,' she said. 'You got here really late and now you have to be up early just for this. I'm sorry now it's such an early wedding. Poor Sam didn't get here till halfway through the evening so the children will be all fractious and cross. And their mother . . .' Thea gulped, feeling tears weren't far away.

'They'll be fine,' Charlotte reassured her. 'At least till the middle of the afternoon and by then it won't matter if they fall asleep. And hey, I can smell toast from across the way. Shall we go and join the others for some? You definitely can't get married on an empty stomach. You'd faint.'

'OK, I'll give it a go but I'm too nervous to eat much.'

'Much wouldn't be good either. Just a teeny bit. Come on, let's get going. You don't want to be rushing the prep.'

Across the path in the manor hallway, Thea was met by a whirling Milly. 'Father Christmas has been! And I can be a *bridesmaid*! And it's *today*!'

'It is!' Thea said, hugging her, rather surprised that there wasn't even a hint of sadness at the lack of her mother; perhaps children really did simply live for the moment.

'Come into the kitchen,' Charlotte said. 'There's a bit more than just toast.'

Curious, Thea followed her in. At first, she didn't quite understand where the baby in the bouncy chair had come from, but then she saw Sam move away from the stove . . .

'Emily!' Thea rushed to hug her sister. 'Oh, Em, I'm so glad!'

Emily's eyes filled with tears. 'Thea, I've been so vile.'

'You have,' Rosie chipped in, looking up from stitching narcissi and ivy leaves on to a cream Alice band.

'It's OK, it's OK. I'm just so *so* glad you're here.' Both of them were crying now and laughing at the same time.

'Thank Charlotte,' Emily said. 'She came and dragged me.'

'Oh, I didn't have to drag you,' Charlotte said kindly. 'You were almost at the point of setting off to hitch-hike. Now, where's that toast? I'm starving and the bride needs something to nibble.'

'Ooh-er . . .' said Patti. 'I can't listen to such smut, girls, not when you're talking about my brother.'

'You daft mucky-minded bat,' her mother said. 'She only means toast.'

There was only one disaster: Rosie's navy velvet hat with pink trim was the same as Susan's. Neither seemed to mind and before the ceremony began they had a very happy chat extolling the great qualities of John Lewis.

Emily and Anna waited in the Pentreath drawing room with Thea, checking over last-minute details. 'Hang on, the headdress has gone sideways,' Emily said. 'It smells divine,' she added, sniffing at it as she pulled it straight and fluffed up Thea's newly streaked blond, golden and hazelnut-coloured hair. As well as Thea's headgear – just a simple band of narcissi and leaves – Rosie had made another one for Milly, who was taking her bridesmaid duties seriously and being still and calm, carefully holding her little bunch of narcissi, ivy and ribbons. Thea's bouquet was the same, but with a clump of mistletoe added.

'You look fabulous, darling,' Anna told Thea. 'Good luck, for everything and for ever,' she said, blowing her a kiss as she went to take her place.

Thea, now ready to go into the orangery beside her father, watched with delight as Elmo took to the piano stool and began to play a beautiful lilting arrangement of 'The Holly and the Ivy' while she and Mike walked through the little gathering to where Sean, gorgeous in chestnut velvet and a cream silk shirt, waited for her.

I'm not going to cry, she thought. I'm not, I'm not. But oh, it was hard not to. Sean reached out and took her hand.

'My beautiful Thea,' he said.

'Well, at least they can't call you the maiden aunt any more,' Sean said to Thea as they sipped champagne on the dunes. There was a fire blazing as well as the barbecue going and everyone was drinking champagne, eating the sausage rolls and admiring the gorgeous day. The sky was the kind of vivid blue that people don't really believe can be real and the sun was as warm as an early spring day.

'I just wanted to ask you something,' Sarah said, coming up to Thea, 'though this probably isn't something you want to think about today. It's just that the teacher in charge of the Meadow School's older group is leaving to go and live in Somerset. I just wondered if you might fancy the job. I mean . . . I could advertise but . . .'

'Oh heavens, yes! I'd love it! I've already given notice at my present school and I can't honestly think of anything I'd like better. It's all coming together: this, and Mum and Dad buying the Marazion house. I'm so darn happy!'

'Let me kiss the bride,' Charlotte interrupted, wielding a full glass of champagne. She hugged Thea and said, 'You scrub up gorgeous, you do.'

'Oh, Charlotte, you are so brilliant. I've got so much to thank you for. This dress, Emily being here—'

'Ha, Sam set that up. He was never just going to leave her there. He knew she needed to be shocked into coming. I was always his back-up plan – that, and the fact he's taking her to see a house in Wiltshire that she's been talking about possibly buying. All I had to do was knock on the door and pick up the pieces of her.'

'Well, whatever you did, you are a complete fairy godmother.'

'Not sure about the "mother" bit of that, but I must tell you, I'm currently dating a vicar and it looks like being a goer, this one. A proper keeper. It's all indirectly from coming here last year and meeting you lot and that Alec.'

'So there's the mistletoe to thank, then,' Sean said. 'On which . . .'

'Ah yes, I want to show you something,' Thea said, leading him a little way from the party.

'So do I,' he said. 'Take the ring off.'

'Is that allowed? I've only just put it on. But I want you to take yours off too.'

'Er . . . OK . . . why?'

'Look inside it.'

'No, *you* look inside yours.'

Laughing, they took their wedding rings off and looked at the inside of the bands.

'Oh, wow, how did you know I'd do the same?' Sean said, staring at his.

'I didn't! How did you know *I* would?'

'I didn't either.'

Inside Thea's ring was the date engraved and a little mistletoe leaf and berries. And inside Sean's was almost exactly the same.

'I think that calls for a toast,' he said, taking her hand and leading her back to the party.

'Everyone?' he called. 'Would you all please raise your glasses to . . . the magic of mistletoe.'

'To the mistletoe!' came the chorus.

'And now,' Sean said, looking down the beach to where black-clad people were assembling at the water's edge, 'it's Christmas Day and one half of this *very* happy couple has something traditional and important to do that is done on this day every year without fail.'

'Let me guess,' Thea said, laughing. 'You're going surfing?'

'I am, my gorgeous wife. If that's OK with you, I'm going surfing.'

Judy Astley became the author of witty, contemporary novels after several years as a dressmaker, illustrator, painter and parent. Her own Christmases are a mad mixture of ever-increasing family, too much food and a panic-stricken last-minute hurtle round the shops for presents. She has usually managed to pay off the resulting expense by the time the next lot of Christmas cards come on the market.

Judy lives in London and Cornwall.